A Little, Aloud for Children

*An anthology of prose and poetry
for reading aloud*

A LITTLE, ALOUD FOR CHILDREN

The Reader Organisation exists to bring books to people, and people together. They are pioneering a Reading Revolution – where great literature is enjoyed as a shared experience – taking books and poems to surprising places and to people who may have lost, or never had, a connection with literature.

The charity works across the UK, delivering weekly read-aloud groups through their Get Into Reading project. Commissioned across a variety of sectors, including mental health, criminal justice, social care, education and elderly care, the Get Into Reading model of weekly read-aloud groups provides a wide range of personal, social and economic benefits.

The Reader Organisation's weekly groups and one-to-one sessions with young people exist to share their love of reading and help them develop their own. Importantly, they offer vital stability for children in the care system, confidence for struggling readers, improved social skills, and a supportive, non-pressured environment for everyone to enjoy reading.

The Reader Organisation believes that reading aloud is not simply a way of getting around reading problems, or something that is only for very young children; it is an experience in its own right, which generates particular and unique responses in individuals and groups, and for people of all ages.

Angela Macmillan is a founding editor of *The Reader* magazine and has worked at The Reader Organisation since its inception.

Michael Morpurgo is one of today's most popular and critically acclaimed children's writers. He has published well over a hundred titles including *Why the Whales Came* (1985), *The Wreck of the Zanzibar* (1995), *The Butterfly Lion* (1996) and *Private Peaceful* (2003). He is perhaps best known as the author of *War Horse* (1982), which the National Theatre has turned into a long-running and internationally successful stage play and which, in 2012, Steven Spielberg made into a film. In 2003, Michael was appointed Children's Laureate and in 2006 was awarded an OBE for services to literature.

A Little, Aloud
for Children

*An anthology of prose and poetry
for reading aloud*

Edited by Angela Macmillan

Foreword by Michael Morpurgo

Illustrations by students of Liverpool
School of Art and Design, LJMU

DOUBLEDAY

A STORIES ALOUD, FOR CHILDREN
DOUBLEDAY BOOK 978 0 857 53417 0

Published in Great Britain by Doubleday,
an imprint of Random House Children's Publishers UK
A Penguin Random House Company

This Doubleday edition published 2014

Copyright © The Reader Organisation, 2012
Forward copyright © Michael Morpurgo, 2012
Illustrations copyright © Liverpool School of Art and Design, LJMU, 2012
and Bonnie Friend, 2012; www.bonniefriend.com

The right of The Reader Organisation to be identified as the author of
this work has been asserted in accordance with the Copyright, Designs and
Patents Act 1988.

The Random House Group Limited supports the Forest Stewardship
Council® (FSC®), the leading international forest-certification organisation.
Our books carrying the FSC label are printed on FSC®-certified paper. FSC
is the only forest-certification scheme supported by the leading environ-
mental organisations, including Greenpeace. Our paper procurement policy
can be found at www.randomhouse.co.uk/environment

MIX
Paper from
responsible sources
FSC® C016897

Set in Adobe Garamond Pro

RANDOM HOUSE CHILDREN'S PUBLISHERS UK
61–63 Uxbridge Road, London W5 5SA

www.**randomhousechildrens**.co.uk
www.**totallyrandombooks**.co.uk
www.**randomhouse**.co.uk

Addresses for companies within The Random House Group Limited can be
found at: www.randomhouse.co.uk/offices.htm

THE RANDOM HOUSE GROUP Limited Reg. No. 954009

A CIP catalogue record for this book is available from the British Library.

Printed and bound in Great Britain by Clays Ltd, St Ives plc

Contents

★★

Foreword

★★

One of my very first memories is of being read to by my mother. It was a magical time when my older brother and I had her to ourselves at the end of the day. Those are the stories that I remember best and love the most to this day. She gave me a precious gift, handed down to me her own love of stories, of the music in the words.

Left to their own devices, with a host of other distractions, a book is the last thing many children will choose to pick up. Many of them have forgotten – or have never been given the idea in the first place – just how pleasurable reading can be. The people at The Reader Organisation want to rediscover or ignite an excitement about reading in children. They want to get them talking about books they've read, swapping and sharing books and stories.

Every week project workers from the organisation go out to read with children and young people in many different settings. Sometimes they read with groups, but often it is simply one-to-one. Their approach is friendly and relaxed with not a hint of a test or an impossible question. Although they go into schools, they rarely sit in a classroom – children need to be shown that first and foremost books are about enjoyment; that learning is a happy, almost effortless by-product.

No one would deny that reading is key to a child's development and fulfilment in life. The benefits of reading, and in particular reading aloud, have been well researched and documented. Reading is the one ability that, once set in motion, has the capacity to feed itself, to grow exponentially, providing a base from which the possibilities are infinite.

Many young children (though by no means all children) enjoy the experience as I did of being read to at bed-time. For all sorts of reasons it is important to carry on reading to children long after they are able to read fluently for themselves. Reading out loud conjures a precious space and a time that is spent exclusively together. A story or a poem can often open up ways of talking about the troubling or the difficult stuff of life. It is sometimes easier to speak of the things that worry or upset us if we can identify them through the character or emotions of a story. Stories help us to feel we are not alone.

A Little, Aloud for Children offers a starting point – a wonderfully varied collection of stories and poems for all ages. Because they are to be read aloud, there is no recommended age – no reason why a parent or grandparent, sister, brother, or friend should not enjoy them as much as the person they are reading to. Neither is there a reason why a child who can read should not turn the tables once in a while and read to an adult.

You will find stories and poems here written two years

ago and a hundred years ago. Some are gripping, some will make you laugh, others might move you to tears. What they all have in common is that they have been tried and tested; read aloud to the delight of children of all ages and backgrounds.

Some of the stories here are extracts from longer novels, which will hopefully tempt the reader to explore the whole work. By reading aloud, you will see how possible it is to embark on great books that might otherwise be considered too difficult for children to tackle themselves.

It is never too early or too late to start. After providing food and shelter, reading to our children and encouraging their own reading is probably the very best thing we can do for them. My own mother showed me that. Reading feeds the imagination, it expands horizons and offers new and exciting ways of seeing and making sense of our lives and of the world around us.

Michael Morpurgo

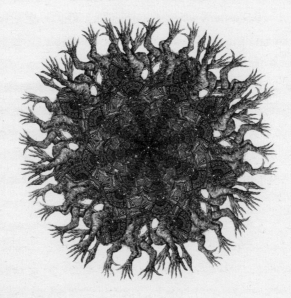

Introduction for Children

★★

I am lucky enough to work for The Reader Organisation, which is all about reading for pleasure. Those of us who work there already know how great reading can be and how amazing it is to lose yourself in the pages of a book. So our job is to go and find the people who don't know about this or who have forgotten about reading or who aren't able to read any more, and then we offer to share great stories and poems, and sometimes cake too.

We began with the idea of having weekly read-aloud groups for adults. It was quite hard to get people to come at first because we wanted the ones who thought they didn't like reading much, and they just said, 'We don't like reading so we don't want to come to your reading group, thank you very much'. But we kept on trying, and even bribed people with tea and cake, and guess what? When we eventually got them to come in and try it, most of them really liked it. I don't mean the cake, though that was very nice, but they liked listening to the stories. They met other people who were also a bit nervous about 'literature', and they made friends. They would say, 'I didn't think I was going to like this but my friend said I should give it a try' or, 'Once I started getting into the story, I just forgot about my bad leg,' or things like that.

More and more groups started; some in libraries or health centres, workplaces, even prisons; some in care homes for the elderly, where very often the residents were not well enough to read for themselves but really enjoyed listening to stories and poems read out loud.

After a while we wondered why we were not doing this for children too. Then we discovered, to our dismay, that hundreds of children do not read for pleasure and have hardly ever been read to (outside school), and were therefore missing out on the best fun. The only thing to do was start a Reading Revolution, which means getting more and more people, adults and children, to read stories and poems, not because they are told to at school or college, but because they want to – for themselves.

Lots of children are suspicious of books. They think books are going to be boring or too difficult. Or they think reading is not cool. I expect you know some of them. Turn to the back of this book and read the Afterword if you would like to hear more about how we start children off on their own reading journeys and how it can change lives.

We want everyone to join our Reading Revolution and read to each other. Just because you can read for yourself doesn't mean that you have to stop listening to stories read by someone else. We want mothers and fathers reading aloud to children, whether their children can read or not; we want sisters and brothers reading together; we want grans and granddads involved, babysitters and family friends. We even want children to read aloud to their friends. Can you imagine that? This anthology is the way to start. It doesn't matter how old you are – nine and a quarter, twelve in two months, seven and two fifths – you will find that the stories and poems in this book can be shared by all ages.

How then, did we go about choosing what went into this special collection? We wanted to include everybody, even the youngest children. Everyone knows they like picture books, but although it wasn't practical for us to include things like *The Hungry Caterpillar* or *Where the Wild Things Are*, it doesn't mean that they can't enjoy stories from this book. A friend of mine has a son of four who is currently obsessed with pirates. His mother is reading *Treasure Island* with him. Of course he can't understand most of it, but it is about pirates, and he recognises things in it – parrots; yo-ho-ho; treasure maps; pirate ships, and Long John Silver of course. All this sitting on his mum's knee with her undivided attention. Wonderful. Another five-year-old girl I know saw the musical film *Oliver!* and decided she wanted to be the Artful Dodger. Her parents read her all the bits about him from the book, which she absolutely loved, and they ended up making a Dodger costume for her which she couldn't bear to take off, not even for school or bed.

Next I asked for recommendations from the people in The Reader Organisation who read with children and young people every day, and they told me the books and poems that their readers enjoy best. Then I asked our publisher, David Fickling, and if anyone should know about great books for children, he should. You will find all these great stories and poems in the anthology. Every one of the pieces had to be good for reading aloud, but even more than that, they had to be brilliant at something. Brilliant at making you laugh, or at making you cry, at making you terrified or making you think something interesting. There are stories about underground worlds, parallel worlds, about monsters, vampires, wolves, some about school or friendship, and one about auditions, not quite like the ones in *The X Factor*, but certainly with the same amount of tears. There are poems about smuggling, convicts, snakes and angels. A few are about feeling sad, lonely or afraid; some are scary and some are joyfully silly.

This book is about sharing. It is full of terrific stories and poems for you to share with someone you like. You can read them by yourself if you want, but sharing a great story out loud can be even better. Try it and see. You could even share some cake too.

Angela Macmillan

P.S. Please will you tell us about how you get on reading to someone or being read to. We would really like to hear about what you read and where, and who shared the book with you and anything else that happened. We have a special website for your messages. Look for www.alittlealoud.com, and when you get there, just click on the 'for children' button. We will answer you.

How to Use This Book

★★

There isn't a right or wrong way to use this book. It is your book, so you can do what you want, read what you want, in the way that you want. I would just like to let you know some of the thinking behind this anthology of stories and poems for reading aloud. We hope that, if you have got out of the habit of reading aloud or listening to stories, or if you have never really done it before, this book will be a good place to begin.

The collection is divided into reading sessions. Each one has a story and a poem that go together under a loose theme. For example, under the heading EXCUSES, EXCUSES, the extract from *Tom Sawyer*, which was written more than one hundred years ago, is all about a boy trying to think of ways of getting out of going to school. The poem that goes with it is modern, and is a conversation between a boy and his teacher in which the boy makes up excuses for not doing his homework. When you have read them both, I hope you will find that one makes you think something more about the other.

None of the stories will take longer than half an hour to read aloud, which makes them perfect for reading before bed or when you are travelling, or just in any spare moments of the day. I have given very approximate reading times, but this will depend on how fast or slow you read, and how often you break off to talk about what is going on. You don't have to keep reading from start to finish. Stopping occasionally to talk to the person you are reading with makes you enjoy it even more.

When you read with someone else, you often end up reading something you would never have read on your own. Say your dad suggests you read *White Fang* together because it is about wolves and he's really interested in wolves, but you think you are not really into books about animals. You may find you like it after all, in which case you have gained something new and un-expected. And if you don't like it that much (but I bet you will) – well, it hasn't taken up much of your day and you have put your dad in a good mood.

If you feel a bit self-conscious about reading aloud, just remember that you are not putting on a grand perform-ance but simply bringing words on a page to life. Think about what you are reading rather than yourself, and the life in the words will come out in your voice. Remember that when you read aloud, slow is best. You can have great fun with these stories and poems, and don't worry if you can't do accents. When I try to do a Scottish accent I usually end up in Wales or Pakistan, and my American accent is rubbish, but it doesn't stop me giving it a go.

Some of the stories in the anthology are extracts from longer books. Hopefully they will act as little tempting morsels, good to read by themselves but so enjoyable that you have to rush off to the library or bookshop and gobble up the rest of the story.

Finally, at the end of the anthology, there is a list of books that have persuaded older children to get into reading.

Angela Macmillan, The Reader Organisation

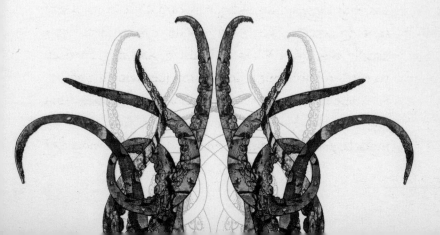

Instructions

★★

Neil Gaiman

Touch the wooden gate in the wall you never saw
    before.
Say 'please' before you open the latch,
go through,
walk down the path.
A red metal imp hangs from
    the green-painted front door,
as a knocker,
do not touch it; it will bite your fingers.
Walk through the house. Take nothing. Eat nothing.
However,
if any creature tells you that it hungers,
feed it.
If it tells you that it is dirty,
clean it.
If it cries to you that it hurts,
if you can,
ease its pain.
From the back garden you will be able to see the
    wild wood.

The deep well you walk past leads to Winter's realm;
there is another land at the bottom of it.
If you turn around here,
you can walk back, safely;
you will lose no face. I will think no less of you.

Once through the garden you will be in the wood.
The trees are old. Eyes peer from the undergrowth.
Beneath a twisted oak sits an old woman.
     She may ask for something;
give it to her. She
will point the way to the castle. Inside it
are three princesses.
Do not trust the youngest. Walk on.
In the clearing beyond the castle the
     twelve months sit about a fire,
warming their feet, exchanging tales.
They may do favors for you, if you are polite.
You may pick strawberries in December's frost.
Trust the wolves, but do not tell them
     where you are going.
The river can be crossed by the ferry.
     The ferryman will take you.
(The answer to his question is this:
If he hands the oar to his passenger, he will be free to
     leave the boat.
Only tell him this from a safe distance.)

If an eagle gives you a feather, keep it safe.

Remember: that giants sleep too soundly; that
witches are often betrayed by their appetites;
dragons have one soft spot, somewhere,
    always;
hearts can be well hidden,
and you betray them with your tongue.
Do not be jealous of your sister:
know that diamonds and roses
are as uncomfortable when they tumble
    from one's lips as toads and frogs:
colder, too, and sharper, and they cut.

Remember your name.
Do not lose hope – what you seek will be
    found.
Trust ghosts. Trust those that you have
    helped to help you in their turn.
Trust dreams.
Trust your heart, and trust your story.

When you come back, return the way you
    came.
Favors will be returned, debts be repaid.
Do not forget your manners.
Do not look back.
Ride the wise eagle (you shall not fall)
Ride the silver fish (you will not drown)
Ride the grey wolf (hold tightly to his fur).

There is a worm at the heart of the tower;
    that is why it will not stand.

When you reach the little house, the
    place your journey started,
you will recognize it, although it will seem
    much smaller than you remember.
Walk up the path, and through the garden
    gate you never saw before but once.
And then go home. Or make a home.

Or rest.

Sailing Away

The Stowaways

★★

EXTRACT

Roger McGough

(approximate reading time 10 minutes)

When I lived in Liverpool, my best friend was a boy called Midge. Kevin Midgeley was his real name, but we called him Midge for short. And he was short, only about three cornflake boxes high (empty ones at that). No three ways about it. Midge was my best friend and we had lots of things in common. Things we enjoyed doing like . . . climbing trees, playing footy, going to the movies, hitting each other really hard. And there were things we didn't enjoy doing like . . . sums, washing behind our ears, eating cabbage.

But there was one thing that really bound us together, one thing we had in common – a love of the sea.

In the old days (but not so long ago), the river Mersey was far busier than it is today. Those were the days of the great passenger liners and cargo boats. Large ships sailed out of Liverpool for Canada, the United States, South Africa, the West Indies, all over the world. My father had been to sea and so had all my uncles, and my grandfather.

Six foot six, muscles rippling in the wind, huge hands grappling with the helm, rum-soaked and fierce as a wounded shark (and that was only my grandmother!). By the time they were twenty, most young men in this city had visited parts of the globe I can't even spell.

In my bedroom each night, I used to lie in bed (best place to lie really), I used to lie there, especially in winter, and listen to the foghorns being sounded all down the river. I could picture the ship nosing its way out of the docks into the channel and out into the Irish Sea. It was exciting. All those exotic places. All those exciting adventures.

Midge and I knew what we wanted to do when we left school . . . become sailors. A captain, an admiral, perhaps one day even a steward. Of course we were only about seven or eight at the time so we thought we'd have a long time to wait. But oddly enough, the call of the sea came sooner than we'd expected.

It was a Wednesday if I remember rightly. I never liked Wednesdays for some reason. I could never spell it for a start and it always seemed to be raining, and there were still two days to go before the weekend. Anyway, Midge and I got into trouble at school. I don't remember what for (something trivial I suppose like chewing gum in class, forgetting how to read, setting fire to the music teacher), I forget now. But we were picked on, nagged, told off and all those boring things that grown-ups get up to sometimes.

And, of course, to make matters worse, my mum and

dad were in a right mood when I got home. Nothing to do with me, of course, because as you have no doubt gathered by now, I was the perfect child: clean, well-mannered, obedient . . . soft in the head. But for some reason I was clipped round the ear and sent to bed early for being childish. Childish! I ask you. I *was* a child. A child acts his age, what does he get? Wallop!

So that night in bed, I decided . . . Yes, you've guessed it. I could hear the big ships calling out to each other as they sidled out of the Mersey into the oceans beyond. The tugs leading the way like proud little guide dogs. That's it. We'd run away to sea, Midge and I. I'd tell him the good news in the morning.

The next two days just couldn't pass quickly enough for us. We had decided to begin our amazing around-the-world voyage on Saturday morning so that in case we didn't like it we would be back in time for school on Monday. As you can imagine there was a lot to think about – what clothes to take, how much food and drink. We decided on two sweaters each and wellies in case we ran into storms around Cape Horn. I read somewhere that sailors lived off rum and dry biscuits, so I poured some of my dad's into an empty pop bottle, and

RUM?
YUCK.

borrowed a handful of half-coated chocolate digestives. I also packed my lonestar cap gun and Midge settled on a magnifying glass.

On Friday night we met round at his house to make the final plans. He lived with his granny and his sister, so there were no nosy parents to discover what we were up to. We hid all the stuff in the shed in the yard and arranged to meet outside his back door next morning at the crack of dawn, or sunrise – whichever came first.

Sure enough, Saturday morning, when the big finger was on twelve and the little one was on six, Midge and I met with our little bundles under our arms and ran up the street as fast as our tiptoes could carry us.

Hardly anyone was about, and the streets were so quiet and deserted except for a few pigeons straddling home after all-night parties. It was a very strange feeling, as if we were the only people alive and the city belonged entirely to us. And soon the world would be ours as well – once we'd stowed away on a ship bound for somewhere far off and exciting.

By the time we'd got down to the Pier Head, though, a lot more people were up and about, including a police-man who eyed us suspiciously. 'Ello, Ello, Ello,' he said, 'and where are you two going so early in the morning?'

'Fishing,' I said.

'Train spotting,' said Midge and we looked at each other.

'Just so long as you're not running away to sea.'

'Oh no,' we chorused. 'Just as if.'

He winked at us. 'Off you go then, and remember to look both ways before crossing your eyes.'

We ran off and straight down on to the landing stage where a lot of ships were tied up. There was no time to lose because already quite a few were putting out to sea, their sirens blowing, the hundreds of seagulls squeaking excitedly, all tossed into the air like giant handfuls of confetti.

Then I noticed a small ship just to the left where the crew were getting ready to cast off. They were so busy doing their work that it was easy for Midge and me to slip on board unnoticed. Up the gang-plank we went and straight up on to the top deck where there was nobody around. The sailors were all busy down below, hauling in the heavy ropes and revving up the engine that turned the great propellers.

We looked around for somewhere to hide. 'I know, let's climb down the funnel,' said Midge.

'Great idea,' I said, taking the mickey. 'Or, better still, let's disguise ourselves as a pair of seagulls and perch up there on the mast.'

Then I spotted them. The lifeboats. 'Quick, let's climb into one of those, they'll never look in there – not unless we run into icebergs anyway.' So in we climbed, and no sooner had we covered ourselves with the tarpaulin than there was a great shuddering and the whole ship seemed to turn round on itself. We were off! Soon we'd be digging for diamonds in the Brazilian jungle or building sandcastles on a tropical island. But we had to be patient, we knew that. Those places are a long way away, it could take days, even months.

So we were patient. Very patient. Until after what seemed like hours and hours we decided to eat our rations, which I divided up equally. I gave Midge all the rum and I had all the biscuits. Looking back on it now, that probably wasn't a good idea, especially for Midge.

What with the rolling of the ship and not having had any breakfast, and the excitement, and a couple of swigs of rum – well you can guess what happened – woooorrppp! All over the place. We pulled back the sheet and decided to give ourselves up. We were too far away at sea now for the captain to turn back. The worst he could do was to clap us in irons or shiver our timbers.

We climbed down on to the deck and as Midge staggered to the nearest rail to feed the fishes, I looked out to sea hoping to catch sight of a whale, a shoal of dolphins, perhaps see the coast of America coming in to view. And what did I see? The Liver Buildings.

Anyone can make a mistake can't they? I mean, we weren't to know we'd stowed away on a ferryboat.

One that goes from Liverpool to Birkenhead and back again, toing and froing across the Mersey. We'd done four trips hidden in the lifeboat and ended up back in Liverpool. And we'd only been away about an hour and a half. 'Ah well, so much for running away to sea,' we thought as we disembarked (although disembowelled might be a better word as far as Midge was concerned). Rum? Yuck.

We got the bus home. My mum and dad were having

their breakfast. 'Aye, aye,' said my dad, 'here comes the early bird. And what have you been up to then?'

'I ran away to sea,' I said.

'Mm, that's nice,' said my mum, shaking out the corn-flakes. 'That's nice.'

The Jumblies

★★

Edward Lear

They went to sea in a Sieve, they did,
  In a Sieve they went to sea:
In spite of all their friends could say,
On a winter's morn, on a stormy day,
  In a Sieve they went to sea!
And when the Sieve turned round and round,
And every one cried, 'You'll all be drowned!'
They called aloud, 'Our Sieve ain't big,
But we don't care a button! we don't care a fig!
  In a Sieve we'll go to sea!'
    Far and few, far and few,
      Are the lands where the Jumblies live;
      Their heads are green, and their hands are blue,
      And they went to sea in a Sieve.

They sailed away in a Sieve, they did,
  In a Sieve they sailed so fast,
With only a beautiful pea-green veil
Tied with a riband by way of a sail,
  To a small tobacco-pipe mast;

And every one said, who saw them go,
'O won't they be soon upset, you know!
For the sky is dark, and the voyage is long,
And happen what may, it's extremely wrong
   In a Sieve to sail so fast!'
      Far and few, far and few,
        Are the lands where the Jumblies live;
       Their heads are green, and their hands are blue,
        And they went to sea in a Sieve.

The water it soon came in, it did,
   The water it soon came in;
So to keep them dry, they wrapped their feet
In a pinky paper all folded neat,
   And they fastened it down with a pin.
And they passed the night in a crockery-jar,
And each of them said, 'How wise we are!
Though the sky be dark, and the voyage be long,
Yet we never can think we were rash or wrong,
   While round in our Sieve we spin!'
      Far and few, far and few,
        Are the lands where the Jumblies live;
       Their heads are green, and their hands are blue,
        And they went to sea in a Sieve.

And all night long they sailed away;
   And when the sun went down,
They whistled and warbled a moony song
To the echoing sound of a coppery gong,

In the shade of the mountains brown.
'O Timballo! How happy we are,
When we live in a sieve and a crockery-jar,
And all night long in the moonlight pale,
We sail away with a pea-green sail,
    In the shade of the mountains brown!'
        Far and few, far and few,
            Are the lands where the Jumblies live;
        Their heads are green, and their hands are blue,
            And they went to sea in a Sieve.

They sailed to the Western Sea, they did,
    To a land all covered with trees,
And they bought an Owl, and a useful Cart,
And a pound of Rice, and a Cranberry Tart,
    And a hive of silvery Bees.
And they bought a Pig, and some green Jack-daws,
And a lovely Monkey with lollipop paws,
And forty bottles of Ring-Bo-Ree,
    And no end of Stilton Cheese.
        Far and few, far and few,
            Are the lands where the Jumblies live;
        Their heads are green, and their hands are blue,
            And they went to sea in a Sieve.

And in twenty years they all came back,
    In twenty years or more,
And every one said, 'How tall they've grown!
For they've been to the Lakes, and the Torrible Zone,

And the hills of the Chankly Bore;'
And they drank their health, and gave them a feast
Of dumplings made of beautiful yeast;
And every one said, 'If we only live,
We too will go to sea in a Sieve, –
To the hills of the Chankly Bore!'
Far and few, far and few,
Are the lands where the Jumblies live;
Their heads are green, and their hands are blue,
And they went to sea in a Sieve.

Be on your Guard

The Wolves of Willoughby Chase

★★

CHAPTER TWO

Joan Aiken

(approximate reading time 19 minutes)

Sylvia was an orphan, both her parents having been carried off by a fever when she was only an infant. She lived with her Aunt Jane, who was now becoming very aged and frail and had written to Sir Willoughby to suggest that he took on the care of the little girl. He had agreed at once to this proposal, for Sylvia, he knew, was delicate, and the country air would do her good. Besides, he welcomed the idea of her gentle companionship for his rather harum-scarum Bonnie.

Aunt Jane and Sylvia shared a room at the top of a house. It was in Park Lane, this being the only street in which Aunt Jane could consider living. Unfortunately, as she was very poor, she could afford to rent only a tiny attic in such a genteel district. The room was divided into two by a very beautiful, but old, curtain of white Chinese brocade. She and Sylvia each had half the room at night, Aunt

Jane sleeping on the divan and Sylvia on the ottoman. During the daytime the curtain was drawn back and hung elegantly looped against the wall. They cooked their meals over the gas jet, and had baths in a large enamelled Chinese bowl, covered with dragons, an heirloom of Aunt Jane's. At other times it stood on a little occasional table by the door and was used for visiting cards.

They were making Sylvia's clothes.

Aunt Jane, with tears running down her face, had taken down the white curtain (which would no longer be needed) and was cutting it up. Fortunately it was large enough to afford material for several chemises, petticoats, pantalettes, dresses, and even a bonnet. Aunt Jane, mopping her eyes with a tiny shred of the material, murmured:

'I do like to see a little girl dressed all in white.'

'I *wish* we needn't cut up your curtain, Auntie,' said Sylvia, who hated to see her aunt so distressed. 'When I'm thirty-five and come into my money, I shall buy you a whole set of white brocade curtains.'

'There's my angel,' her aunt replied, embracing her. 'But when you are thirty-five I shall be a hundred and three,' and she set to work making the tucks in a petticoat with thousands of tiny stitches. Sylvia sighed, and bent her fair head over another, with stitches almost equally tiny. She was a little depressed – though she would not dream of saying so – at the idea of wearing nothing but white, especially at her cousin Bonnie's, where everything was sure to be grand and handsome.

'Now let me think,' muttered Aunt Jane, sewing away like lightning. 'What can we use to make you a travelling-cloak?'

She paused for a moment and glanced round the room, at the lovingly tended pieces of Sheraton and Hepplewhite furniture, the antimacassars, the Persian screen across the gas-jet kitchen. The window curtains were too threadbare to use – and in any case one must have window curtains. At last she recollected an old green velvet shawl which they sometimes used as an extra bed-cover when it was very cold and they slept together on the ottoman.

'I can use my jet-trimmed mantle instead,' she said reassuringly to Sylvia. 'After all, one person cannot be so cold as two.'

By the day of departure, all the clothes had been finished. Nothing much could be done about Sylvia's shoes, which were deplorably shabby, but Aunt Jane blacked them with a mixture of soot and candle grease, and Sylvia's bonnet was trimmed with a white plume from the ostrich-feather fan which her aunt had carried at her coming-out ball. All Sylvia's belongings were neatly packed into an old carpet-bag, and Aunt Jane had made her up a little packet of provisions for the journey, though with strict injunctions not to eat them if there were anyone else in the compartment.

'For ladies *never* eat in public.'

They were too poor to take a hackney-carriage to the station, and Aunt Jane always refused to travel in omnibuses, so they walked, carrying the bag between them. Fortunately the station was not far, nor the bag heavy.

Aunt Jane secured a corner seat for her charge, and put her under the care of the guard.

'Now remember, my dear child,' she said, kissing Sylvia and looking suspiciously round the empty compartment, 'never speak to strangers, tip all the servants immediately (I have put all the farthings from my reticule at the bottom of your valise); do not model yourself on your cousin Bonnie, who I believe is a dear good child but a little wild; give my fond regards to my brother Willoughby and tell him that I am in the pink of health and *amply* provided for; and if anyone except the guard speaks to you, pull the communication cord.'

'Yes, Auntie,' replied Sylvia dutifully, embracing her. She felt a pang as she saw the frail old figure struggling away through the crowd, and wondered how her Aunt Jane would manage that evening without her little niece to adjust her curl-papers and read aloud a page of Dr Johnson's Dictionary.

Then all Sylvia's fears were aroused, for a strange man entered the compartment and sat down. He did not speak, however, and took no notice of her, and, the train shortly afterwards departing, her thoughts were diverted into a less apprehensive vein as she watched the unfamiliar houses with their lighted windows flying past.

It was to be a long journey – a night and a day. The hour of departure was six o'clock in the evening, and Sylvia knew that she did not arrive at her destination until about eight of the following evening. What strange forests, towns, mountains, and stretches of countryside would they not have passed by then, as the train proceeded at its steady fifteen miles an hour! She had never been out of London before, and watched eagerly from her window until they had left the houses behind, and she was driven to study the toes of her own shoes, so lovingly polished by Aunt Jane.

The thought of the old lady, carefully preparing for her solitary slumbers, was too much for Sylvia, and tears began to run silently down her cheeks, which she endeavoured to mop with her tiny handkerchief (made from a spare two inches of white brocade).

'Here, this won't do,' said a voice in her ear suddenly, and she looked up in alarm to see that the man at the other end of the compartment had moved along and was sitting opposite and staring at her. Sylvia gave her eyes a final dab and haughtily concentrated on her reflection in the dark window, but her heart was racing. Should she pull the communication cord? She stole a cautious glance at the man's reflection and saw that he was standing up, apparently extracting something from a large leather portmanteau. Then he turned towards her, holding something out: she looked round enough to see that it was a box of chocolates about a foot square by six inches deep, swathed around with violet ribbons.

'No, thank you,' said Sylvia, in as ladylike a tone as she could muster. 'I never touch chocolate.' All the same, she had to swallow rapidly a couple of times, for the tea which she had shared with Aunt Jane before the journey, although very refined, had not been substantial – two pieces of thin bread-and-butter, a cinnamon wafer, and a sliver of caraway cake.

She knew better, however, than to accept food from strangers, and as to opening her own little packet while he was in the carriage – that was out of the question. She shook her head again.

'Now come along – do,' said the man coaxingly. 'All little girls like sweeties, *I* know.'

'Sir,' said Sylvia coldly, 'if you speak to me again I shall be obliged to pull the communication cord.'

He sighed and put away the box. Her relief over this was premature, however, for he turned round next minute with a confectioners' pasteboard carton filled with every imaginable variety of little cakes – there were jam tarts, maids of honour, lemon cheese cakes, Chelsea buns, and numerous little iced confections in brilliant and enticing colours.

'I always put up a bit of tiffin for a journey,' he murmured as if to himself, and, placing the box on the seat directly opposite Sylvia, he selected a cake covered with violet icing and bit into it. It appeared to be filled with jam. Sylvia looked straight ahead and ignored him, but again she had to swallow.

'Now my dear, how about one of these little odds and ends?' said the man. 'I can't possibly eat them all by myself – can I?'

Sylvia stood up and looked for the communication cord. It was out of her reach.

'Shall I pull it for you?' inquired her fellow-traveller politely, following the direction of her eyes upwards. Sylvia did not reply to him. She did not feel, though, that it would be ladylike to climb up on the seat or arm-rest to pull the cord herself, so she sat down again, biting her lip with anxiety. To her inexpressible relief the stranger, after eating three or four more cakes with every appearance of enjoyment, put the box back in his portmanteau, wrapped himself in a richly furred cloak, retired to his own corner, and shut his eyes. A subdued but regular snore soon issuing from his partly-opened mouth presently convinced Sylvia that he was asleep, and she began to breathe more freely. At length she brought out from concealment under her mantle her most treasured possession, and held it lovingly in her arms.

This was a doll named Annabelle, made of wood, not much larger than a candle, and plainly dressed, but extremely dear to Sylvia. She and Annabelle had no secrets from one another, and it was a great comfort to her to have this companion as the train rocked on through the unfamiliar dark.

Presently she grew drowsy and fell into uneasy slumber, but not for long; it was bitterly cold and her feet in their thin shoes felt like lumps of ice. She huddled into her corner and wrapped herself in the green cloak, envying her companion his thick furs and undisturbed repose, and wishing it were ladylike to curl her feet up beneath her on the seat. Unfortunately she knew better than that.

She dreamed, without being really asleep, of arctic seas,

of monstrous tunnels through hillsides fringed with icicles. Her travelling companion, who had grown a long tail and a pair of horns, offered her cakes the size of grand pianos and coloured scarlet, blue and green; when she bit into them she found they were made of snow.

She woke suddenly from one of these dreams to find that the train had stopped with a jerk.

'Oh! What is it? Where are we?' she exclaimed before she could stop herself.

'No need to alarm yourself, miss,' said her companion, looking unavailingly out of the black square of window. 'Wolves on the line, most likely – they often have trouble of that kind hereabouts.'

'Wolves!' Sylvia stared at him in terror.

'They don't often get into the train, though,' he added reassuringly. 'Two years ago they managed to climb into the guard's van and eat a pig, and once they got the engine-driver – another had to be sent in a relief-engine – but they don't often eat a passenger, I promise you.'

As if in contradiction of his words a sad and sinister howling now arose beyond the windows, and Sylvia, pressing her face against the dark pane, saw that they were passing through a thickly wooded region where snow lay deep on the ground. Across this white carpet she could just discern a ragged multitude pouring, out of which arose, from time to time, this terrible cry. She was almost petrified with fear and sat clutching Annabelle in a cold and trembling hand. At length she summoned up strength to whisper:

'Why don't we go on?'

'Oh, I expect there are too many of 'em on the line ahead,' the man answered carelessly. 'Can't just push through them, you see – the engine would be derailed in no time, and then we *should* be in a bad way. No, I expect we'll have to wait here till daylight now – the wolves get scared then, you know, and make for home. All that matters is that the driver shan't get eaten in the meantime – he'll keep 'em off by throwing lumps of coal at them I dare say.'

'Oh!' Sylvia exclaimed in irrepressible alarm, as a heavy body thudded suddenly against the window, and she had a momentary view of a pointed grey head, red slavering jaws, and pale eyes gleaming with ferocity.

'Oh, don't worry about that,' soothed her companion. 'They'll keep up that jumping against the windows for hours. They're not much danger, you know, singly; it's only in the whole pack you've got to watch out for 'em.'

Sylvia was not much comforted by this. She moved along to the middle of the seat and huddled there, glancing fearfully first to one side and then to the other. The strange man seemed quite undisturbed by the repeated onslaught of the wolves which followed. He took a pinch of snuff, remarked that it was all a great nuisance and they would be late, and composed himself to sleep again.

He had just begun to snore when a discomposing incident occurred. The window beside him, which must have been insecurely fastened, was not proof against the continuous impact of the frenzied and ravenous animals. The catch suddenly slipped, and the window fell open with a crash, its glass shivering into fragments.

Sylvia screamed. Another instant, and a wolf pre-
cipitated itself through the aperture thus formed. It turned
snarling on the sleeping stranger, who started awake with
an oath, and very adroitly flung his cloak over the animal.
He then seized one of the shattered pieces of glass lying on
the floor and stabbed the imprisoned beast through the
cloak. It fell dead.

'Tush,' said Sylvia's companion, breathing heavily and
passing his hand over his face. 'Unexpected – most.'

He extracted the dead wolf from the folds of the cloak
and tipped its body, with some exertion, out through the
broken window. There was a chorus of snarling and yelp-
ing outside, and then the wolves seemed to take fright at
the appearance of their dead comrade, for Sylvia saw them
coursing away over the snow.

'Come, that's capital,' said the man. 'We'd better shift
before they come back.'

'Shift?'

'Into another compartment,' he explained. 'Can't stay
in this one now – too cold for one thing, and for another,
have wolves popping in the whole time – nuisance. No,
come along, now's the time to do it.'

Sylvia was most reluctant, and indeed almost too
terrified to accompany him, but she saw the force of his
proposal and watched anxiously as he opened the door and
glanced this way and that.

'Right! Just pass me out those bags, will you?' He had
placed both his and hers ready on the seat. She passed

them out. Holding them in one hand, he made his way sideways along the footboard to the next carriage door, which he opened. He tossed in the bags, returned for his cloak and rug, and finally reappeared and held out his hand to Sylvia.

'Come along now, my dear, if you don't want to be made into wolf-porridge,' he exclaimed with frightening joviality, and Sylvia timorously permitted him to assist her along the narrow ledge and into the next carriage. It was with a sense of unbounded relief and thankfulness that she heard him slam the door and make sure that the windows were securely fastened.

'Excellent,' he remarked with a smile at Sylvia which bared every tooth in his head. 'Now we can have another forty winks,' and he wrapped himself up again in his cloak, careless of any wolf gore that might remain on its folds, and shut his eyes.

Sylvia was too cold and terrified to sleep. She crouched, as before, in the middle of the seat – icy, shivering, and expecting at any minute to hear the wolves recommence their attack against the window.

'Here, we can't have this,' said a disapproving voice, and she turned to see the man awake again and scrutinizing her closely. 'Not warm enough, eh? Here . . .' and then as he saw her wince away from his cloak, he unstrapped a warm plaid travelling rug and insisted on wrapping her in it. Tired, frozen, and frightened, Sylvia was unable to resist him any longer.

'Put your feet up and lie down,' he ordered. 'That's right. Now shut your eyes. No more wolves for the time being – they've been scared away. Off to sleep with you.'

Sylvia was beginning to be deliciously warm. Her last recollection was of hearing his snores begin again.

In Black Chasms

★★

Leslie Norris

In black chasms, in caves where water
Drops and drips, in pits deep under the ground,
The ogres wait. A thousand years will not
Alter them. They are hideous, bad-tempered,
Bound only to be cruel, enemies of all.
Slow-moving, lazy, their long hard arms
Are strong as bulldozers, their red eyes
Gleam with deceit. When they smile,
It is not with kindness. In their language
They have no words for friendship, honesty,
Loyalty, generosity. Their names are
Bully, Slyness, Greed, Vandal and Cunning.
They hate light, and quarrel among themselves.
A single ogre will pass by, or only threaten
In his loud, rough voice, but they are dangerous
In packs. Be on your guard against them, keep
Always a brave front, value your friends,
For they are needed against ogres.

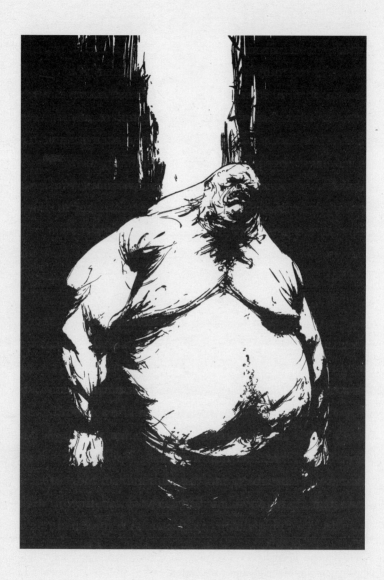

Diving Deep

Broken Toys

★★

FROM *TALES FROM OUTER SUBURBIA*

Shaun Tan

(approximate reading time 7 minutes)

I know you think you saw him first, but I'm pretty sure it was me – he was over there by the underpass, feeling his way along the graffiti-covered wall and, I said, 'Look, there's something you don't see every day.'

Well, we'd certainly seen crazy people before – 'shell-shocked by life' as you once put it. But something pretty strange must have happened to this guy to make him decide to wander about in a spacesuit on a dead-quiet public holiday. We hid behind a postbox to get a better look. Up close it was even more perplexing, the spacesuit was covered in barnacles and sea-stuff, and dripping wet in spite of the fierce summer heat.

'It's not a spacesuit, stupid,' you whispered. 'It's that old-fashioned diving gear, from the pearlers up north. You know, in the olden days, when they got the *bends* because they didn't know about decompressification and how it turns your blood into lemonade.' You sighed loudly at my blank look and said, 'Never mind.'

But, as we stealthily followed our crazy person, I could tell you were right, because of the helmet, and the long air hose dragging behind.

He shuffled aimlessly across the empty football oval, past the petrol station and up and down people's driveways. He plodded around the edge of the closed corner deli, feeling along walls and windows as if sleepwalking, leaving big wet glove-prints that dried to ghostly patches of salt.

You said, 'I'll give you *ten bucks* to go and say hello.'

I said, 'No way.'

'We'll both go then.'

'Okay.'

We crept closer. The smell was weird, like the ocean, I suppose, but with some other sweet odour that was hard to identify. Red dust had collected in the creases of the suit, as though he had been through a desert as well as an ocean.

We were strategically planning our opening remarks when the dull, scratched face-plate turned towards us and said something we couldn't make out. The diver moved forwards, creaking, babbling. We backed off.

'Crazy talk,' I said.

But you listened carefully and shook your head. 'Nah, I think it's . . . *Japanese*.'

He was saying the same sentence over and over – ending with something like 'tasoo-ke-te, tasoo-ke-te.' And he was holding out one hand to show us a little wooden horse, which might once have been golden and shiny, but was now cracked and sun-bleached, held together with string.

'Maybe we should take him to Mrs Bad News,' you suggested, meaning old Mrs Katayama, the only Japanese person we knew in our neighbourhood.

'No way,' I said, and my raised eyebrows referred to our all-too-recent confrontation over the back fence, best described as a barrage of incomprehensible abuse followed by the return of our model aeroplane sliced neatly in half – a further addition to our box of stray toys that had fallen into the old crone's backyard and come back dissected. These were the only times we ever saw her, hence, 'Mrs Bad News'.

Your raised eyebrows referred to exactly the same thing, but also signalled the flash of a brilliant idea. Why not lead a crazy man in a diving suit to Mrs Katayama's front yard, and lock him in? Nothing more needed to be said. We did the Special Handshake of Unbreakable Agreement.

You reached out to take the diver's enormous gloved hand, then suddenly recoiled – 'It was so weird and slimy,' you explained later – yet our guy understood enough to follow, shuffling along footpaths, across roads and down back-alley short-cuts. His long, wheezy breathing grew louder each time we stopped to let him catch up. He plodded behind us as if every joint ached, with that big hose dragging behind, trickling a seemingly endless supply of water from its frayed end. It gave me the creeps.

Finally we arrived at the dreaded house with the overgrown cherry trees. We ushered our guest through the front gate, which we had long ago figured out how to unlock. The weathered steps creaked under his weight. You rattled the flyscreen door, and then we both got the hell out of there. We snapped the gate shut behind us, barely able to suppress our giggles, and ran behind the phone booth on the other side of the road to behold the unfolding drama.

We waited and waited.

And waited.

'This sucks,' you eventually admitted, remembering that Mrs Bad News never opened her door, even though she was always home. We had often joked that the door was painted onto the front wall. We had tried knocking once before, and she had just yelled, 'Who Is There?' and then 'Go Away!' Such was the experience of our diver friend on this occasion. But he did not move, perhaps because he did not understand, so there was still hope for entertainment.

Suddenly the diver reached up, removed his heavy helmet and let it slip from his hands to the wooden boards with a loud bang that make us jump. Even from behind we could see he was a young man with neatly combed hair, shiny black. A far more surprising sight was the front door opening, and the frail silhouette of Mrs Bad News peeking through.

The diver said those Japanese words again and held out the toy horse. He was blocking our view so we couldn't see much, except Mrs Bad News covering her mouth with both hands. She looked like she was about to faint from terror. We couldn't believe our luck.

'Hang on a sec,' you said, squinting, 'I think she's . . . *crying*!' And indeed she was – standing in her doorway, sobbing uncontrollably.

Had we gone too far?

We actually started feeling *bad* for her . . . But then her pale matchstick arms flew out and wrapped around the wet, barnacled figure on her doorstep. We didn't see what happened next because we were too busy comparing our raised eyebrows of disbelief. Then the flyscreen door slapped shut and there was only the dark rectangle of the doorway, with the diving helmet sitting in a puddle of water.

We waited a long time, but nothing else happened.

'I guess she knew him,' I said as we walked home around the corner.

We never found out who the diver was, or what happened to him. But we had started hearing old-style jazz wafting over the back fence late in the evenings, and we noticed funny cooking smells and soft-spoken voices in animated conversation. And we stopped hating Mrs Katayama after that, because she would come all the way around to our front door with a quiet nod and a quick smile, returning our stray toys just as we had lost them – all in one piece.

Ariel's Song

★★

FROM *THE TEMPEST*

William Shakespeare

Full fathom five thy father lies:
   Of his bones are coral made;
Those are pearls that were his eyes;
   Nothing of him that doth fade,
But doth suffer a sea-change
Into something rich and strange,
Sea-nymphs hourly ring his knell:
   Ding-dong.
Hark! now I hear them, ding-dong, bell.

Charming Creatures

How the Rhinoceros Got His Skin

★★

FROM *JUST SO STORIES*

Rudyard Kipling

(approximate reading time 5 minutes)

Once upon a time, on an uninhabited island on the shores of the Red Sea, there lived a Parsee from whose hat the rays of the sun were reflected in more-than-oriental splendour. And the Parsee lived by the Red Sea with nothing but his hat and his knife and a cooking-stove of the kind that you must particularly never touch. And one day he took flour and water and currants and plums and sugar and things, and made himself one cake which was two feet across and three feet thick. It was indeed a Superior Comestible (*that's* magic), and he put it on the stove because *he* was allowed to cook on that stove, and he baked it and he baked it till it was all done brown and smelt most sentimental. But just as he was going to eat it there came down to the beach from the Altogether Uninhabited Interior one Rhinoceros with a horn on his nose, two piggy eyes, and few manners. In those days the

Rhinoceros's skin fitted him quite tight. There were no wrinkles in it anywhere. He looked exactly like a Noah's Ark Rhinoceros, but of course much bigger. All the same, he had no manners then, and he has no manners now, and he never will have any manners. He said, 'How!' and the Parsee left that cake and climbed to the top of a palm-tree with nothing on but his hat; from which the rays of the sun were always reflected in more-than-oriental splendour. And the Rhinoceros upset the oil-stove with his nose, and the cake rolled on the sand, and he spiked that cake on the horn of his nose, and he ate it, and he went away, waving his tail, to the desolate and Exclusively Uninhabited Interior which abuts on the islands of Mazanderan, Socotra, and Promontories of the Larger Equinox. Then the Parsee came down from his palm-tree and put the stove on its legs and recited the following *Sloka*, which, as you have not heard, I will now proceed to relate –

'Them that takes cakes
Which the Parsee-man bakes
Makes dreadful mistakes.'

And there was a great deal more in that than you
would think.

Because, five weeks later, there was a heatwave in the
Red Sea, and everybody took off all the clothes they had.
The Parsee took off his hat; but the Rhinoceros took off
his skin and carried it over his shoulder as he came down
to the beach to bathe. In those days it buttoned
underneath with three buttons and looked like a
waterproof. He said nothing whatever about the Parsee's
cake, because he had eaten it all; and he never had any
manners, then, since, or henceforward. He waddled
straight into the water and blew bubbles through his nose,
leaving his skin on the beach.

Presently the Parsee came by and found the skin, and
he smiled one smile that ran all round his face two times.
Then he danced three times round the skin and rubbed his
hands. Then he went to his camp and filled his hat with
cake-crumbs, for the Parsee never ate anything but cake,
and never swept out his camp. He took that skin, and he
shook that skin, and he scrubbed that skin, and he rubbed
that skin just as full of old, dry, stale, tickly cake-crumbs
and some burned currants as ever it could *possibly* hold.
Then he climbed to the top of his palm-tree and waited for
the Rhinoceros to come out of the water and put it on.

And the Rhinoceros did. He buttoned it up with the

three buttons, and it tickled like cake-crumbs in bed. Then he wanted to scratch, but that made it worse; and then he lay down on the sands and rolled and rolled and rolled, and every time he rolled the cake-crumbs tickled him worse and worse and worse. Then he ran to the palm-tree and rubbed and rubbed and rubbed himself against it. He rubbed so much and so hard that he rubbed his skin into a great fold over his shoulders, and another fold underneath, where the buttons used to be (but he rubbed the buttons off), and he rubbed some more folds over his legs. And it spoiled his temper, but it didn't make the least difference to the cake-crumbs. They were inside his skin and they tickled. So he went home, very angry indeed and horribly scratchy; and from that day to this every rhinoceros has great folds in his skin and a very bad temper, all on account of the cake-crumbs inside.

But the Parsee came down from his palm-tree, wearing his hat, from which the rays of the sun were reflected in more-than-oriental splendour, packed up his cooking-stove, and went away in the direction of Orotavo, Amygdala, the Upland Meadows of Anantarivo, and the Marshes of Sonaput.

I Had a Hippopotamus

★★

Patrick Barrington

I had a hippopotamus; I kept him in a shed
And fed him upon vitamins and vegetable bread;
I made him my companion on many cheery walks,
And had his portrait done by a celebrity in chalks.

His charming eccentricities were known on every side,
The creature's popularity was wonderfully wide;
He frolicked with the Rector in a dozen friendly tussles,
Who could not but remark on his hippopotamuscles.

If he should be afflicted by depression or the dumps,
By hippopotameasles or the hippopotamumps,
I never knew a particle of peace till it was plain
He was hippopotamasticating properly again.

I had a hippopotamus; I loved him as a friend;
But beautiful relationships are bound to have an end;
Time takes, alas! our joys from us and robs us of our blisses;
My hippopotamus turned out to be a hippopotamissis.

My housekeeper regarded him with jaundice in her eye;
She did not want a colony of hippopotami;
She borrowed a machine-gun from from her soldier-
    nephew, Percy,
And showed my hippopotamus no hippopotamercy.

My house now lacks that glamour that the charming
    creature gave,
The garage where I kept him is as silent as the grave;
No longer he displays among the motor-tyres and
    spanners
His hippopotamastery of hippopotamanners.

No longer now he gambols in the orchards in the spring;
No longer do I lead him through the village on a string;
No longer in the mornings does the neighbourhood
    rejoice
To his hippopotamusically-modulated voice.

I had a hippopotamus; but nothing upon earth
Is constant in its happiness or lasting in its mirth;
No joy that life can give me can be strong enough to
    smother
My sorrow for that might-have-been-a-hippopotamother.

Mice is Nice

The Mouse and His Child

★★

CHAPTER ONE

Russell Hoban

(approximate reading time 21 minutes)

The tramp was big and squarely built, and he walked with the rolling stride of the long road, his steps too big for the little streets of the little town. Shivering in his thin coat, he passed aimlessly through the crowd while rosy-faced Christmas shoppers quickened their steps and moved aside to give him room.

The sound of music made him stop at a toyshop where the door, continually swinging open and shut in a moving stream of people, jangled its bell and sent warm air and Christmas carols out into the street. 'Deck the halls with boughs of holly,' sang the loudspeakers in the shop, and the tramp smelled Christmas in the pine wreaths, in the bright paint and varnish, in the shining metal and fresh pasteboard of the new toys.

He put his face close to the window, and looking past the toys displayed there, peered into the shop. Under the

wreaths and winking coloured lights a little train clattered through sparkling tunnels and over painted mountains on a green table, the tiny clacking of its wheels circling in and out of the music. Beyond it the shelves were packed with tin toys and wooden toys and plush toys – dolls, teddy bears, games and puzzles, fire engines and boats and wagons, and row on row of closed boxes, each printed with a fascinating picture of the toy it hid from sight.

On the counter, rising grandly above the heads of the children clustered before it, was a splendid dolls' house. It was very large and expensive, a full three storeys high, and a marvel of its kind. The porches and balconies were elegant with scrollwork brackets, and the mansard roof with its dormers and cross gables was topped by tall brick chimneys and a handsome lookout. In front of the house stood a clockwork elephant wearing a purple head-cloth, and when the saleslady wound her up for the watching children, she walked slowly up and down, swinging her trunk and flapping her ears. Near the elephant a little tin seal balanced a red and yellow ball on her nose and kept it spinning while her reflection in the glass counter top smiled up at her and spun its own red and yellow ball.

As the tramp watched, the saleslady opened a box and took out two toy mice, a large one and a small one, who stood upright with outstretched arms and joined hands. They wore blue velveteen trousers and patent leather shoes, and they had glass-bead eyes, white thread whiskers, and

black rubber tails. When the saleslady wound the key in the mouse father's back he danced in a circle, swinging his little son up off the counter and down again while the children laughed and reached out to touch them. Around and around they danced gravely, and more and more slowly as the spring unwound, until the mouse father came to a stop holding the child high in his upraised arms.

The saleslady, looking up as she wound the toy again, saw the tramp's whiskered, staring, face on the other side of the glass. She pursed her mouth and looked away, and the tramp turned from the window back to the street. The grey sky had begun to let down its snow, and the ragged man stood in the middle of the pavement while the soft flakes fell around him and the people quick-stepped past him.

Then, with his big broken shoes printing his footsteps in the fresh snow, he solemnly danced in a circle, swinging his empty arms up and down. A little black-and-white spotted dog trotting past stopped and sat down to look at him, and for a moment the man and the dog were the only two creatures on the street not moving in a fixed direction. People laughed, shook their heads, and hurried on. The tramp stopped with arms upraised. Then he lowered his head, jammed his hands into his pockets, and lurched away down the street, around a corner, and into the evening and the lamplight on the snow. The dog sniffed at his footprints, then trotted on where they led.

The store closed. The customers and clerks went home. The music was silent. The wreaths were dim, the shop was dark except for the dolls' house on the counter. Light streamed from all its windows out into the shadows around it, and the toys before it stood up silhouetted black and motionless as the hours slowly passed.

Then, 'Midnight!' said the old store clock. Its pendulum swung gleaming in the shadows as it counted twelve thin chimes into the silence, folded its hands together, and stared out through the dark window at the thick snow sifting through the light of the street lamp. Far away and muffled by the snow the town hall clock struck midnight with its deeper note.

'Where are we?' the mouse child asked his father. His voice was tiny in the stillness of the night.

'I don't know,' the father answered.

'*What* are we, Papa?'

'I don't know. We must wait and see.'

'What astonishing ignorance!' said the clockwork elephant. 'But of course you're new. I've been here such a long time that I'd forgotten how it was. Now, then,' she said, 'this place is a toyshop, and you are toy mice. People are going to come and buy you for children, because it's almost a time called Christmas.'

'Why haven't they bought you?' asked the little tin seal. 'How come you've stayed here so long?'

'It isn't quite the same for me, my dear,' replied the ele-

phant. 'I'm part of the establishment, you see, and this is my house.'

The house was certainly grand enough for her, or indeed for anyone. The very cornices and carven brackets bespoke a residence of dignity and style, and the dolls never set foot outside it. They had no need to; everything they could possibly want was there, from the covered platters and silver chafing dishes on the sideboard to the ebony grand piano among the potted ferns in the conservatory. No expense had been spared, and no detail was wanting. The house had rooms for every purpose, all opulently furnished and appropriately occupied: there were a piano-teacher doll and a young-lady-pupil doll in the conservatory, a nursemaid doll for the children dolls in the nursery, and a cook and butler doll in the kitchen. Interminable-weekend-guest dolls lay in all the guest room beds, sporting dolls played billiards in the billiard room, and a scholar doll in the library never ceased perusal of the book he held, although he kept in touch with the world by the hand he lightly rested on the globe that stood beside him. There was even an astronomer doll in the lookout observatory, who tirelessly aimed his little telescope at one of the automatic fire sprinklers in the ceiling of the shop. In the dining room, beneath a glittering chandelier, a party of lady and gentleman dolls sat perpetually around a table. Whatever the cook and butler might hope to serve them, they had never taken anything but tea, and that from

empty cups, while plaster cakes and pastry, defying time, stood by the silver teapot on the white damask cloth.

It was the elephant's constant delight to watch that tea party through the window, and as the hostess she took great pride in the quality of her hospitality. 'Have another cup of tea,' she said to one of the ladies. 'Try a little pastry.'

'HIGH-SOCIETY SCANDAL, changing to cloudy, with a possibility of BARGAINS GALORE!' replied the lady. Her papier-mâché head being made of paste and newsprint, she always spoke in scraps of news and advertising, in whatever order they came to mind.

'Bucket seats,' remarked the gentleman next to her. 'Power steering optional. GOVERNMENT FALLS.'

The mouse child was still thinking of what the elephant had said before. 'What happens when they buy you?' he asked her.

'That, of course, is outside of my experience,' said the elephant, 'but I should think that one simply goes out into the world and does whatever one does. One dances or balances a ball, as the case may be.'

The child remembered the bitter wind that had blown in through the door, and the great staring face of the tramp at the window with the grey winter sky behind him. Now that sky was a silent darkness beyond the street lamp and the white flakes falling. The dolls' house was bright and warm; the teapot gleamed upon the dazzling cloth. 'I don't want to go out into the world,' he said.

'Obviously the child isn't properly brought up,' said the elephant to the gentleman doll nearest her. 'But then how could he be, poor thing, without a mother's guidance?'

'PRICES SLASHED,' said the gentleman. 'EVERYTHING MUST GO.'

'You're quite right,' said the elephant. 'Everything must, in one way or another, go. One does what one is wound to do. It is expected of me that I walk up and down in front of my house; it is expected of you that you drink tea. And it is expected of this young mouse that he go out into the world with his father and dance in a circle.'

'But I don't want to,' said the mouse child, and he began to cry. It was an odd, little, tinny, rasping, sound, and father and son both rattled with it.

'There, there,' said the father, 'don't cry. Please don't.' Toys all around the shop were listening. 'He'd better stop that,' they said.

It was the clock that spoke next, startling them with his flat brass voice. 'I might remind you of the rules of clockwork,' he said. 'No talking before midnight and after dawn, and no crying on the job.'

'He's not on the job,' said the seal. 'We're on our own time now.'

'Toys that cry on their own time sometimes cry on the job,' said the clock, 'and no good ever comes of it. A word to the wise.'

'Do be quiet,' said the elephant to the mouse child. 'I'll sing you a lullaby. Pay attention now.' The mouse child stopped crying, and listened while the elephant sang:

>Hush, hush, little plush,
>Mama's near you through the night.
>Hush, hush, little plush,
>Everything will be all right.

'Are you my mama?' asked the child. He had no idea what a mama might be, but he knew at once that he needed one badly.

'Good heavens!' said the elephant. 'Of course I'm not your mama. I was simply singing words I once heard a large teddy bear sing to a small one.'

'Will you *be* my mama,' said the child, 'and will you sing to me all the time? And can we all stay here together and live in the beautiful house where the party is and not go out into the world?'

'Certainly not!' snorted the elephant. 'Really,' she said to the gentleman doll, 'this is intolerable. One is polite to the transient element on the counter, and see what comes of it.'

'Twenty-one-inch colour television,' offered the gentleman. 'Nagging backaches and muscle tension. A HEART-WARMING LOVE STORY THE WHOLE FAMILY WILL ENJOY.'

'You're an idiot,' snapped the elephant, and no one on the counter said another word for the rest of the night.

Outside the window the snowflakes whirled into the lamp-light and out into the darkness again; inside the shop the clock ticked slowly through the slow dim hours, and the tea party in the dolls' house silently continued.

The next day the mouse and his child were sold. While the elephant walked back and forth and the seal balanced her ball and the ladies and gentleman sat over their tea-cups, the father and son were put into a box, wrapped up, and carried off.

They came out of their wrappings to find the store gone and themselves under a Christmas tree with other toys around them. The tree was hung with lights and angels, and smelled of the pine woods. The fire crackled and sang on the hearth, and the children curled up on the

rug with the family cat to watch the toys perform. A furry white rabbit struck his cymbals together with a tiny clash; a tin monkey played 'La Golondrina' on a little violin; a tin bird pecked steadily at the floor. And the mouse and his child danced.

Presents in bright wrappings were piled all around them, but the windup toys were not presents for the children; the grown-ups brought them down from the attic every year with the Christmas ornaments, and every year after Christmas they were packed away again. 'You may look at them,' said the grown-ups to the children, 'but we must wind them for you. Then they will not be broken, and we can enjoy them for many Christmases.'

So the mouse and his child danced under the tree every evening, and every night when the family was asleep they talked with the other toys. The monkey complained of being made to play the same tune over and over on a cheap fiddle; the bird complained of having to peck at a bare floor; the rabbit complained that there was no meaning in his cymbals. And soon the mouse and his child complained of the futility of dancing in an endless circle that led nowhere.

Every evening the toys performed, and every day the pine tree shed more needles on the floor around them until Christmas was gone. Then the tree was thrown out and the toys were packed off to the attic with the ornaments. There they lay jumbled in a box together, in the

warm, sharp, dry smell of the attic beams and the dim light
of the clouded, cobwebbed windows. Through long days
and nights they listened to the rain on the roof and the
wind in the trees, but the sound of the living room clock
striking midnight could not reach them; they never had
permission to speak at all, and they lay in silence until
another year had passed and they stood once more beneath
the tree.

So it was that four Christmases came and went, until
there came a fifth Christmas that was different from the
others.

'Wind up the toys for us!' said the children as they lay on
the rug by the fire and leaned their cheeks on their hands.

When the mouse father was wound up, he danced in a
circle as he always did, swinging the child up and down.
The room, the tree, and the faces in the firelight whirled
past the child as always, but this time he saw something
new: among the other presents stood a dolls' house, a little
one-room affair with a red-brick pattern printed on its
fibreboard walls.

As the mouse child danced by with his father, he
looked through the dolls' house window and saw a very
small teddy bear and a pink china baby doll sitting at a
table on which was a tea set bigger than both of them.
Around and around the mouse child danced, rising and
falling as his father swung him up and down, while the

little tea party in the window circled past him.

How far away that other dolls' house seemed now! How far away that other tea party with its elegant ladies and gentlemen, and the elephant he had wanted for a mama! The mouse child was on the job and he knew it, but he began to cry.

No one noticed his outbreak but the family cat. She had grown used to the mechanical toys and no longer paid any attention to them, but the strange little sound of the mouse child's sobbing startled and upset her. She dabbed at the toy, arched her back, jumped suddenly sidewise, and leaping on to a table, knocked over a heavy vase of flowers. It fell with a crash, landing squarely on the mouse and his child. The vase was shattered to bits, and the toy was smashed.

Early the next morning the tramp came through the town, as he did each winter. With the little dog still at his heels he walked the snowy street past the house where the children and the grown-ups lived. He looked into the dust-bin to see what he might be able to use, took an empty coffee can and a bundle of newspapers, and went back to the junkyard where he had slept the night before in a wrecked car. Only then did he find the mouse and his child inside the papers, crushed almost flat but still holding fast to each other.

The tramp looked at the battered wrecks around him

in the cold, clear sunlight. He looked down at himself in his ragged clothes. Then he sat down in the car he had slept in, and reached into his pocket for a little screwdriver. While the dog watched quietly, he took the mouse and his child apart to see if he could make them dance again. The junkyard lay silent, its wrecks upheaved like rusty islands in the sparkling snow; the only sounds were the bells of Christmas ringing in the town and the cawing of some crows, hoarse and sharp in the cold air.

All that day the tramp sat in the junkyard labouring over the broken toy, stopping only to eat some bread and meat that he took from his pocket and shared with the dog. He was able to bend the tin bodies almost back into their original shapes, but he had a great deal of trouble with the clockwork motor. When he wound it up, the mechanism jammed, and in trying to clear it he broke some of the little cogs and bars that had made the mouse father dance in a circle and swing the child up and down. The tramp removed those parts and put the toy together as well as he could. Their patent leather shoes had been lost in the dust-bin; their blue velveteen trousers hung wrinkled and awry; their fur had come unglued in several places, but the mouse and his child were whole again.

Now when it was wound up the motor worked without jamming, but the mouse and his child danced no more. The father, his legs somewhat bent, lurched straight ahead with a rolling stride, pushing the child backwards

before him. The little dog sat and watched them with his head cocked to one side. The ragged man smiled and threw away the leftover parts. Then he put the toy in his pocket and walked out to the highway.

High on a ridge above the town where snowy fields sloped off on either side, the road crossed a bridge over the railway tracks, went past the town rubbish dump, and stretched away to the horizon. The tramp set the mouse and his child down at the edge of the road and wound up the father.

'Be tramps,' he said, and turned and walked away with the dog at his heels.

White Ones

★★

Philip Gross

With small scritchety claws
and pink
shortsighted blink-
ing-in-the-sunlight
eyes that looked raw
as if they'd cried all night . . .

One morning they were gone.

On holiday,
says Dad. *Gone to stay*
*with their friend*s
in the pet shop. And so I pretend
I don't know about the cage door
He left open. I try to ignore

the look on the face of the cat.

It isn't that
wakes me up in the darkness. No,
it's the scritch and the scratch
at the bars, those pink-eyed
lies. They're only little
white ones, oh

but watch them breed and grow.

Round About
the Cauldron

Jorinda and Jorindel

★★

Brothers Grimm

(approximate reading time 7 minutes)

There was once an old castle, that stood in the middle of a deep gloomy wood, and in the castle lived an old fairy. Now this fairy could take any shape she pleased. All the day long she flew about in the form of an owl, or crept about the country like a cat; but at night she always became an old woman again. When any young man came within a hundred paces of her castle, he became quite fixed, and could not move a step till she came and set him free; which she would not do till he had given her his word never to come there again. But when any pretty maiden came within that space she was changed into a bird, and the fairy put her into a cage, and hung her up in a chamber in the castle. There were seven hundred of these cages hanging in the castle, and all with beautiful birds in them.

Now there was once a maiden whose name was Jorinda. She was prettier than all the pretty girls that ever were seen before, and a shepherd lad, whose name was Jorindel, was very fond of her, and they were soon to be married.

One day they went to walk in the wood, that they might be alone; and Jorindel said, 'We must take care that we don't go too near to the fairy's castle.' It was a beautiful evening; the last rays of the setting sun shone bright through the long stems of the trees upon the green underwood beneath, and the turtle-doves sang from the tall birches.

Jorinda sat down to gaze upon the sun; Jorindel sat by her side; and both felt sad, they knew not why; but it seemed as if they were to be parted from one another for ever. They had wandered a long way; and when they looked to see which way they should go home, they found themselves at a loss to know what path to take.

The sun was setting fast, and already half of its circle had sunk behind the hill. Jorindel on a sudden looked behind him, and saw through the bushes that they had, without knowing it, sat down close under the old walls of the castle. Then he shrank for fear, turned pale, and trembled. Jorinda was just singing,

> 'The ring-dove sang from the willow spray,
>   Well-a-day! Well-a-day!
> He mourn'd for the fate of his darling mate,
>   Well-a-day!'

when her song stopped suddenly. Jorindel turned to see the reason, and beheld his Jorinda changed into a nightingale, so that her song ended with a mournful 'jug, jug'. An owl with fiery eyes flew three times round them, and three times screamed: 'Tu whu! Tu whu! Tu whu!'

Jorindel could not move; he stood fixed as a stone, and could neither weep, nor speak, nor stir hand or foot. And now the sun went quite down; the gloomy night came; the owl flew into a bush; and a moment after the old fairy came forth pale and meagre, with staring eyes, and a nose and chin that almost met one another.

She mumbled something to herself, seized the nightingale, and went away with it in her hand. Poor Jorindel saw the nightingale was gone – but what could he do? He could not speak, he could not move from the spot where he stood. At last the fairy came back and sang with a hoarse voice:

'Till the prisoner is fast,
And her doom is cast,
There stay! Oh, stay!
When the charm is around her,
And the spell has bound her,
Hie away! away!'

On a sudden Jorindel found himself free. Then he fell on his knees before the fairy, and prayed her to give him back his dear Jorinda; but she laughed at him, and said he should never see her again; then she went her way.

He prayed, he wept, he sorrowed, but all in vain. 'Alas!' he said, 'what will become of me?' He could not go back to his own home, so he went to a strange village, and employed himself in keeping sheep. Many a time did he walk round and round as near to the hated castle as he dared go, but all in vain; he neither heard nor saw anything of Jorinda.

At last he dreamt one night that he found a beautiful purple flower, and that in the middle of it lay a costly pearl; and he dreamt that he plucked the flower, and went with it in his hand into the castle, and that everything he touched with it was disenchanted, and that there he found his Jorinda again.

In the morning when he awoke, he began to search over hill and dale for this pretty flower. For eight long days he sought for it in vain, but on the ninth day, early in the morning, he found the beautiful purple flower; and in the middle of it was a large dewdrop, as big as a costly pearl. Then he plucked the flower, and set out and travelled day and night till he came again to the castle.

He walked nearer than a hundred paces to it, and yet he did not become fixed as before, but found that he could go quite close up to the door. Jorindel was very glad indeed to see this. Then he touched the door with the flower, and it sprang open; so that he went in through the court, and listened when he heard so many birds singing. At last he came to the chamber where the fairy sat, with the seven hundred birds singing in the seven hundred cages. When she saw Jorindel she was very angry, and screamed with rage; but she could not come within two yards of him, for the flower he held in his hand was his safeguard. He looked around at the birds, but alas! there were many, many nightingales, and he was at a loss to find out which was his Jorinda. While he was thinking what to

do, he saw the fairy had taken down one of the cages, and was making off with it through the door. He ran – or flew – after her, touched the cage with the flower, and Jorinda stood before him, and threw her arms round his neck looking as beautiful as ever, as beautiful as when they walked together in the wood.

Then he touched all the other birds with the flower, so that they all took their old forms again; and he took Jorinda home, where they were married, and lived happily together many years: and so did a good many other lads, whose maidens had been forced to sing in the old fairy's cages by themselves much longer than they liked.

Witch's Chant

★★

FROM *MACBETH*

William Shakespeare

Round about the cauldron go;
In the poison'd entrails throw.
Toad, that under cold stone
Days and nights has thirty-one
Swelter'd venom, sleeping got,
Boil thou first i' the charmed pot.

Double, double, toil and trouble;
Fire, burn; and cauldron, bubble.

Fillet of a fenny snake,
In the cauldron boil and bake;
Eye of newt, and toe of frog,
Wool of bat, and tongue of dog,
Adder's fork, and blind-worm's sting,
Lizard's leg, and owlet's wing,
For a charm of powerful trouble,
Like a hell-broth boil and bubble.

Double, double, toil and trouble;
Fire, burn; and cauldron, bubble.

Go to Bed

The Snooks Family

★★

Harcourt Williams

(approximate reading time 4 minutes)

One night Mr and Mrs Snooks were going to bed as usual. It so happened that Mrs Snooks got into bed first, and she said to her husband, 'Please, Mr Snooks, would you blow the candle out?' And Mr Snooks replied, 'Certainly, Mrs Snooks.' Whereupon he picked up the candlestick and began to blow, but unfortunately he could only blow by putting his under lip over his upper lip, which meant that his breath went up to the ceiling instead of blowing out the candle flame.

And he puffed and he puffed, but he could not blow it out.

So Mrs Snooks said, 'I will do it, my dear,' and she got out of bed and took the candlestick from her husband and began to blow. But unfortunately she could only blow by putting her upper lip over her under lip, so that all her breath went down to the floor. And she puffed and she puffed, but she could not blow the candle out.

So Mrs Snooks called their son John. John put on his sky-blue dressing gown and slipped his feet into his primrose-coloured slippers and came down into his parents' bedroom.

'John, dear,' said Mrs Snooks, 'will you please blow out the candle for us?' And John said, 'Certainly, Mummy.'

But unfortunately John could only blow out of the right corner of his mouth, so that all his breath hit the wall of the room instead of the candle.

And he puffed and he puffed, but he could not blow out the candle.

So they all called for his sister, little Ann. And little Ann put on her scarlet dressing-gown and slipped on her pink slippers and came down to her parents' bedroom.

'Ann, dear,' said Mr Snooks, 'will you please blow the candle out for us?' And Ann said, 'Certainly, Daddy.'

But unfortunately Ann could only blow out of the left side of her mouth, so that all her breath hit the wall instead of the candle.

And she puffed and she puffed, but she could not blow out the candle.

It was just then that they heard in the street below a heavy steady tread coming along the pavement. Mr Snooks threw open the window and they all craned their necks out. They saw a policeman coming slowly towards the house.

'Oh, Mr Policeman,' said Mrs Snooks, 'will you come up and blow out our candle? We do so want to go to bed.'

'Certainly, Madam,' replied the policeman, and he entered and climbed the stairs – blump, blump, blump. He came into the bedroom where Mr Snooks, Mrs

Snooks, John Snooks and little Ann Snooks were all standing round the candle which they could *not* blow out.

The policeman then picked up the candlestick in a
very dignified manner and, putting his mouth into the
usual shape for blowing, puffed out the candle at the first
puff. Just like this – PUFF!

The Snooks family all said, 'Thank you, Mr Policeman.' And the policeman said, 'Don't mention it,' and
turned to go down the stairs again.

'Just a moment, Policeman,' said Mr Snooks. 'You
mustn't go down the stairs in the dark. You might fall.'
And taking a box of matches, he LIT THE CANDLE
AGAIN!

Mr Snooks went down the stairs with the policeman
and saw him out of the door. His footsteps went blump,
blump, blump along the quiet street.

John Snooks and little Ann Snooks went back to bed.
Mr and Mrs Snooks got into bed again. There was silence
for a moment.

'Mr Snooks,' said Mrs Snooks, 'would you blow out
the candle?'

Mr Snooks got out of bed. 'Certainly, Mrs Snooks,'
he said . . .

And so on *ad infinitum.*

Escape at Bedtime

★★

R. L. Stevenson

The lights from the parlour and kitchen shone out
   Through the blinds and the windows and bars;
And high overhead and all moving about,
   There were thousands of millions of stars.
There ne'er were such thousands of leaves on a tree,
   Nor of people in church or the Park,
As the crowds of the stars that looked down upon me,
   And that glittered and winked in the dark.
The Dog, and the Plough, and the Hunter, and all,
   And the star of the sailor, and Mars,
These shown in the sky, and the pail by the wall
   Would be half full of water and stars.
They saw me at last, and they chased me with cries,
   And they soon had me packed into bed;
But the glory kept shining and bright in my eyes,
   And the stars going round in my head.

Secrets

The Secret Garden

★★

EXTRACT FROM CHAPTER THIRTEEN
Frances Hodgson Burnett

(approximate reading time 20 minutes)

Mary Lennox is a spoiled and sickly child who has been brought up in India. After her parents die in a cholera epidemic, she is sent to live with her uncle, Mr Craven, in Misselthwaite Manor in Yorkshire. Here, left to herself for most of the day, she wanders the grounds and has discovered a locked, walled garden. At night time, she has sometimes heard the sound of crying.

She had been lying awake turning from side to side for about an hour, when suddenly something made her sit up in bed and turn her head toward the door listening. She listened and she listened.

'It isn't the wind now,' she said in a loud whisper. 'That isn't the wind. It is different. It is that crying I heard before.'

The door of her room was ajar and the sound came down the corridor, a far-off faint sound of fretful crying. She listened for a few minutes and each minute she became more and more sure. She felt as if she must find out what it was. It seemed even stranger than the secret garden and the buried key. Perhaps the fact that she was in a rebellious mood made her bold. She put her foot out of bed and stood on the floor.

'I am going to find out what it is,' she said. 'Everybody is in bed and I don't care about Mrs Medlock – I don't care!'

There was a candle by her bedside and she took it up and went softly out of the room. The corridor looked very long and dark, but she was too excited to mind that. So she went on with her dim light, almost feeling her way, her heart beating so loud that she fancied she could hear it. The far-off faint crying went on and led her. Sometimes it stopped for a moment or so and then began again. Was this the right corner to turn? Yes, there was the tapestry door.

She pushed it open very gently and closed it behind her, and she stood in the corridor and could hear the crying quite plainly, though it was not loud. It was on the other side of the wall at her left and a few yards farther on there was a door. She could see a glimmer of light coming from beneath it. The Someone was crying in that room, and it was quite a young Someone.

So she walked to the door and pushed it open, and there she was standing in the room!

It was a big room with ancient, handsome furniture in it. There was a low fire glowing faintly on the hearth and a night-light burning by the side of a carved four-posted bed hung with brocade, and on the bed was lying a boy, crying pitifully.

Mary wondered if she was in a real place or if she had fallen asleep again and was dreaming without knowing it.

The boy had a sharp, delicate face, the colour of ivory and he seemed to have eyes too big for it. He had also a lot of hair which tumbled over his forehead in heavy locks and made his thin face seem smaller. He looked like a boy who had been ill, but he was crying more as if he were tired and cross than as if he were in pain.

'Who are you?' he said at last in a half-frightened whisper. 'Are you a ghost?'

'No, I am not,' Mary answered, her own whisper sounding half frightened. 'Are you one?'

He stared and stared and stared. Mary could not help noticing what strange eyes he had. They were agate-grey and they looked too big for his face because they had black lashes all round them.

'No,' he replied after waiting a moment or so. 'I am Colin.'

'Who is Colin?' she faltered.

'I am Colin Craven. Who are you?'

'I am Mary Lennox. Mr Craven is my uncle.'

'He is my father,' said the boy.

'Your father!' gasped Mary. 'No one ever told me he had a boy! Why didn't they?'

'Come here,' he said.

She came close to the bed and he put out his hand and touched her.

'You are real, aren't you?' he said. 'I have such real dreams very often. You might be one of them.'

Mary had slipped on a woollen wrapper before she left her room and she put a piece of it between his fingers.

'Rub that and see how thick and warm it is,' she said. 'I will pinch you a little if you like, to show you how real I am. For a minute I thought you might be a dream, too.'

'Where did you come from?' he asked.

'From my own room. The wind wuthered so I couldn't go to sleep and I heard someone crying and wanted to find out who it was. What were you crying for?'

'Because I couldn't go to sleep either and my head ached. Tell me your name again.'

'Mary Lennox. Did no one ever tell you I had come to live here?'

He was still fingering the fold of her wrapper.

'No,' he answered. 'They daren't.'

'Why?' asked Mary.

'Because I should have been afraid you would see me. I won't let people see me and talk me over.'

'Why?' Mary asked again, feeling more mystified every moment.

'Because I am like this always, ill and having to lie down. My father won't let people talk me over either. The servants are not allowed to speak about me. If I live I may be a hunchback, but I shan't live. My father hates to think I may be like him.'

'Oh, what a queer house this is!' Mary said. 'Everything

is a kind of secret. Rooms are locked up and gardens are locked up – and you! Have you been locked up?'

'No. I stay in this room because I don't want to be moved out of it. It tires me too much.'

'Does your father come and see you?' Mary ventured.

'Sometimes. Generally when I am asleep. He doesn't want to see me.'

'Why?' Mary could not help asking again.

A sort of angry shadow passed over the boy's face.

'My mother died when I was born and it makes him wretched to look at me. He thinks I don't know, but I've heard people talking. He almost hates me.'

'He hates the garden, because she died,' said Mary, half speaking to herself.

'What garden?' the boy asked.

'Oh! Just – just a garden she used to like,' Mary stammered. 'Have you been here always?'

'Nearly always. Sometimes I have been taken to places at the seaside, but I won't stay because people stare at me. I used to wear an iron thing to keep my back straight, but a grand doctor came from London to see me and said it was stupid. He told them to take it off and keep me out in the fresh air. I hate fresh air and I don't want to go out.'

'I didn't when first I came here,' said Mary. 'Why do you keep looking at me like that?'

'Because of the dreams that are so real,' he answered rather fretfully. 'Sometimes when I open my eyes I don't believe I'm awake.'

'We're both awake,' said Mary. She glanced round the

room with its high ceiling and shadowy corners and dim firelight. 'It looks quite like a dream, and it's the middle of the night, and everybody in the house is asleep – everybody but us. We are wide awake.'

'I don't want it to be a dream,' the boy said restlessly.

Mary thought of something all at once.

'If you don't like people to see you,' she began, 'do you want me to go away?'

He still held the fold of her wrapper and he gave it a little pull.

'No,' he said. 'I want to hear about you.'

Mary put down her candle on the table near the bed and sat down on the cushioned stool. She did not want to go away at all. She wanted to stay in the mysterious hidden-away room and talk to the mysterious boy.

He wanted to know a great deal about India and about her voyage across the ocean. She found out that because he had been an invalid he had not learned things as other children had. One of his nurses had taught him to read when he was quite little and he was always reading and looking at pictures in splendid books.

Though his father rarely saw him when he was awake, he was given all sorts of wonderful things to amuse himself with. He never seemed to have been amused, however. He could have anything he asked for and was never made to do anything he did not like to do. 'Everyone is obliged to do what pleases me,' he said indifferently. 'It makes me ill to be angry. No one believes I shall live to grow up.'

He said it as if he was so accustomed to the idea that it

had ceased to matter to him at all. He seemed to like the sound of Mary's voice.

'How old are you?' he asked.

'I am ten,' answered Mary, forgetting herself for the moment, 'and so are you.'

'How do you know that?' he demanded in a surprised voice.

'Because when you were born the garden door was locked and the key was buried. And it has been locked for ten years.'

Colin half sat up, turning toward her, leaning on his elbows.

'What garden door was locked? Who did it? Where was the key buried?' he exclaimed as if he were suddenly very much interested.

'It – it was the garden Mr Craven hates,' said Mary nervously. 'He locked the door. No one – no one knew where he buried the key.'

'What sort of a garden is it?' Colin persisted eagerly.

'No one has been allowed to go into it for ten years,' was Mary's careful answer.

But it was too late to be careful. He was too much like herself. He too had had nothing to think about and the idea of a hidden garden attracted him as it had attracted her. He asked question after question. Where was it? Had she never looked for the door? Had she never asked the gardeners?

'They won't talk about it,' said Mary. 'I think they have been told not to answer questions.'

'I would make them,' said Colin.

'Could you?' Mary faltered, beginning to feel frightened. If he could make people answer questions, who knew what might happen?

'Everyone is obliged to please me. I told you that,' he said.

Mary had not known that she herself had been spoiled, but she could see quite plainly that this mysterious boy had been. He thought that the whole world belonged to him. How peculiar he was and how coolly he spoke of not living.

'Do you think you won't live?' she asked, partly because she was curious and partly in hope of making him forget the garden.

'I don't suppose I shall. Ever since I remember anything I have heard people say I shan't. At first they thought I was too little to understand and now they think I don't hear. But I do. My doctor is my father's cousin. He is quite poor and if I die he will have all Misselthwaite when my father is dead. I should think he wouldn't want me to live.'

'Do you want to live?' inquired Mary.

'No,' he answered, in a cross, tired fashion. 'But I don't want to die. When I feel ill I lie here and think about it until I cry and cry.'

'I have heard you crying three times,' Mary said, 'but I did not know who it was. Were you crying about that?' She did so want him to forget the garden.

'I dare say,' he answered. 'Let us talk about something else. Talk about that garden. Don't you want to see it?'

'Yes,' answered Mary in quite a low voice.

'I do,' he went on persistently. 'I don't think I ever really wanted to see anything before, but I want to see that garden. I want the key dug up. I want the door unlocked. I would let them take me there in my chair. That would be getting fresh air. I am going to make them open the door.'

'Oh, don't – don't – don't – don't do that!' she cried out.

He stared as if he thought she had gone crazy!

'Why?' he exclaimed. 'You said you wanted to see it.'

'I do,' she answered, almost with a sob in her throat, 'but if you make them open the door and take you in like that it will never be a secret again.'

He leaned still farther forward.

'A secret,' he said. 'What do you mean? Tell me.'

Mary's words almost tumbled over one another.

'You see – you see,' she panted, 'if no one knows but ourselves – if there was a door, hidden somewhere under the ivy – if there was – and we could find it; and if we could slip through it together and shut it behind us, and no one knew anyone was inside and we called it our garden—'

'Is it dead?' he interrupted her.

'It soon will be if no one cares for it,' she went on. 'The bulbs will live but the roses—'

He stopped her again as excited as she was herself.

'What are bulbs?' he put in quickly.

'They are daffodils and lilies and snowdrops. They are

working in the earth now – pushing up pale-green points because the spring is coming.'

'Is the spring coming?' he said. 'What is it like? You don't see it in rooms if you are ill.'

'It is the sun shining on the rain and the rain falling on the sunshine, and things pushing up and working under the earth,' said Mary. 'If the garden was a secret and we could get into it we could watch the things grow bigger every day, and see how many roses are alive. Don't you see? Oh, don't you see how much nicer it would be if it was a secret?'

He dropped back on his pillow and lay there with an odd expression on his face.

'I never had a secret,' he said, 'except that one about not living to grow up. They don't know I know that, so it is a sort of secret. But I like this kind better.'

'If you won't make them take you to the garden,' pleaded Mary, 'perhaps – I feel almost sure I can find out how to get in sometime.'

'I should – like – that,' he said very slowly, his eyes looking dreamy. 'I should like that. I should not mind fresh air in a secret garden.'

Mary began to recover her breath and feel safer, because the idea of keeping the secret seemed to please him.

'I'll tell you what I *think* it would be like, if we could go into it,' she said. 'It has been shut up so long things have grown into a tangle perhaps.'

He lay quite still and listened while she went on

talking about the roses which *might* have clambered from tree to tree and hung down – about the many birds which *might* have built their nests there because it was so safe.

'I did not know birds could be like that,' he said. 'But if you stay in a room you never see things.'

'I am going to let you look at something,' he said. 'Do you see that rose-coloured silk curtain hanging on the wall over the mantelpiece?'

'Yes,' she answered.

'There is a cord hanging from it,' said Colin. 'Go and pull it.'

Mary got up, much mystified, and found the cord. When she pulled it the silk curtain ran back on rings and when it ran back it uncovered a picture. It was the picture of a girl with a laughing face. She had bright hair tied up with a blue ribbon and her gay, lovely eyes were exactly like Colin's unhappy ones, agate-grey and looking twice as big as they really were because of the black lashes all round them.

'She is my mother,' said Colin complainingly. 'I don't see why she died. Sometimes I hate her for doing it.'

'How queer!' said Mary.

'If she had lived I believe I should not have been ill always,' he grumbled. 'I dare say I should have lived, too. And my father would not have hated to look at me. I dare say I should have had a strong back. Draw the curtain again.'

Mary did as she was told and returned to her foot-stool.

'She is much prettier than you,' she said, 'but her eyes are just like yours – at least they are the same shape and colour. Why is the curtain drawn over her?'

He moved uncomfortably.

'I made them do it,' he said. 'Sometimes I don't like to see her looking at me. She smiles too much when I am ill and miserable. Besides, she is mine and I don't want everyone to see her.'

There were a few moments of silence and then Mary spoke.

'What would Mrs Medlock do if she found out that I had been here?' she inquired.

'She would do as I told her to do,' he answered. 'And I should tell her that I wanted you to come here and talk to me every day. I am glad you came.'

'So am I,' said Mary. 'I will come as often as I can, but' – she hesitated – 'I shall have to look every day for the garden door.'

'Yes, you must,' said Colin, 'and you can tell me about it afterward.'

'I have been here a long time,' said Mary. 'Shall I go away now? Your eyes look sleepy.'

'I wish I could go to sleep before you leave me,' he said rather shyly.

'Shut your eyes,' said Mary, drawing her footstool closer, 'and I will do what my *ayah* used to do in India. I will pat your hand and stroke it and sing something quite low.'

'I should like that perhaps,' he said drowsily.

Somehow she was sorry for him and did not want him to lie awake, so she leaned against the bed and began to stroke and pat his hand and sing a very low little chanting song in Hindustani.

'That is nice,' he said more drowsily still, and she went on chanting and stroking, but when she looked at him again his black lashes were lying close against his cheeks, for his eyes were shut and he was fast asleep. So she got up softly, took her candle and crept away without making a sound.

The Secret

★★

Anon

We have a secret, just we three,
The robin, and I, and the sweet cherry-tree;
The bird told the tree, and the tree told me,
And nobody knows it but just us three.

But of course the robin knows it best,
Because she built the – I shan't tell the rest;
And laid the four little – something in it –
I'm afraid I shall tell it every minute.

But if the tree and the robin
    don't peep,
I'll try my best the secret to
    keep;
Though I know when the
    little birds fly about
Then the whole secret will be
    out.

Excuses, Excuses

The Adventures of Tom Sawyer

★★

EXTRACT FROM CHAPTER SIX
Mark Twain

(approximate reading time 6 minutes)

Tom Sawyer is a mischievous boy with a rich imagination. He lives with his Aunt Polly and his half-brother Sid in the Mississippi River town of St Petersburg, Missouri, USA.

Monday morning found Tom Sawyer miserable. Monday morning always found him so, because it began another week's slow suffering in school. He generally began that day with wishing he had had no intervening holiday, it made the going into captivity and fetters again so much more odious.

Tom lay thinking. Presently it occurred to him that he wished he was sick; then he could stay home from school. Here was a vague possibility. He canvassed his system. No ailment was found, and he investigated again. This time he thought he could detect colicky symptoms, and he began to encourage them with considerable hope. But they soon grew feeble, and presently died wholly away. He reflected further. Suddenly he discovered something. One of his upper teeth was loose. This was lucky; he was about to begin to groan, as a 'starter,' as he called it, when it occurred to him that if he came into court with that argument his aunt would pull it out, and that would hurt. So he thought he would hold the tooth in reserve for the present, and seek further. Nothing offered for some little time, and then he remembered hearing the doctor tell about a certain thing that laid up a patient for two or three weeks and threatened to make him lose a finger. So the boy eagerly drew his sore toe from under the sheet and held it up for inspection. But now he did not know the necessary symptoms. However, it seemed well worth while to chance it, so he fell to groaning with considerable spirit.

But Sid slept on, unconscious.

Tom groaned louder, and fancied that he began to feel pain in the toe.

No result from Sid.

Tom was panting with his exertions by this time. He took a rest and then swelled himself up and fetched a succession of admirable groans.

Sid snored on.

Tom was aggravated. He said, 'Sid, Sid!' and shook him. This course worked well, and Tom began to groan again. Sid yawned, stretched, then brought himself up on his elbow with a snort, and began to stare at Tom. Tom went on groaning. Sid said:

'Tom! say, Tom!'

No response.

'Here, Tom! TOM! What is the matter, Tom?' And he shook him and looked in his face anxiously.

Tom moaned out:

'Oh, don't, Sid. Don't joggle me.'

'Why, what's the matter, Tom? I must call Auntie.'

'No, never mind. It'll be over by and by, maybe. Don't call anybody.'

'But I must! Don't groan so, Tom, it's awful. How long you been this way?'

'Hours. Ouch! Oh, don't stir so, Sid, you'll kill me.'

'Tom, why didn't you wake me sooner? Oh, Tom, don't! It makes my flesh crawl to hear you. Tom, what is the matter?'

'I forgive you everything, Sid. [Groan.] Everything you've ever done to me. When I'm gone—'

'Oh, Tom, you ain't dying, are you? Don't, Tom. Oh, don't. Maybe—'

'I forgive everybody, Sid. [Groan.] Tell 'em so, Sid. And, Sid, you give my window-sash, and my cat with one eye to that new girl that's come to town, and tell her—'

But Sid had snatched his clothes and gone. Tom was suffering in reality now, so handsomely was his imagination working, and so his groans had gathered quite a genuine tone.

Sid flew downstairs and said:

'Oh, Aunt Polly, come! Tom's dying!'

'Dying!'

'Yes'm. Don't wait, come quick!'

'Rubbage! I don't believe it!'

But she fled upstairs nevertheless, with Sid and Mary at her heels. And her face grew white, too, and her lips trembled. When she reached the bedside she gasped out:

'You, Tom! Tom, what's the matter with you?'

'Oh, Auntie, I'm—'

'What's the matter with you – what *is* the matter with you, child?'

'Oh, Auntie, my sore toe's mortified!'

The old lady sank down into a chair and laughed a little, then cried a little, then did both together. This restored her, and she said:

'Tom, what a turn you did give me. Now you shut up that nonsense and climb out of this.'

The groans ceased, and the pain vanished from the toe. The boy felt a little foolish, and he said:

'Aunt Polly, it *seemed* mortified, and it hurt so I never minded my tooth at all.'

'Your tooth, indeed! What's the matter with your tooth?'

'One of them's loose, and it aches perfectly awful.'

'There, there now, don't begin that groaning again. Open your mouth. Well, your tooth *is* loose, but you're not going to die about that. Mary, get me a silk thread, and a chunk of fire out of the kitchen.'

Tom said:

'Oh, please, Auntie, don't pull it out, it don't hurt any more. I wish I may never stir if it does. Please don't,

Auntie, *I* don't want to stay home from school.'

'Oh, you don't, don't you? So all this row was because you thought you'd get to stay home from school and go a-fishing? Tom, Tom, I love you so, and you seem to try every way you can to break my old heart with your out-rageousness.'

By this time the dental instruments were ready. The old lady made one end of the silk thread fast to Tom's tooth with a loop and tied the other to the bedpost. Then she seized the chunk of fire and suddenly thrust it almost into the boy's face. The tooth hung dangling by the bed-post, now.

But all trials bring their compensations. As Tom wended to school after breakfast, he was the envy of every boy he met because the gap in his upper row of teeth enabled him to expectorate in a new and admirable way. He gathered quite a following of lads interested in the exhibition; and one that had cut his finger and had been a centre of fascination and homage up to this time, now found himself suddenly without an adherent, and shorn of his glory. His heart was heavy, and he said with a disdain which he did not feel, that it wasn't anything to spit like Tom Sawyer; but another boy said, 'Sour grapes!' and he wandered away a dismantled hero.

Conversation Piece

★★

Gareth Owen

Late again Blenkinsop?
What's the excuse this time?
Not my fault sir.
Whose fault is it then?
Grandma's sir.
Grandma's. What did she do?
She died sir.
Died?
She's seriously dead all right sir.
That makes four grandmothers this term
And all on PE days Blenkinsop.
I know. It's very upsetting sir.
How many grandmothers have you got
    Blenkinsop?
Grandmothers sir? None sir.
None?
All dead sir.
And what about yesterday Blenkinsop?
What about yesterday sir?
You missed maths.

That was the dentist sir.

The dentist died?

No sir. My teeth sir.

You missed the test Blenkinsop?

I'd been looking forward to it too sir.

Right line up for PE.

Can't sir.

No such word as can't. Why can't you?

No kit sir.

Where is it?

Home sir.

What's it doing at home?

Not ironed sir.

Couldn't you iron it?

Can't do it sir.

Why not?

My hand sir.

Who usually does it?

Grandma sir.

Why couldn't she do it?

Dead sir.

Being Teacher

Cosmic

★★

Frank Cottrell Boyce

(approximate reading time 8 minutes)

Liam Digby is an ordinary boy, except for the fact that he is very very tall.

On my very first day at Waterloo High, I was the tallest person on the lower-school site.

The new uniform Mum had bought at the beginning of the summer didn't fit any more and they had to send off for an extra-large lower-school blazer. I got a special dispensation to wear my own clothes for the first half-term.

When we went to get my travel pass for the bus to school, the woman in the office wouldn't believe I was school age so we had to go home and get my birth certificate. And then the next morning, when I showed it to the bus driver, she wouldn't believe it was mine, and I had to get off the bus and text Mum, and she came down and explained to the driver of the next bus that I was unusually tall for my age.

'It's not the height, love,' said the driver. 'It's the stubble.'

Mum said, 'Am I going to have to do this every morning?'

'Only till we all get used to him.'

In the end, Mum sent off for a passport for me. I kept it in my pocket in case I got questioned again. Dad said, 'That'll keep you out of trouble.'

How wrong can a person be, by the way?

Dad also gave me his old mobile phone, so that if he ever lost me again – like in Enchantment Land – he would be able to find me. His phone's got DraxWorld on it. In case you don't know, that's this cosmic application that shows you your present location, directions to anywhere from anywhere, and also live satellite photographs of anything in the world. You can use it to look at volcanoes erupting. Tidal waves. Forest fires. Anything. Dad uses it to make sure the traffic is flowing smoothly on the bypass.

That first day at Waterloo High, I was on DraxWorld all the way to school on the 61. I used it to look at theme parks and thrill rides. I found Oblivion in Alton Towers, Space Mountain in EuroDisney, the Terror in Camelot, Thunder Dolphin, Air . . . all of them. As the bus was crawling along Waterloo Road I typed in Waterloo, wondering if I'd be able to get a satellite view of me on the bus. Instead the screen filled up with ten thousand options. There were Waterloos everywhere. Waterloo Station in London. Waterloo the port in Sierra Leone. Waterloo in Belgium. You could go round the whole planet, just jumping from Waterloo to Waterloo.

I found Waterloos with waterfalls, Waterloos in the jungle, Waterloos in snowy mountains and Waterloos with sandy white beaches. I couldn't figure out why anyone who wanted to live in a Waterloo would think – yes, Waterloo, but not the one with the big beach, or the one in the limitless white wastes of Siberia; no, the one with the flyover, handy for the New Strand Shopping Centre.

DraxWorld gives you directions to anywhere, so it's not like it would be hard. If you were a proper grown-up and not just a stubbly boy – if you were my dad, for instance – all you'd have to do is fill your car with petrol, turn left, turn right, go straight on and next thing you know: white beaches, snowy mountains, coral reefs. Truly, grown-upness is wasted on grown-ups.

When I got to school, Mrs Sass (the head) saw me in reception and said, 'Ah . . . Tom?'

'Liam.'

'Yes, of course. I'm Lorraine – come this way.'

I remember thinking, Fancy her telling me her first name. Isn't that friendly? Mrs Kendall never told us her first name when we were in Joan of Arc.

So 'Lorraine' took me off to the staffroom and started telling me the names of all the teachers. They all shook hands with me and said they were pleased to meet me. I was thinking, What a polite school! I wonder if they do this to every new kid. It must take ages. Then Lorraine said, 'Everybody, this is Tom – sorry, Liam – Middleton, our new head of media studies.' And she was pointing at me.

I know I should've put her right there and then, but someone gave me a mug of coffee and a custard cream and sat me down in a nice big easy chair. So I thought, I'll tell her later when I've eaten the biscuit.

Then Lorraine said, 'We've got assembly this morning. I'll bring you up on to the stage and introduce you to the whole school. Do you have anything you'd like me to say about you – like what football team you support, or any special interests?'

I suppose that would have been a good time to say, 'Very interestingly I'm not a teacher. I'm a Year Seven.' But she just seemed so happy, so I said, 'I like massively multi-player online computer games.'

She looked a bit blank.

'Like World of Warcraft. You know, where you have an avatar, and your avatar has skills and goes on quests?'

'Ah,' said Lorraine, 'skills. We are great believers in promoting skills here at Waterloo High.'

'I've got a lot of skills,' I said. 'Of course, some of them aren't that useful in real life – like dragon taming. Some of them are illegal – like knife-throwing. I think that's illegal.'

'I think it probably is.'

'I did try to persuade the head in my last school to start a World of Warcraft club, but she just looked at me like I was an idiot.'

Lorraine looked at me like I was an idiot.

Then the bell went. 'We'd better go through to assembly. Maybe you should just introduce yourself. Don't worry about being interesting.'

* * *

So that's how I ended up on the stage, standing just behind Mrs Sass while she talked to the whole school. There were about eight people in the front row who knew me because they'd been at Joan of Arc Primary too, including Florida Kirby who kept waving and making faces. Mrs Sass said everyone was welcome and she hoped everyone had had a good summer and then something about a new registration procedure and then she said, 'And now I'd like to introduce you to a new member of staff. He's going to be teaching media studies and he'll be form tutor for Class Nine Mandela. This is Mr Middleton . . .'

And she pointed at me.

I stepped up to the microphone and said, 'Thanks, Lorraine – sorry, Mrs Sass.' But everyone in the hall was already muttering, 'Lorraine . . . her name's Lorraine . . .' and Lorraine was looking cross.

All these faces were looking up at me. Part of me was thinking, I really should think more about the consequences of my actions. Then this wouldn't happen to me. But another part of me was thinking, This is good.

I said, 'Morning, everybody.'

And everybody said, 'Morning, sir.'

Sir!

I said, 'Has anyone here been to Waterloo near Liverpool?'

Twelve hundred hands shot up and waggled in the air like a salute. Looking out at them, I felt like the bad emperor in *Star Wars*. I took a breath and said, 'Has anyone been to Waterloo in Belgium, scene of the original Battle of Waterloo in 1815?' No one. I said, 'Siberia. Siberia is as big as Europe. It's got the largest freshwater lake in the world. A lake so big it has its own species of dolphin. The ice is so thick that the railway runs over it. It's also got a town called Waterloo. Has anyone here been to Waterloo, Siberia?'

No one put their hand up.

'Why not?'

No one answered, but they all squirmed in their seats, as though going to Siberia was homework and they hadn't done it.

'Waterloo in Sierra Leone?'

No one had.

'Sierra Leone has lush rainforests and amazing history. Anyone?'

No one.

'Why!?'

They all squirmed again. 'Why have we all been to the Waterloo with the bypass and the shopping precinct when none of us has ever been to the Waterloo with the water-fall, the Waterloo in the jungle, the Waterloo by the frozen lake? Why? These places – they're not in Narnia. You don't have to find a magic wardrobe to get to them. They're not in Azeroth. You don't have to create an avatar and climb inside a computer. They're real places. You can go there by bus. Sometimes it'll take a lot of buses. But they're just there. They're part of your world.'

Someone shouted, 'Yes!'

I was amazed to see it wasn't one of the children; it was Mrs Sass. I realize now that she thought I was being a bit metaphorical. She thought I was going to say something about how education opens up new worlds for you or something. But I didn't. I said, 'Let's go!' No one moved. They all thought I was being metaphorical too. I said, 'Come on. What are we doing here? Let's go. Come on. Follow me.'

I don't know where that last bit came from. It just came out. It was part of the flow of the thing. I walked down the middle of the hall towards the doors at the back. It took a minute, but somebody followed me. Then someone else. Then someone else and someone else and everyone followed me out of the hall, through the lower-school exit and into the playground.

The sun was shining. The birds were singing. I walked up to the gates and pushed. Nothing happened. Waterloo High is a high-security school. The gates are locked at 9 a.m. and no one can get in or out without a swipe card. That's why there was a man in a leather jacket standing on the other side of the gates, talking into the intercom.

'I'm the new head of media studies,' he was saying.

And over the intercom the secretary was saying, 'I don't understand. You're already here. You're taking assembly.'

By then Mrs Sass was at the gate. She looked at the actual new head of media studies. Then she looked at me and she hissed, 'Who are you?'

I did try to explain it all to her. I said, 'I'm really sorry, Lorraine.'

'Don't call me Lorraine any more. It's Mrs Sass.'

'Yes, Mrs Sass.'

'Why didn't you tell me your real name?'

'I did.'

'But . . . well, you should have more sense, a big lad like you.'

When I got home Mum said, 'So how did it go? First day at big school?'

I said, 'All right.'

'Is that all you've got to say? All right?'

'No.'

'What else?'

'I'm starving.' Sometimes it's better not to go into too much detail.

Skimpily Red

★★

Celia Gentles

I've never seen Miss Nixon
so flustered or so vexed
as when I saw her picking up
a pair of pants in Next.

Miss Nixon's rather strict and prim.
She teaches us R.E.
The knickers she was purchasing
were silk and r-e-d.

I grinned at her. She put them back,
looked guilty as a thief.
I couldn't help but notice
they were very, very brief.

Her eyes met mine. She gave me such
a long hard icy stare,
and said 'Will Johnson! Why are you
in Ladies Underwear?'

As scarlet as those skimpy pants
I felt my face grow red.
Then Mum looked up, peered round
    the stand.
'My son's with me,' she said.

Worst Christmas
Puddings

The New
Treasure Seekers

★★

EXTRACT FROM CHAPTER TWO

E. Nesbit

(approximate reading time 16 minutes)

*Oswald, Dora, Dicky, Alice, H.O. and Noël are the Bastable
children. Just before Christmas their father is called away. As
their mother is dead, the children are left in the care of
Matilda, a housekeeper.*

Before Father went away he took Dora and Oswald into
his study, and said –

'I'm awfully sorry I've got to go away, but it is very serious business, and I must go. You'll be good while I'm away,
kiddies, won't you?'

We promised faithfully. Then he said –

'There are reasons – you wouldn't understand if I
tried to tell you – but you can't have much of a Christmas
this year. But I've told Matilda to make you a good plain
pudding. Perhaps next Christmas will be brighter.'

When Father had been seen off at Lewisham Station

with his bags, and a plaid rug in a strap, we came home again, and it was horrid. There were papers and things littered all over his room where he had packed. We tidied the room up – it was the only thing we could do for him. It was Dicky who accidentally broke his shaving-glass, and H.O. made a paper boat out of a letter we found out afterwards Father particularly wanted to keep. This took us some time, and when we went into the nursery the fire was black out, and we could not get it alight again, even with the whole *Daily Chronicle*. Matilda, who was our general then, was out, as well as the fire, so we went and sat in the kitchen. There is always a good fire in kitchens. The kitchen hearthrug was not nice to sit on, so we spread newspapers on it.

It was sitting in the kitchen, I think, that brought to our minds my father's parting words – about the pudding, I mean.

The plain pudding instantly cast its shadow over the deepening gloom of our young minds.

'I wonder *how* plain she'll make it?' Dicky said.

'As plain as plain, you may depend,' said Oswald.

'I believe I could make a pudding that *wasn't* plain, if I tried,' Alice said. 'Why shouldn't we?'

'No chink,' said Oswald, with brief sadness.

'How much would it cost?' Noël asked, and added that Dora had twopence and H.O. had a French halfpenny.

Dora got the cookery-book out of the dresser drawer, where it lay doubled up among clothes-pegs, dirty dusters, scallop shells, string, penny novelettes, and the dining-room corkscrew. The general we had then – it seemed as if she did all the cooking on the cookery-book instead of on the baking-board, there were traces of so many bygone meals upon its pages.

'It doesn't say Christmas pudding at all,' said Dora.

'Try plum,' the resourceful Oswald instantly counselled.

Dora turned the greasy pages anxiously.

' "Plum-pudding, 518.

' "A rich, with flour, 517.

' "Christmas, 517.

' "Cold brandy sauce for, 241.'

'We shouldn't care about that, so it's no use looking.

' "Good without eggs, 518.

' "Plain, 518.'

'We don't want *that* anyhow. "Christmas, 517" – that's the one.'

It took her a long time to find the page. Oswald got a shovel of coals and made up the fire. It blazed up like the devouring elephant the *Daily Telegraph* always calls it. Then Dora read –

' "Christmas plum-pudding. Time six hours." '

'To eat it in?' said H.O.

'No, silly! to make it.'

'Forge ahead, Dora,' Dicky replied.

Dora went on –

' "2072. One pound and a half of raisins; half a pound of currants; three quarters of a pound of breadcrumbs; half a pound of flour; three-quarters of a pound of beef suet;

nine eggs; one wine glassful of brandy; half a pound of citron and orange peel; half a nutmeg; and a little ground ginger." I wonder *how* little ground ginger.'

'A teacupful would be enough, I think,' Alice said; 'we must not be extravagant.'

'We haven't got anything yet to be extravagant *with*,' said Oswald, who had toothache that day. 'What would you do with the things if you'd got them?'

'You'd "chop the suet as fine as possible" – I wonder how fine that is?' replied Dora and the book together – ' "and mix it with the breadcrumbs and flour; add the currants washed and dried." '

'Not starched, then,' said Alice.

' "The citron and orange peel cut into thin slices" – I wonder what they call thin? Matilda's thin bread-and-butter is quite different from what I mean by it – "and the raisins stoned and divided." How many heaps would you divide them into?'

'Seven, I suppose,' said Alice; 'one for each person and one for the pot – I mean pudding.'

' "Mix it all well together with the grated nutmeg and ginger. Then stir in nine eggs well beaten, and the brandy" – we'll leave that out, I think – "and again mix it thoroughly together that every ingredient may be moistened; put it into a buttered mould, tie over tightly, and boil for six hours. Serve it ornamented with holly and brandy poured over it." '

'I should think holly and brandy poured over it would be simply beastly,' said Dicky.

'I expect the book knows. I daresay holly and water would do as well though. "This pudding may be made a month before" – it's no use reading about that though, because we've only got four days to Christmas.'

'It's no use reading about any of it,' said Oswald, with thoughtful repeatedness, 'because we haven't got the things, and we haven't got the coin to get them.'

'We might get the tin somehow,' said Dicky.

'There must be lots of kind people who would subscribe to a Christmas pudding for poor children who hadn't any,' Noël said.

'Well, I'm going skating at Penn's,' said Oswald. 'It's no use thinking about puddings. We must put up with it plain.'

So he went, and Dicky went with him.

When they returned to their home in the evening the fire had been lighted again in the nursery, and the others were just having tea. Alice said –

'Matilda is in a frightful rage about your putting those coals on the kitchen fire, Oswald. She's locked the coal-cellar door, and she's got the key in her pocket. I don't see how we can boil the pudding.'

'What pudding?' said Oswald dreamily. He was thinking of a chap he had seen at Penn's who had cut the date 1899 on the ice with four strokes.

'*The* pudding,' Alice said. 'Oh, we've had such a time, Oswald! First Dora and I went to the shops to find out exactly what the pudding would cost – it's only two and elevenpence halfpenny, counting in the holly. We've got eight-and-sevenpence.'

Alice and Dora went out and bought the things next morning. They bought double quantities, so that it came to five shillings and elevenpence, and was enough to make a noble pudding. There was a lot of holly left over for decorations. We used very little for the sauce. The money that was left we spent very anxiously in other things to eat, such as dates and figs and toffee.

We did not tell Matilda about it. She was a red-haired girl, and apt to turn shirty at the least thing.

Concealed under our jackets and overcoats, we carried the parcels up to the nursery, and hid them in the treasure-chest we had there. It was the bureau drawer. It was locked up afterwards because the treacle got all over the green baize and the little drawers inside it while we were waiting to begin to make the pudding. It was the grocer told us we ought to put treacle in the pudding, and also about not so much ginger as a teacupful.

When Matilda had begun to pretend to scrub the floor (she pretended this three times a week so as to have an excuse not to let us in the kitchen, but I know she used to read novelettes most of the time, because Alice and I had a squint through the window more than once), we barricaded the nursery door and set to work. We were very careful to be quite clean. We washed our hands as well as the currants. I have sometimes thought we did not get all the soap off the currants. The pudding smelt like a washing-day when the time came to cut it open. And we washed a corner of the table to chop the suet on. Chopping suet looks easy till you try.

Father's machine he weighs letters with did to weigh out the things. We did this very carefully, in case the grocer had not done so. Everything was right except the raisins. H.O. had carried them home. He was very young then, and there was a hole in the corner of the paper bag and his mouth was sticky.

Lots of people have been hanged to a gibbet in chains on evidence no worse than that, and we told H.O. so till he cried. This was good for him. It was not unkindness to H.O., but part of our duty.

Chopping suet as fine as possible is much harder than any one would think, as I said before. So is crumbling bread – especially if your loaf is new, like ours was. When we had done them the breadcrumbs and the suet were both very large and lumpy, and of a dingy grey colour, something like pale slate pencil.

They looked a better colour when we had mixed them with the flour. The girls had washed the currants with Brown Windsor soap and the sponge. Some of the currants got inside the sponge and kept coming out in the bath for days afterwards. I see now that this was not quite nice. We cut the candied peel as thin as we wish people would cut our bread-and-butter. We tried to take the stones out of the raisins, but they were too sticky, so we just divided them up in seven lots. Then we mixed the other things in the wash-hand basin from the spare bedroom that was always spare. We each put in our own lot of raisins and turned it all into a pudding-basin, and tied it up in one of Alice's pinafores, which was the nearest thing to a proper pudding-cloth we could find – at any rate clean. What was left sticking to the wash-hand basin did not taste so bad.

'It's a little bit soapy,' Alice said, 'but perhaps that will boil out; like stains in table-cloths.'

It was a difficult question how to boil the pudding. Matilda proved furious when asked to let us, just because some one had happened to knock her hat off the scullery door and Pincher had got it and done for it. However, part of the embassy nicked a saucepan while the others were being told what Matilda thought about the hat, and we got hot water out of the bath-room and made it boil over our nursery fire. We put the pudding in – it was now getting on towards the hour of tea – and let it boil. It boiled for an hour and a quarter. Then Matilda came suddenly in and said, 'I'm not going to have you messing about in here with my saucepans'; and she tried to take it off the fire. I think I have forgotten who caught hold of her first to make her chuck it. I am sure no needless violence was used. Anyway, while the struggle progressed, Alice and Dora took the saucepan away and put it in the boot-cupboard under the stairs and put the key in their pocket.

This sharp encounter made every one very hot and cross. We got over it before Matilda did, but we brought her round before bedtime.

All the house was still. The gas was out all over the house except on the first landing, when several darkly shrouded figures might have been observed creeping down-stairs to the kitchen.

We got out our saucepan. The kitchen fire was red, but

low; the coal-cellar was locked, and there was nothing in the scuttle but a little coal-dust and the piece of brown paper that is put in to keep the coals from tumbling out through the bottom where the hole is. We put the saucepan on the fire and plied it with fuel – two *Chronicles*, a *Telegraph*, and two *Family Herald* novelettes were burned in vain. I am almost sure the pudding did not boil at all that night.

'Never mind,' Alice said. 'We can each nick a piece of coal every time we go into the kitchen tomorrow.'

This daring scheme was faithfully performed, and by night we had nearly half a waste-paper basket of coal, coke, and cinders.

There was more fire left in the grate that night, and we fed it with the fuel we had collected. This time the fire blazed up, and the pudding boiled like mad. This was the time it boiled two hours – at least I think it was about that, but we dropped asleep on the kitchen tables and dresser. You dare not be lowly in the night in the kitchen, because of the beetles. We were aroused by a horrible smell. It was the pudding-cloth burning. All the water had secretly boiled itself away. We filled it up at once with cold, and the saucepan cracked. So we cleaned it and put it back on the shelf and took another and went to bed. You see what a lot of trouble we had over the pudding. Every evening till Christmas, which had now become only the day after tomorrow, we sneaked down in the inky midnight and boiled that pudding for as long as it would.

On Christmas morning we chopped the holly for the sauce, but we put hot water (instead of brandy) and moist sugar. Some of them said it was not so bad.

Christmas Pudding

★★

Charles Thomson

It lay on the table
proudly displayed.
'The best Christmas pudding,'
said Mum, 'ever made.

You'll all find out
just how good in a minute,
for I've put some special
ingredients in it.'

It did seem sort
of strange somehow.
I couldn't quite
describe it now –

like something from
the fourth dimension.
'It is,' said Mum,
'my own invention.'

'You'll all remember
this – don't doubt it!'
Gran peered. 'There's something
odd about it.'

'Well, here we go,'
smiled Mum with pride
and grasped the knife
that lay beside.

'This is how puddings
should be made.'
The candlelight
gleamed off the blade.

There was a hush.
Time seemed to stop.
The knife blade touched
the pudding top.

The room shook in
a blinding flash,
a huge bang
and a mighty crash.

'Aliens!' I thought.
'Is my laser loaded?'
But no – the pudding
had exploded.

We sat there stunned
in frozen poses.
Bits of it
were up our noses.

Mum looked very
close to tears.
Bits of it
were in our ears.

Bits of it
dropped down the chair.
Bits of it
were in our hair.

Still no one moved
from where we sat.
Bits of it
were on the cat.

'Well then,' said Dad,
'no need to wait.'
Yes – bits of it
were on the plate.

'You're right, dear. Each
year in December,
this is a dish
that we'll remember.'

Bits covered the table
like lumpy lacquer.
'Very clever – a Christmas
pudding cracker.'

Going Up and Coming Down

Double Act

★★

CHAPTER NINE
Jacqueline Wilson

(approximate reading time 16 minutes)

Ruby and Garnet are identical ten-year-old twins. Sadly their mother died three years ago, and since then they have done everything together. They have gone to an audition for a television version of Enid Blyton's book Twins at St Clare's. *Perhaps this is their chance to be famous actresses.*

It was so *weird* seeing so many twins. Ruby and I have seen identical twins before, obviously, but never *hundreds* of pairs. It was as if the whole world had split into two. I felt as if I was splitting too. We've always felt so different. Unique. Special. It's what made us *us*. But standing there in that street we were just part of the crowd. Totally ordinary. With nothing at all to make us stand out.

'Let's go back home,' I said to Ruby. 'Look at them all. We don't stand a chance.'

'Don't be so ridiculous,' said Ruby furiously. 'I keep telling and telling and telling you, this is our big chance.

We're not giving up now. We'll show them all. We'll act better than any of them.'

'But I can't act at *all*, Ruby.'

She just gave me this terrible look, took hold of my arm, and marched me to the end of the very long queue.

We passed big twins, little twins, pretty twins, plain twins, showy twins, shabby twins, girly-girly twins, tomboy twins, even real boy twins.

'They obviously haven't even read the book!' said Ruby dismissively. 'Unless they're going to put on frocks and wigs and play the part in drag.'

'But look at some of the others. The ones with the big smiles and loud voices. I bet they've been to acting school,' I said.

'Well, so what. I've done my best to school you in acting. Now come on, let's go over our parts.'

'Not out here, in front of everyone,' I said, agonized.

'Look, you're the one who needs heaps of practice, not me,' said Ruby. Then she pulled me close and muttered in my ear, 'We'll just do it in whispers, OK? And I've been thinking – we'll have to inject a little oomph into our act to make us stand out in front of all these others. So we'll still do the scene with the twins having a battle with Mam'zelle, but we'll act Mam'zelle too. Don't look so scared, I'll do her. I am good at doing zee French accent, ma chérie, oh la la, très bon.'

But as it turned out we didn't get a chance to do any of our act. We had to wait hours and hours in the queue and I was desperate to go to the loo so when we did eventually get inside the building I had to walk around with my legs crossed and we had to give our names and addresses and date of birth and school to this lady at a desk and then we went upstairs and I was scared I might really wet myself and it would be the sheep situation all over again only worse but there were toilets along the corridor and a big cloakroom where you were supposed to change only we didn't have anything to change into, 'cos we were wearing it. But Ruby pinched my cheeks to give me a bit more colour and I tidied our hair although my hands were trembling so I could barely tie a knot and then we got into *another* queue, waiting to get into the actual audition room.

It got scarier and scarier and I had to dash back to the loo once or twice and even Ruby got a bit fidgety and she kept staring round at all the other twins. They were rehearsing their routines and they all seemed so brilliant that Ruby started to frown and bite her nails.

'I didn't figure we might have to dance,' she mumbled. 'They don't do any dancing in the story do they? Although maybe they're turning it into a musical version? So if we're asked, we'll sing . . . er . . . not a pop song, they'll all do that. We could do "My Bonnie Lies Over the Ocean" with hand gestures.'

'I'm not singing, especially not with hand gestures!' I said. 'You know we can't sing in tune, either of us.'

'Well, we could just sort of say the words, with lots of expression,' said Ruby relentlessly. 'And if we have to dance well . . . we'll just have to jump and jiggle a bit. Improvise. You copy me, OK?'

This was so obviously not OK that I didn't even bother to protest.

'We could work on a routine now, you know,' said Ruby, hopping and skipping and kicking out one leg.

She kicked a little too enthusiastically, and there was an argument with the twins in front of us.

They were dressed up in wonderfully old-fashioned school uniform – gymslips and baggy blouses and lisle stockings and strappy shoes. One of the lisle stockings had a little ladder now where it had connected with Ruby's kick, and the mother of the laddered-lisle was very cross indeed.

'Look, it was an accident – anyway, it just adds to her general schoolgirl . . . *authenticity*,' said Ruby, pronouncing this big word with pride.

The mother didn't seem convinced, and the schoolgirl twins were still getting all shirty too, but then they were called into the audition room so they rushed off in a fluster.

'Us next,' said Ruby. She took hold of me by the shoulders. 'We're going to do great, Garnet. Better than any of this dopey stupid showy-offy lot. You and me. Ruby and Garnet. We'll act it all out and it won't be scary at all, it'll just be like us playing in private at home. Trust me.'

I tried. And then it was our turn. And it wasn't at all like playing in private. We were shown on to this stage and there were lots of people watching us and a camera filming us and I was so frightened I nearly fell over. Ruby grabbed me by the hand and hissed 'Twin-grin' and marched us into the middle of the stage.

'Hi, twins,' said this woman with short hair and a smock.

'Hi there,' said Ruby, imitating her voice, trying to sound all cool and casual, though I could see little beads of sweat on her forehead.

She nudged me, and I squeaked 'Hi' too.

'We've got our audition piece all prepared,' Ruby said brightly, trying to show them we were dead professional. 'I'm Pat and she's Isabel and I'm also Mam'zelle and at the end I'm Janet as well.'

They all laughed, for some reason. I blushed, because I was scared they thought Ruby was silly, but Ruby didn't seem to mind. She laughed too.

'We'd love to see your little number some time, twins, but right now we just want to test out your voices,' said the woman with the short hair. 'Sooo – twin number one. Tell me what you had to eat yesterday.'

Ruby blinked at her. But then she threw back her hair, put her hand on one hip, and got started.

'OK, you want to know what I had to eat yesterday. Well, breakfast was boring old muesli again. Garnet and I used to have Coco Pops and jam sandwiches and they were yummy, but now we have this awful woman living with us, our dad's girlfriend, and she's into health foods so it's bye-bye Coco Pops, hello muesli – all this oat and bran that makes your face ache munching and then there are these little raisins like rabbit droppings, yuck.'

They were all laughing again, but this time even I could see that this was good. They loved Ruby.

'Right, now, twin two, tell us what you had for lunch,' said the woman with short hair.

They stopped looking at Ruby. They looked at me. And Ruby looked at me too. Desperately. Terrified I was going to let us down.

I tried to pretend to myself that I wasn't shy stupid scaredy-cat Garnet. I made out I was Ruby. I threw back my hair. I put my hand on my hip. I opened my mouth to start.

I had it all worked out what I was going to do. I was going to tell about Rose's garlic crumble and how it not only tasted absolutely disgusting, but people ducked and dodged for days afterwards whenever we breathed in their direction and we'd worn out six toothbrushes already trying to take the taste away. I could be funny too if I really tried. I could be just as good as Ruby. I *could*.

But then someone came bursting through the door and stood there, staring. *Dad!*

And I couldn't. I simply couldn't.

He didn't say anything to stop me.

But he didn't need to. I couldn't get started, not in front of him. I opened my mouth – but nothing came out. I tried to speak, but I couldn't even squeak.

'Come *on*, Garnet,' said Ruby.

I gulped, I opened my mouth, I tried. But all I managed was a goldfish impersonation.

'Look, I'll say what we had for lunch,' said Ruby.

'No, sweetie, we've already heard you. We want your twin to talk now. Let's skip lunch. And tea and supper.

What time did you go to bed, twin two?'

I saw Ruby flash her eyes at me. I knew she was willing me to tell a funny story about our bed-delaying tactics, our constant unnecessary trips to the bathroom, our midnight raids on the fridge, our frequent nocturnal ramblings – all deliberately done to unnerve Dad and Rose, so that they could never totally relax into unwedded bliss.

I could tell it, but not in front of *Dad*.

So, after several centuries had gone by and I actually saw the short-haired woman glance at her watch, I started a stupid mumble about 'Well, we're supposed to start getting ready for bed at nine, ten at weekends, but we often try to stay up.'

My voice was this sad expressionless little squeak. I saw Ruby close her eyes in agony. I saw Dad hang his head. I saw the short-haired woman and all her colleagues shaking their heads. I saw it all and I shrank down to mouse-size to match my squeak.

'Thank you, sweetie. Off you go, twins. Next!' said the short-haired woman. She was already staring past us, smiling at the new set of twins.

'No, hang on a minute!' said Ruby. 'Look, my sister isn't very well, she's been sick, she's not normally like this, she can speak up and be ever so funny, I swear she can. How about if we just do a couple of minutes of our prepared piece? Give us a chance. We've used up all our savings getting here and we're going to get in terrible trouble with our dad when we get back . . .'

'Yes, it's a shame, sweetie, but we don't really have the

time,' said the short-haired woman, and she put her arm round both of us. It wasn't just sympathy. She propelled us gently but firmly to the edge of the stage.

Even in the midst of her despair Ruby remembered the camera, twisting round and grimacing in agony, and then she sighed and waved her hand.

I could hear a few chuckles.

'That kid's a caution,' said someone.

'Yeah. Pity about her twin.'

It was only a murmur. But it was like a giant roaring in my ears. It wouldn't soften or stop.

I couldn't seem to hear properly even when Dad caught up with us.

'You bet you're in terrible trouble,' he said furiously. 'How *dare* you run off here like this, when I expressly forbade it. I couldn't believe it when we woke up and found you both gone. I was so worried I was going to call the police, but Rose insisted you'd both be all right and that you'd obviously gone for this idiotic audition.'

'Well, it was a complete waste of time anyway,' said Ruby. 'You really blew it for us, Dad. We were doing just great and then you had to come barging in and put us off our stroke.'

'Put *me* off. Not you,' I said. 'And it wasn't Dad's fault. He waited. He gave us a chance. But I mucked it up. That's what they said. You were great, Ruby, yeah. But I was useless. They said so.'

'No they didn't,' said Ruby. 'And anyway, they didn't give you a proper chance. It wasn't fair.'

'You don't want to be an actress anyway, Garnet,' said Dad. 'And even if you'd both been offered the parts, I wouldn't have let you take them. Ruby can act when she grows up, but I don't want my girls turning into ghastly little child stars, thank you very much.'

'There's no chance of me being any sort of star,' I said, and I started crying. I couldn't bear it. They were both so sorry for me. Dad was still mega-mad because we'd sneaked off up to London by ourselves, but he was holding back his anger for a bit to try to comfort me.

And Ruby wasn't cross with me. She should hate me for ever because I did muck it up. I should have said all that stuff and never mind about Dad being there. I *could* have done. Only I didn't. I let her down. I'll always let her down.

She's the biggest and the brightest and the best.

She's the caution.

She's the star.

It's a pity she's stuck with me.

Pity about her twin.

Pity about her twin.

Pity about her twin.

Give Yourself a Hug

★★

Grace Nichols

Give yourself a hug
when you feel unloved

Give yourself a hug
when people put on airs
to make you feel a bug

Give yourself a hug
when everyone seems to give you
a cold-shoulder shrug

Give yourself a hug –
a big big hug

And keep on singing,
'Only one in a million like me
Only one in a million-billion-trillion-zillion
like me.'

Kings and Things

The Death of King Arthur

★★

FROM *STORIES OF KING ARTHUR'S KNIGHTS*

Mary MacGregor

(approximate reading time 10 minutes)

King Arthur ruled Britain from his royal palace at Camelot where the bravest of his knights were allowed to sit at the Round Table – a symbol of equality. For many years the kingdom prospered, but when Arthur's best friend Sir Lancelot fell in love with Arthur's wife, Queen Guinevere, everything began to go wrong. Lancelot fled to Brittany and Arthur went after him, leaving the country in the charge of his scheming nephew, Modred.

It was not to win renown that King Arthur had gone far across the sea, for he loved his own country so well, that to gain glory at home made him happiest of all.

But a false knight with his followers was laying waste the country across the sea, and Arthur had gone to wage war against him.

'And you, Sir Modred, will rule the country while I am gone,' the King had said. And the knight smiled as he thought of the power that would be his.

At first the people missed their great King Arthur, but as the months passed they began to forget him, and to talk only of Sir Modred and his ways.

And he, that he might gain the people's praise, made easier laws than ever Arthur had done, till by and by there were many in the country who wished that the King would never come back.

When Modred knew what the people wished, he was glad, and he made up his mind to do a cruel deed.

He would cause letters to be written from beyond the sea, and the letters would tell that the great King Arthur had been slain in battle.

And when the letters came the people read, 'King Arthur is dead,' and they believed the news was true.

And there were some who wept because the noble King was slain, but some had no time to weep. 'We must find a new King,' they said. And because his laws were easy, these chose Sir Modred to rule over them.

The wicked knight was pleased that the people wished him to be their King. 'They shall take me to Canterbury to crown me,' he said proudly. And the nobles took him there, and amid shouts and rejoicings he was crowned.

But it was not very long till other letters came from across the sea, saying that King Arthur had not been slain, and that he was coming back to rule over his own country once more.

When Sir Modred heard that King Arthur was on his way home, he collected a great army and went to Dover to try to keep the King from landing.

But no army would have been strong enough to keep Arthur and his knights away from the country they loved so well. They fought fiercely till they got on shore and scattered all Sir Modred's men.

Then the knight gathered together another army, and chose a new battlefield.

But King Arthur fought so bravely that he and his men were again victorious, and Sir Modred fled to Canterbury.

Many of the people began to forsake the false knight now, and saying that he was a traitor, they went back to King Arthur.

But still Sir Modred wished to conquer the King. He would go through the counties of Kent and Surrey and raise a new army.

Now King Arthur had dreamed that if he fought with Sir Modred again he would be slain. So when he heard that the knight had raised another army, he thought, 'I will meet this traitor who has betrayed me. When he looks in my face, he will be ashamed and remember his vow of obedience.'

And he sent two bishops to Sir Modred. 'Say to the knight that the King would speak with him alone,' said Arthur.

And the traitor thought, 'The King wishes to give me gold or great power, if I send my army away without fighting.' 'I will meet King Arthur,' he said to the bishops.

But because he did not altogether trust the King he said he would take fourteen men with him to the meeting-place, 'and the King must have fourteen men with him too,' said Sir Modred. 'And our armies shall keep watch when we meet, and if a sword is lifted it shall be the signal for battle.'

Then King Arthur arranged a feast for Sir Modred and his men. And as they feasted all went merrily till an adder glided out of a little bush and stung one of the knight's men. And the pain was so great, that the man quickly drew his sword to kill the adder.

And when the armies saw the sword flash in the light, they sprang to their feet and began to fight, 'for this is the signal for battle,' they thought.

And when evening came there were many thousand slain and wounded, and Sir Modred was left alone. But Arthur had still two knights with him, Sir Lucan and Sir Bedivere.

When King Arthur saw that his army was lost and all his knights slain but two, he said, 'Would to God I could find Sir Modred, who has caused all this trouble.'

'He is yonder,' said Sir Lucan, 'but remember your dream, and go not near him.'

'Whether I die or live,' said the King, 'he shall not escape.' And seizing his spear he ran to Sir Modred, crying, 'Now you shall die.'

And Arthur smote him under the shield, and the spear passed through his body, and he died.

Then, wounded and exhausted, the King fainted, and

his knights lifted him and took him to a little chapel not far from a lake.

As the King lay there, he heard cries of fear and pain from the distant battlefield.

'What causes these cries?' said the King wearily. And to soothe the sick King, Sir Lucan said he would go to see.

And when he reached the battlefield, he saw in the moonlight that robbers were on the field stooping over the slain, and taking from them their rings and their gold. And those that were only wounded, the robbers slew, that they might take their jewels too.

Sir Lucan hastened back, and told the King what he had seen.

'We will carry you farther off, lest the robbers find us here,' said the knights. And Sir Lucan lifted the King on one side and Sir Bedivere lifted him on the other.

But Sir Lucan had been wounded in the battle, and as he lifted the King he fell back and died.

Then Arthur and Sir Bedivere wept for the fallen knight.

Now the King felt so ill that he thought he would not live much longer, and he turned to Sir Bedivere: 'Take Excalibur, my good sword,' he said, 'and go with it to the lake, and throw it into its waters. Then come quickly and tell me what you see.'

Sir Bedivere took the sword and went down to the lake. But as he looked at the handle with its sparkling gems and the richness of the sword, he thought he could not throw it away. 'I will hide it carefully here among the rushes,' thought the knight. And when he had hidden it, he went slowly to the King and told him he had thrown the sword into the lake.

'What did you see?' asked the King eagerly.

'Nothing but the ripple of the waves as they broke on the beach,' said Sir Bedivere.

'You have not told me the truth,' said the King. 'If you love me, go again to the lake, and throw my sword into the water.'

Again the knight went to the water's edge. He drew the sword from its hiding-place. He would do the King's will, for he loved him. But again the beauty of the sword made him pause. 'It is a noble sword; I will not throw it away,' he murmured, as once more he hid it among the rushes. Then he went back more slowly, and told the King that he had done his will.

'What did you see?' asked the King.

'Nothing but the ripples of the waves as they broke on the beach,' repeated the knight.

'You have betrayed me twice,' said the King sadly, 'and yet you are a noble knight! Go again to the lake, and do not betray me for a rich sword.'

Then for the third time Sir Bedivere went to the water's edge, and drawing the sword from among the rushes, he flung it as far as he could into the lake.

And as the knight watched, an arm and a hand appeared above the surface of the lake. He saw the hand seize the sword, and shaking it three times, disappear again under the water. Then Sir Bedivere went back quickly to the King, and told him what he had seen.

'Carry me to the lake,' entreated Arthur, 'for I have been here too long.'

And the knight carried the King on his shoulders down to the water's side. There they found a barge lying, and seated in it were three Queens, and each Queen wore a black hood. And when they saw King Arthur they wept.

'Lay me in the barge,' said the King. And when Sir Bedivere had laid him there, King Arthur rested his head on the lap of the fairest Queen. And they rowed from land.

Sir Bedivere, left alone, watched the barge as it drifted out of sight, and then he went sorrowfully on his way, till he reached a hermitage. And he lived there as a hermit for the rest of his life.

And the barge was rowed to a vale where the King was healed of his wound.

And some say that now he is dead, but others say that King Arthur will come again, and clear the country of its foes.

William I
1066

★★

Eleanor Farjeon

William the First was the first of our kings,
Not counting Ethelreds, Egberts and things
And he had himself crowned and anointed and blest
In Ten-Sixty-I-Needn't-Tell-You-The-Rest.

But being a Norman, King William the First
By the Saxons he conquered was hated and cursed,
And they planned and they plotted far into the night,
Which William could tell by the candles alight.

Then William decided these rebels to quell
By ringing the Curfew, a sort of a bell,
And if any Saxon was found out of bed
After eight o'clock sharp, it was Off With His Head!

So at BONG NUMBER ONE they all started to run
Like a warren of rabbits upset by a gun;

At BONG NUMBER TWO they were all in a stew,
Flinging cap after tunic and hose after shoe;

At BONG NUMBER THREE they were bare to the
    knee,
Undoing the doings as quick as can be;
At BONG NUMBER FOUR they were stripped to the
    core,
And pulling on nightshirts the wrong side before;
At BONG NUMBER FIVE they were looking alive,
And bizzing and buzzing like bees in a hive.

At BONG NUMBER SIX they gave themselves kicks,
Tripping over the rushes to snuff out the wicks;
At BONG NUMBER SEVEN from Durham to Devon,
They slipped up a prayer to Our Father in Heaven;
And at BONG NUMBER EIGHT it was fatal to wait,
So with hearts beating all at a terrible rate,
In a deuce of a state, I need hardly relate,
They jumped BONG into bed like a bull at a gate.

Disappearing Acts

The London Eye Mystery

★★

CHAPTERS ONE AND EIGHT
Siobhan Dowd

(approximate reading time 15 minutes)

My favourite thing to do in London is to fly the Eye.

On a clear day you can see for twenty-five miles in all directions because you are in the largest observation wheel ever built. You are sealed into one of the thirty-two capsules with the strangers who were next to you in the queue, and when they close the doors, the sound of the city is cut off. You begin to rise. The capsules are made of glass and steel and are hung from the rim of the wheel. As the wheel turns, the capsules use the force of gravity to stay upright. It takes thirty minutes to go a full circle.

From the top of the ride, Kat says London looks like toy-town and the cars on the roads below look like abacus beads going left and right and stopping and starting. I think London looks like London and the cars like cars, only smaller.

The best thing to see from up there is the river Thames. You can see how it loops and curves but when you are on the ground you think it is straight.

The next best thing to look at is the spokes and metallic hawsers of the Eye itself. You are looking at the only cantilevered structure of its kind on earth. It is designed like a giant bicycle wheel in the sky, supported by a massive A-frame.

It is also interesting to watch the capsules on either side of yours. You see strangers looking out, just like you are doing. The capsule that is higher than yours becomes lower than yours and the capsule that is lower becomes higher. You have to shut your eyes because it makes a strange feeling go up your oesophagus. You are glad the movement is smooth and slow.

And then your capsule goes lower and you are sad because you do not want the ride to end. You would like to go round one more time, but it's not allowed. So you get out feeling like an astronaut coming down from space, a little lighter than you were.

We took Salim to the Eye because he'd never been up before. A stranger came up to us in the queue, offering us a free ticket. We took it and gave it to Salim. We shouldn't have done this, but we did. He went up on his own at 11.32, 24 May, and was due to come down at 12.02 the same day. He turned and waved to Kat and me as he boarded, but you couldn't see his face, just his shadow. They sealed him in with twenty other people whom we didn't know.

Kat and I tracked Salim's capsule as it made its orbit. When it reached its highest point, we both said, 'NOW!' at the same time and Kat laughed and I joined in. That's how we knew we'd been tracking the right one. We saw the people bunch up as the capsule came back down, facing northeast towards the automatic camera for the souvenir photograph. They were just dark bits of jackets, legs, dresses and sleeves.

Then the capsule landed. The doors opened and the passengers came out in twos and threes. They walked off in different directions. Their faces were smiling. Their paths probably never crossed again.

But Salim wasn't among them.

We waited for the next capsule and the next and the one after that. He still didn't appear. Somewhere, somehow, in the thirty minutes of riding the Eye, in his sealed capsule, he had vanished off the face of the earth. This is how having a funny brain that runs on a different operating system from other people's helped me to figure out what had happened.

We walked over to where Mum and Aunt Gloria were having coffee.

'Let's lie,' hissed Kat. 'About taking that ticket from a stranger.' She grabbed me by the wrist so hard it hurt.

'Lie,' I repeated. 'Hrumm. Lie.'

'We could say that Salim got lost in the crowds, that he—' She let my wrist go. 'Oh, forget it,' she said. 'I know telling a lie with you is useless. And stop doing that duck-that's-forgotten-how-to-quack look!'

We reached the table where Aunt Gloria and Mum sat talking up another storm. We stood by them in silence. A pounding started up in my ears, as if my blood pressure had shot up above normal, which is what Mum says happens to her when Kat drives her distracted.

'There you are,' Aunt Gloria said. 'Have you got the tickets?'

Kat waited for me to say something.

I waited for Kat to say something.

'Where's Salim?' asked Mum. 'Not still in the queue?'

'Hrumm,' I said. 'No.'

Mum looked as if Salim might be behind us. 'Where then?'

'We don't know!' Kat blurted. 'This man – he came up and offered us a ticket. For free. He'd bought it and then decided he couldn't face the ride.'

'He had claustrophobia,' I said.

'That's right. And the queue was terrible. So we took the ticket. And gave it to Salim. And Salim went up on his own. And he didn't come down.'

Aunt Gloria shaded her eyes and looked up. 'So he's up there somewhere,' she said, smiling.

Kat had a hand to her mouth and her fingers were wriggling like worms. I'd never seen her act like this before. 'No,' she said. 'He went up ages ago. Ted and I tracked his pod. But when it came down – he wasn't on it.'

Mum's face scrunched up, which meant she was a) puzzled or b) cross or c) both. 'What on earth do you mean, he wasn't on it?'

'He went up, Mum,' I repeated. 'But he didn't come

down.' My hand flapped and Mum's mouth went round like an O. 'He defied the law of gravity, Mum. He went up but he didn't come down. Which means Newton got it wrong. Hrumm.'

Mum looked more cross than puzzled by now. But Aunt Gloria's face remained smooth like paper without a crease. 'Bet I know what happened,' she said, smiling.

'What?' we all said.

'He probably went round one more time.'

The simplicity of this solution struck Kat and me at once.

'That's it. He just stayed on,' said Kat.

I looked at my watch. 'In which case he'll land at twelve thirty-two.'

We went back to the Eye, this time with Mum. Aunt Gloria said she would stay where she was, because Salim would know where to find her if we missed him.

We watched several pods open and close, but no Salim. 12.32 came and went. No Salim. Mum asked the staff if they could help. A woman from customer services came to talk to us. She said she'd like to help but couldn't. She said that the London Eye management policy states that children are not supposed to ride without an adult accompanying them.

Mum's eyebrows met in the middle. 'Kat,' she said, 'I relied on you. You should never have accepted that ticket. You should never have let Salim go up on his own.'

Something terrible happened then. Kat started crying. She hadn't done that in ages. She pressed her knuckles up against her cheekbones. 'It's always my fault. Never Ted's. I'm always to blame. Ted never does anything wrong.'

'You're older, Kat. But obviously not much wiser.'

Mum bit her lip and they both stared at each other.

'Why don't we call his mobile?' I said.

Mum frowned as if I'd said something stupid; then her face cleared (which is what you say when someone's been looking unhappy and then they suddenly cheer up, and I like this phrase because it is another weather metaphor. A face can clear just like the sky can when a dark cumulonimbus cloud has passed over and the sun comes out again). 'Of course! Ted,' Mum said, smiling, 'you're a genius. We should have thought of that right away.'

We hurried back to where Aunt Gloria was waiting at the table. There was no sign of Salim. When she saw us come back without him, she gave a big sigh. 'Where has that boy *got* to?' she said.

Mum picked up Aunt Gloria's handbag. 'Call him. Get your mobile out. Give him a call.'

'OK,' Aunt Gloria said. 'He's probably only a few yards away.'

She pressed some buttons and put the phone to her ear with a smile and a nod of her head. Then her expression did the opposite of 'clear'. It clouded over.

'*The mobile phone you are calling has been switched off,*' she repeated. '*Please try later.*'

She dropped the phone down on the table. Her lips trembled.

'Why's his phone off?' she whispered. 'Why?'

Kat said later that we spent the next hour darting around the South Bank like headless chickens. It is a puzzling fact that chickens can run around in a frenzy for some seconds after being decapitated, but I do not think they do this for a whole hour. We looked everywhere but there was no sign of Salim. We went back to the staff, who called in the police. A constable took our names and addresses. He asked if we thought Salim knew his way back to our house. Probably, we said. Then he told us to do three things:

a) keep trying his phone

b) go home and wait, and

c) try not to worry.

He said he would report Salim's disappearance to the rest of the squad on duty in the area. If he hadn't re-appeared in a few hours, an officer would visit us. Kat tried to explain about how Salim had vanished sometime after getting *on* the wheel and before getting *off*. He looked at her as if she was imagining it.

'Children don't evaporate into thin air,' he said. 'Not in my experience.'

So then we did b) and went home to wait. We were hoping to see Salim in our front garden but he wasn't there. So Aunt Gloria did a), that is, she pressed and repressed the redial button on her mobile phone. Mum got her inside and made tea. Kat fetched a china plate and arranged some chocolate fingers on it. This was Mum and Kat's way of trying to do c). But nobody ate any. We all tried not to worry but nobody succeeded.

Then Mum called Dad and told him what had happened. He said he was round the corner at the Barracks and nearly finished for the day. He'd come home to see if there was anything he could do to help. Mum hung up. Immediately the phone rang. Aunt Gloria grabbed it.

'Salim!' she said loudly.

She listened for a few seconds and her face turned into a mini ice age (that's my own expression and I hope you can guess what it means). She slammed the phone down.

'Some man,' she said, 'selling conservatory windows.' She made it sound as if selling conservatory windows was a crime against humanity. She looked at the clock on the mantelpiece.

'Three hours,' she said. 'He's been gone three hours. This hasn't happened before.'

Then she started pacing up and down the room, punching one fist into the palm of another. It was very interesting to watch. I wondered what kind of weather she could be compared to and decided on a thunderstorm, very localized, with forked lightning.

'Salim,' she said, as if he were in the room, 'I'll have your guts for garters.'

I had never heard this before and wondered what garters were. Kat told me later that they are what women used to wear around their thighs to keep their stockings up and they are elasticated. I do not think guts would be a tidy way of doing this.

Then Aunt Gloria said, 'Oh, my boy, what have they done to you?'

I wondered whom she meant by 'they'.

Then, 'You'd better be back by Wednesday or we'll miss our flight to New York.'

Then, 'That stupid policeman. Saying not to worry. I'll bet *he* doesn't have children.'

Then, 'Supposing some terrible gang has abducted him? Oh, mercy, mercy, no!'

Then she noticed me watching her.

'What are *you* staring at?' She pointed a pink-lacquered fingernail at me and jabbed the air. 'If you hadn't suggested going to the London Eye, this would never have happened. You and your bloody bicycle wheel in the sky!' She flopped onto the sofa and made a wailing sound. 'Oh, Ted. I'm sorry. I didn't mean that.'

'Glo!' Mum said, rushing to sit beside her. 'Calm down, love.' She flapped her hand at me as if I was an annoying fly. I figured out that this meant she didn't want me anywhere nearby.

I went to see Kat, who was in the kitchen sitting at the table. She had her headphones on and her head down on her arms so she couldn't see me or hear me.

So I went up to my room.

How to Disappear

★★

Amanda Dalton

First rehearse the easy things.
Lose your words in a high wind,
walk in the dark on an unlit road,
observe how other people mislay keys,
their diaries, new umbrellas.
See what it takes to go unnoticed
in a crowded room. Tell lies:
I love you. I'll be back in half an hour.
I'm fine.

The childish things.
Stand very still behind a tree,
become a cowboy, say you have died,
climb into wardrobes, breathe on a mirror
until there's no one there, and practise magic
tricks with smoke and fire –
a flick of the wrist and the victim's lost
his watch, his wife, his ten pound note.
    Perfect it.
Hold your breath a little longer every time.

The hardest things.
Eat less, much less, and take a vow of silence.
Learn the point of vanishing, the moment
embers turn to ash, the sun falls down,
the sudden white-out comes.
And when it comes again – it will –
just walk at it, walk into it, and walk,
until you know that you're no longer
anywhere.

Toads

The Wind in the Willows

★★

EXTRACT FROM CHAPTER TEN

Kenneth Grahame

(approximate reading time 11 minutes)

Mr Toad of Toad Hall is jolly, rich, boastful and absolutely loves motor cars. In our extract he has been sent to prison for twenty years for stealing a car. Disguised as a washerwoman, he manages to escape and is now on the run from the police.

He sang as he walked, and he walked as he sang, and got more inflated every minute. But his pride was shortly to have a severe fall.

After some miles of country lanes he reached the high road, and as he turned into it and glanced along its white length, he saw approaching him a speck that turned into a dot and then into a blob, and then into something very familiar; and a double note of warning, only too well known, fell on his delighted ear.

'This is something like!' said the excited Toad. 'This is real life again, this is once more the great world from which I have been missed so long! I will hail them, my brothers of the wheel, and pitch them a yarn, of the sort that has been so successful hitherto; and they will give me a lift, of course, and then I will talk to them some more; and, perhaps, with luck, it may even end in my driving up to Toad Hall in a motor-car! That will be one in the eye for Badger!'

He stepped confidently out into the road to hail the motor-car, which came along at an easy pace, slowing down as it neared the lane; when suddenly he became very pale, his heart turned to water, his knees shook and yielded under him, and he doubled up and collapsed with a sickening pain in his interior. And well he might, the unhappy animal; for the approaching car was the very one he had stolen out of the yard of the Red Lion Hotel on that fatal day when all his troubles began! And the people in it were the very same people he had sat and watched at luncheon in the coffee-room!

He sank down in a shabby, miserable heap in the road, murmuring to himself in despair, 'It's all up! It's all over now! Chains and policemen again! Prison again! Dry bread and water again! O, what a fool I have been! What did I want to go strutting about the country for, singing conceited songs, and hailing people in broad day on the high road, instead of hiding till nightfall and slipping home quietly by back ways! O hapless Toad! O ill-fated animal!'

The terrible motor-car drew slowly nearer and nearer till at last he heard it stop just short of him. Two gentlemen got out and walked round the trembling heap of crumpled misery lying in the road, and one of them said, 'O dear! this is very sad! Here is a poor old thing – a washerwoman apparently – who has fainted in the road! Perhaps she is overcome by the heat, poor creature; or possibly she has not had any food to-day. Let us lift her into the car and take her to the nearest village, where doubtless she has friends.'

They tenderly lifted Toad into the motor-car and propped him up with soft cushions, and proceeded on their way.

When Toad heard them talk in so kind and sympathetic a manner, and knew that he was not recognized, his courage began to revive, and he cautiously opened first one eye and then the other.

'Look!' said one of the gentlemen, 'she is better already. The fresh air is doing her good. How do you feel now, ma'am?'

'Thank you kindly, sir,' said Toad in a feeble voice, 'I'm feeling a great deal better!'

'That's right,' said the gentleman. 'Now keep quite still, and, above all, don't try to talk.'

'I won't,' said Toad. 'I was only thinking, if I might sit on the front seat there, beside the driver, where I could get the fresh air full in my face, I should soon be all right again.'

'What a very sensible woman!' said the gentleman. 'Of course you shall.' So they carefully helped Toad into the front seat beside the driver, and on they went again.

Toad was almost himself again by now. He sat up, looked about him, and tried to beat down the tremors, the yearnings, the old cravings that rose up and beset him and took possession of him entirely.

'It is fate!' he said to himself. 'Why strive? Why struggle?' and he turned to the driver at his side.

'Please sir,' he said, 'I wish you would kindly let me try and drive the car for a little. I've been watching you carefully, and it looks so easy and so interesting, and I should like to be able to tell my friends that once I had driven a motor-car!'

The driver laughed at the proposal, so heartily that the gentleman inquired what the matter was. When he heard, he said, to Toad's delight, 'Bravo, ma'am! I like your spirit. Let her have a try, and look after her. She won't do any harm.'

Toad eagerly scrambled into the seat vacated by the driver, took the steering-wheel in his hands, listened with affected humility to the instructions given him, and set the car in motion, but very slowly and carefully at first, for he was determined to be prudent.

The gentlemen behind clapped their hands and applauded, and Toad heard them saying, 'How well she does it! Fancy a washerwoman driving a car as well as that, the first time!'

Toad went a little faster; then faster still, and faster.

He heard the gentlemen call out warningly, 'Be careful, washerwoman!' And this annoyed him, and he began to lose his head.

The driver tried to interfere, but he pinned him down in his seat with one elbow, and put on full speed. The rush of air in his face, the hum of the engine, and the light jump of the car beneath him intoxicated his weak brain. 'Washerwoman, indeed!' he shouted recklessly. 'Ho! ho! I am the Toad, the motor-car snatcher, the prison-breaker, the Toad who always escapes! Sit still and you shall know what driving really is, for you are in the hands of the famous, the skilful, the entirely fearless Toad!'

With a cry of horror the whole party rose and flung themselves on him. 'Seize him!' they cried, 'seize the Toad, the wicked animal who stole our motor-car! Bind him, chain him, drag him to the nearest police-station. Down with the desperate and dangerous Toad!'

Alas! they should have thought, they ought to have been more prudent, they should have remembered to stop the motor-car somehow before playing any pranks of that sort. With a half-turn of the wheel the Toad sent the car crashing through the low hedge that ran along the road-side. One mighty bound, a violent shock, and the wheels of the car were churning up the thick mud of a horse-pond.

Toad found himself flying through the air with the strong upward rush and delicate curve of a swallow. He liked the motion, and was just beginning to wonder whether it would go on until he developed wings and turned into a Toad-bird, when he landed on his back with a thump, in the soft, rich grass of a meadow. Sitting up, he could just see the motor-car in the pond, nearly sub-merged; the gentlemen and the driver, encumbered by their long coats, were floundering helplessly in the water.

He picked himself up rapidly, and set off running across country as hard as he could, scrambling through hedges, jumping ditches, pounding across fields, till he was breathless and weary, and had to settle down into an easy walk. When he had recovered his breath somewhat, and was able to think calmly, he began to giggle, and from giggling he took to laughing, and he laughed till he had to sit down under a hedge. 'Ho, ho!' he cried, in ecstasies of self-admiration, 'Toad again! Toad, as usual comes out on the top! Who was it got them to give him a lift? Who managed to get on the front seat for the sake of fresh air? Who persuaded them into letting him see if he could drive? Who landed them all in a horse-pond? Who escaped, flying gaily and unscathed through the air, leaving the narrow-minded, grudging, timid excursionists in the mud where they should rightly be? Why, Toad, of course; clever Toad, great Toad, *good* Toad!'

Then he burst into song again, and chanted with uplifted voice:

'The motor-car went Poop-poop-poop,
As it raced along the road.
Who was it steered it into a pond?
Ingenious Mr Toad!

O, how clever I am! How clever, how clever how very clev—'

A slight noise at a distance behind him made him turn his head and look. O horror! O misery! O despair!

About two fields off, a chauffeur in his leather gaiters and two large rural policemen were visible, running towards him as hard as they could go!

Poor Toad sprang to his feet and pelted away again, his heart in his mouth. 'O my!' he gasped, as he panted along, 'what an *ass* I am! What a *conceited* and heedless ass! Swaggering again! Shouting and singing songs again! Sitting still and gassing again! O my! O my! O my!'

He glanced back, and saw to his dismay that they were gaining on him. On he ran desperately, but kept looking back and saw that they still gained steadily. He did his best, but he was a fat animal, and his legs were short, and still they gained. He could hear them close behind him now. Ceasing to heed where he was going, he struggled on blindly and wildly, looking back over his shoulder at the now triumphant enemy, when suddenly the earth failed under his feet, he grasped at the air, and, splash! he found himself head over ears in deep water, rapid water, water that bore him along with a force he could not contend with; and he knew that in his blind panic he had run straight into the river!

He rose to the surface and tried to grasp the reeds and the rushes that grew along the water's edge close under the bank, but the stream was so strong that it tore them out of his hands. 'O my!' gasped poor Toad, 'if ever I steal a motor-car again! If ever I sing another conceited song' – then down he went, and came up breathless and spluttering. Presently he saw that he was approaching a big dark hole in the bank, just above his head, and as the stream bore him past he reached up with a paw and caught hold of the edge and held on. Then slowly and with difficulty he drew himself up out of the water, till at last he was able to rest his elbows on the edge of the hole. There he remained for some minutes, puffing and panting, for he was quite exhausted.

A Song of Toad

★★

Kenneth Grahame

The world has held great Heroes,
　As history-books have showed;
But never a name to go down to fame
　Compared to that of Toad!

The clever men at Oxford
　Know all that there is to be knowed.
But they none of them know one half as much
　As intelligent Mr Toad!

The animals sat in the ark and cried,
　Their tears in torrents flowed.
Who was it said, 'There's land ahead'?
　Encouraging Mr Toad!

The Army all saluted
　As they marched along the road.
Was it the King? Or Kitchener?
　No. It was Mr Toad.

The Queen and her ladies-in-waiting
    Sat at the window and sewed.
She cried, 'Look! Who's that *handsome* man?'
    They answered, 'Mr Toad.'

The motor-car went Poop-poop-poop
    As it raced along the road.
Who was it steered it into a pond?
    Ingenious Mr Toad!

Bad Boys and Bad Girls

The Knight at Arms

★★

CHAPTER FOUR FROM *MORE WILLIAM*

Richmal Crompton

(approximate reading time 14 minutes)

'A knight,' said Miss Drew, who was struggling to inspire her class with enthusiasm for Tennyson's 'Idylls of the King', 'a knight was a person who spent his time going round succouring the oppressed.'

'Suckin' wot?' said William, bewildered.

'Succour means to help. He spent his time helping anyone who was in trouble.'

'How much did he get for it?' asked William.

'Nothing, of course,' said Miss Drew, appalled by the base commercialism of the twentieth century. 'He helped the poor because he *loved* them, William. He had a lot of adventures and fighting and he helped beautiful, per-secuted damsels.'

William's respect for the knight rose.

'Of course,' said Miss Drew hastily, 'they needn't necess-arily be beautiful, but, in most of the stories we have, they were beautiful.'

Followed some stories of fighting and adventure and

the rescuing of beautiful damsels. The idea of the thing began to take hold of William's imagination.

'I say,' he said to his chum Ginger after school, 'that knight thing sounds all right. Suckin' – I mean helpin' people an' fightin' an' all that. I wun't mind doin' it an' you could be my squire.'

'Yes,' said Ginger slowly, 'I'd thought of doin' it, but I'd thought of *you* bein' the squire.'

'Well,' said William after a pause, 'let's be squires in turn. You first,' he added hastily.

'Wot'll you give me if I'm first?' said Ginger, displaying again the base commercialism of his age.

William considered.

'I'll give you first drink out of a bottle of ginger-ale wot I'm goin' to get with my next money. It'll be three weeks off 'cause they're takin' the next two weeks to pay for an ole window wot my ball slipped into by mistake.'

He spoke with the bitterness that always characterised his statements of the injustice of the grown-up world.

'All right,' said Ginger.

'I won't forget about the drink of ginger-ale.'

'No, you won't,' said Ginger simply. 'I'll remind you all right. Well, let's set off.'

' 'Course,' said William, 'it would be *nicer* with armour an' horses an' trumpets, but I 'spect folks ud think anyone a bit soft wot went about in the streets in armour now, 'cause these times is different. She said so. Anyway, she said we could still be knights an' help people, di'n't she? Anyway, I'll get my bugle. That'll be *something*.'

William's bugle had just returned to public life after one of its periodic terms of retirement into his father's keeping.

William took his bugle proudly in one hand and his pistol (the glorious result of a dip in the bran tub at a school party) in the other, and, sternly denying themselves the pleasures of afternoon school, off the two set upon the road of romance and adventure.

'I'll carry the bugle,' said Ginger, ''cause I'm squire.'

William was loth to give up his treasure.

'Well, I'll carry it now,' he said, 'but when I begin fightin' folks, I'll give it you to hold.'

They walked along for about a mile without meeting anyone. William began to be aware of a sinking feeling in the region of his waist.

'I wonder wot they *eat*,' he said at last. 'I'm gettin' so's I wouldn't mind sumthin' to eat.'

'We di'n't ought to have set off before dinner,' said the squire with after-the-event wisdom. 'We ought to have waited till *after* dinner.'

'You ought to have *brought* sumthin',' said William severely. 'You're the squire. You're not much of a squire not to have brought sumthin' for me to eat.'

'An' me,' put in Ginger. 'If I'd brought any I'd have brought it for me more'n for you.'

William fingered his minute pistol.

'If we meet any wild animals . . .' he said darkly.

A cow gazed at them mournfully over a hedge.

'You might go an' milk that,' suggested William. 'Milk

'ud be better'n nothing.'

'*You* go an' milk it.'

'No, I'm not squire. I bet squires did the milkin'. Knights wu'n't of done the milkin'.'

'I'll remember,' said Ginger bitterly, 'when you're squire, all the things wot you said a squire ought to do when I was squire.'

They entered the field and gazed at the cow from a respectful distance. She turned her eyes upon them sadly.

'Go on!' said the knight to his reluctant squire.

'I'm not good at cows,' objected that gentleman.

'Well, I will, then!' said William with reckless bravado, and advanced boldly upon the animal. The animal very slightly lowered its horns (perhaps in sign of greeting) and emitted a sonorous mo-o-o-o-o. Like lightning the gallant pair made for the road.

'Anyway,' said William gloomily, 'we'd got nothin' to put it in, so we'd only of got tossed for nothin', p'raps, if we'd gone on.'

They walked on down the road till they came to a pair of iron gates and a drive that led up to a big house. William's spirits rose. His hunger was forgotten.

'Come on!' he said. 'We might find someone to rescue here. It looks like a place where there might be someone to rescue.'

There was no one in the garden to question the right of entry of two small boys armed with a bugle and a toy pistol. Unchallenged they went up to the house. While the knight was wondering whether to blow his bugle at the front door or by the open window, they caught sight suddenly of a vision inside the window. It was a girl as fair and slim and beautiful as any wandering knight could desire. And she was speaking fast and passionately.

William, ready for all contingencies, marshalled his forces.

'Follow me!' he whispered and crept on all fours nearer the window. They could see a man now, an elderly man with white hair and a white beard.

'And how long will you keep me in this vile prison?' she was saying in a voice that trembled with anger, 'base wretch that you are!'

'Crumbs!' ejaculated William.

'Ha! Ha!' sneered the man. 'I have you in my power. I will keep you here a prisoner till you sign the paper which will make me master of all your wealth, and beware, girl, if you do not sign, you may answer for it with your life!'

'Golly!' murmured William.

Then he crawled away into the bushes, followed by his attendant squire.

'Well,' said William, his face purple with excitement, 'we've found someone to rescue all *right*. He's a base wretch, wot she said, all *right*.'

'Will you kill him?' said the awed squire.

'How big was he? Could you see?' said William the discreet.

'He was ever so big. Great big face he had, too, with a beard.'

'Then I won't try killin' him – not straight off. I'll

think of some plan – somethin' cunnin'.'

He sat with his chin on his hands, gazing into space, till they were surprised by the opening of the front door and the appearance of a tall, thick-set, elderly man. William quivered with excitement. The man went along a path through the bushes. William and Ginger followed on all fours with elaborate caution. At every almost inaudible sound from Ginger, William turned his red, frowning face on to him with a resounding 'Sh!' The path ended at a small shed with a locked door. The man opened the door – the key stood in the lock – and entered.

Promptly William, with a snarl expressive of cunning and triumph, hurled himself at the door and turned the key in the lock.

'Here!' came an angry shout from inside. 'Who's that? What the devil—'

'You low ole caitiff!' said William through the keyhole.

'Who the deuce—?' exploded the voice.

'You base wretch, like wot she said you was,' bawled William, his mouth still applied closely to the keyhole.

'Let me out at once, or I'll—'

'You mean ole oppressor!'

'Who the deuce are you? What's the tomfool trick? Let me *out*! Do you hear?'

A resounding kick shook the door.

'I've gotter pistol,' said William sternly. 'I'll shoot you dead if you kick the door down, you mangy ole beast!'

The sound of kicking ceased and a scrambling and scraping, accompanied by oaths, proceeded from the interior.

'I'll stay on guard,' said William with the tense expression of the soldier at his post, 'an' you go an' set her free. Go an' blow the bugle at the front door, then they'll know something's happened,' he added simply.

Miss Priscilla Greene was pouring out tea in the drawing-room. Two young men and a maiden were the recipients of her hospitality.

'Dad will be here in a minute,' she said. 'He's just gone to the dark-room to see to some photos he'd left in toning or fixing, or something. We'll get on with the rehearsal as soon as he comes. We'd just rehearsed the scene he and I have together, so we're ready for the ones where we all come in.'

'How did it go off?'

'Oh, quite well. We knew our parts, anyway.'

'I think the village will enjoy it.'

'Anyway, it's never very critical, is it? And it loves a melodrama.'

'Yes. I wonder if Father knows you're here. He said he'd come straight back. Perhaps I'd better go and find him.'

'Oh, let me go, Miss Greene,' said one of the youths ardently.

'Well, I don't know whether you'd find the place. It's a shed in the garden that he uses. We use half as a dark-room and half as a coal-cellar.'

'I'll go—'

He stopped. A nightmare sound, as discordant as it was

ear-splitting, filled the room. Miss Greene sank back into her chair, suddenly white. One of the young men let a cup of tea fall neatly from his fingers on to the floor and there crash into fragments. The young lady visitor emitted a scream that would have done credit to a factory siren. Then at the open French window appeared a small boy holding a bugle, purple-faced with the effort of his performance.

One of the young men was the first to recover speech. He stepped away from the broken crockery on the floor as if to disclaim all responsibility for it and said sternly:

'Did you make that horrible noise?'

Miss Greene began to laugh hysterically.

'Do have some tea now you've come,' she said to Ginger.

Ginger remembered the pangs of hunger, of which excitement had momentarily rendered him oblivious, and, deciding that there was no time like the present, took a cake from the stand and began to consume it in silence.

'You'd better be careful,' said the young lady to her hostess; 'he might have escaped from the asylum. He looks mad. He had a very mad look, I thought, when he was standing at the window.'

'He's evidently hungry, anyway. I can't think why Father doesn't come.'

Here Ginger, fortified by a walnut bun, remembered his mission.

'It's all right now,' he said. 'You can go home. He's shut up. Me an' William shut him up.'

'You see!' said the young lady, with a meaning glance around. 'I *said* he was from the asylum. He looked mad. We'd better humour him and ring up the asylum. Have another cake, darling boy,' she said in a tone of honeyed sweetness.

Nothing loth, Ginger selected an ornate pyramid of icing.

At this point there came a bellowing and crashing and tramping outside and Miss Priscilla's father, roaring fury and threats of vengeance, hurled himself into the room. Miss Priscilla's father had made his escape by a small window at the other end of the shed. To do this he had had to climb over the coals in the dark. His face and hands and clothes and once-white beard were covered with coal. His eyes gleamed whitely.

'An abominable attack … utterly unprovoked … dastardly ruffians!'

Here he stopped to splutter because his mouth was full of coal dust. While he was spluttering, William, who had just discovered that his bird had flown, appeared at the window.

'He's got out,' he said reproachfully. 'Look at him. He's got out. An' all our trouble for nothing. Why di'n't someone *stop* him gettin' out?'

*   *   *

William and Ginger sat on the railing that separated their houses.

'It's not really much *fun* bein' a knight,' said William slowly.

'No,' agreed Ginger. 'You never know when folks *is* oppressed. An' anyway, wot's one afternoon away from school to make such a fuss about?'

'Seems to me from wot Father said,' went on William gloomily, 'you'll have to wait a jolly long time for that drink of ginger-ale.'

An expression of dejection came over Ginger's face.

'An' you wasn't even ever squire,' he said. Then he brightened.

'They were jolly good cakes, wasn't they?' he said.

William's lips curved into a smile of blissful reminiscence.

'*Jolly* good!' he agreed.

Matilda Who Told Lies, and Was Burned to Death

★★

Hilaire Belloc

Matilda told such dreadful lies,
It made one gasp and stretch one's eyes;
Her Aunt, who, from her earliest youth,
Had kept a strict regard for truth,
Attempted to believe Matilda:
The effort very nearly killed her,
And would have done so, had not she
Discovered this infirmity.
For once, towards the close of day,
Matilda, growing tired of play,
And finding she was left alone,
Went tiptoe to the telephone
And summoned the immediate aid
Of London's noble fire-brigade.
Within an hour the gallant band
Were pouring in on every hand,
From Putney, Hackney Downs, and Bow
With courage high and hearts a-glow

They galloped, roaring through the town,
'Matilda's house is burning down!'
Inspired by British cheers and loud
Proceeding from the frenzied crowd,
They ran their ladders through a score
Of windows on the ballroom floor;
And took peculiar pains to souse
The pictures up and down the house,
Until Matilda's Aunt succeeded
In showing them they were not needed;
And even then she had to pay
To get the men to go away!
It happened that a few weeks later
Her Aunt was off to the theatre
To see that interesting play
The Second Mrs Tanqueray,
She had refused to take her niece
To hear this entertaining piece:
A deprivation just and wise
To punish her for telling lies.
That night a fire *did* break out –
You should have heard Matilda shout!
You should have heard her scream and bawl,
And throw the window up and call
To people passing in the street –
(The rapidly increasing heat
Encouraging her to obtain
Their confidence) – but all in vain!
For every time she shouted 'Fire!'

They only answered 'Little liar!'
And therefore when her Aunt returned,
Matilda, and the house, were burned.

White Bird

The Silver Swan

★★

Michael Morpurgo

(approximate reading time 14 minutes)

The silver swan, who living had no note,
When death approached, unlocked her silent throat:
Leaning her breast against the reedy shore
Thus sung her first and last, and sung no more.

Orlando Gibbons

A swan came to my loch one day, a silver swan. I was fishing for trout in the moonlight. She came flying in above me, her wings singing in the air. She circled the loch twice, and then landed, silver, silver in the moonlight.

I stood and watched her as she arranged her wings behind her and sailed out over the loch, making it entirely her own. I stayed as late as I could, quite unable to leave her.

I went down to the loch every day after that, but not to fish for trout, simply to watch my silver swan.

In those early days I took great care not to frighten her away, keeping myself still and hidden in the shadow of the alders. But even so, she knew I was there – I was sure of it.

Within a week I would find her cruising along the lochside, waiting for me when I arrived in the early mornings. I took to bringing some bread crusts with me. She would look sideways at them at first, rather disdainfully. Then, after a while, she reached out her neck, snatched them out of the water, and made off with them in triumph.

One day I dared to dunk the bread crusts for her, dared to try to feed her by hand. She took all I offered her and came back for more. She was coming close enough now for me to be able to touch her neck. I would talk to her as I stroked her. She really listened, I know she did.

I never saw the cob arrive. He was just there swimming beside her one morning out on the loch. You could see the love between them even then. The princess of the loch had found her prince. When they drank they dipped their necks together, as one. When they flew, their wings beat together, as one.

She knew I was there, I think, still watching. But she did not come to see me again, nor to have her bread crusts. I tried to be more glad for her than sad for me, but it was hard.

As winter tried, and failed, to turn to spring, they began to make a home on the small island, way out in the middle of the loch. I could watch them now only through my binoculars. I was there every day I could be – no matter what the weather.

Things were happening. They were no longer busy just preening themselves, or feeding, or simply gliding out over the loch taking their reflections with them. Between them they were building a nest – a clumsy messy excuse for a nest it seemed to me – set on a reedy knoll near the shore of their island.

It took them several days to construct. Neither ever seemed quite satisfied with the other's work. A twig was too big, or too small, or perhaps just not in the right place. There were no arguments as such, as far as I could see. But my silver swan would rearrange things, tactfully, when her cob wasn't there. And he would do the same when she wasn't there.

Then, one bright cold morning with the ground beneath my feet hard with a late and unexpected frost, I arrived to see my silver swan enthroned at last on her nest, her cob proudly patrolling the loch close by.

I knew there were foxes about even then. I had heard

their cries often enough echoing through the night. I had seen their footprints in the snow. But I had never seen one out and about, until now.

It was dusk. I was on my way back home from the loch, coming up through the woods, when I spotted a family of five cubs, their mother sitting on guard near by. Unseen and unsmelt, I crouched down where I was and watched.

I could see at once that they were starving, some of them already too weak even to pester their mother for food. But I could see too that she had none to give – she was thin and rangy herself. I remember thinking then: That's one family of foxes that's not likely to make it, not if the spring doesn't come soon, not if this winter goes on much longer.

But the winter did go on that year, on and on.

I thought little more of the foxes. My mind was on other things, more important things. My silver swan and her cob shared the sitting duties and the guarding duties, never leaving the precious nest long enough for me even to catch sight of the eggs, let alone count them. But I could count the days, and I did.

As the day approached I made up my mind I would go down to the loch, no matter what, and stay there until it happened – however long that might take. But the great day dawned foggy. Out of my bedroom window, I could barely see across the farmyard.

I ran all the way down to the loch. From the lochside I could see nothing of the island, nothing of the loch, only a few feet of limpid grey water lapping at the muddy shore.

I could hear the muffled *aarking* of a heron out in the fog, and the distant piping of a moorhen. But I stayed to keep watch, all that day, all the next.

I was there in the morning two days later when the fog began at last to lift and the pale sun to come through. The island was there again. I turned my binoculars at once on the nest. It was deserted. They were gone. I scanned the loch, still mist-covered in places. Not a ripple. Nothing.

Then out of nothing they appeared, my silver swan, her cob and four cygnets, coming straight towards me. As they came towards the shore they turned and sailed right past me. I swear she was showing them to me, parading them. They both swam with such easy power, the cygnets bobbing along in their wake. But I had counted wrong. There was another one, hitching a ride amongst his mother's folded wings. A snug little swan, I thought, littler than the others perhaps. A lucky little swan.

That night the wind came in from the north and the loch froze over. It stayed frozen. I wondered how they would manage. But I need not have worried. They swam about, keeping a pool of water near the island clear of ice. They had enough to eat, enough to drink. They would be fine. And every day the cygnets were growing. It was clear now that one of them was indeed much smaller, much weaker. But he was keeping up. He was coping. All was well.

Then, silently, as I slept one night, it snowed outside. It snowed on the farm, on the trees, on the frozen loch. I took bread crusts with me the next morning, just in case, and hurried down to the loch. As I came out of the woods I saw the fox's paw prints in the snow. They were heading down towards the loch.

I was running, stumbling through the drifts, dreading all along what I might find.

The fox was stalking around the nest. My silver swan was standing her ground over her young, neck lowered in attack, her wings beating the air frantically, furiously. I shouted. I screamed. But I was too late and too far away to help.

Quick as a flash the fox darted in, had her by the wing and was dragging her away. I ran out onto the ice. I felt it crack and give suddenly beneath me. I was knee-deep in the loch then, still screaming; but the fox would not be put off. I could see the blood, red, bright red, on the snow. The five cygnets were scattering in their terror. My silver swan was still fighting. But she was losing, and there was nothing I could do.

I heard the sudden singing of wings above me. The cob! The cob flying in, diving to attack. The fox took one look upwards, released her victim, and scampered off over the ice, chased all the way by the cob.

For some moments I thought my silver swan was dead. She lay so still on the snow. But then she was on her feet and limping back to her island, one wing flapping feebly, the other trailing, covered in blood and useless. She was gathering her cygnets about her. They were all there. She was enfolding them, loving them, when the cob came flying back to her, landing awkwardly on the ice.

He stood over her all that day and would not leave her side. He knew she was dying. So, by then, did I. I had nothing but revenge and murder in my heart. Time and again, as I sat there at the lochside, I thought of taking my father's gun and going into the woods to hunt down the killer fox. But then I would think of her cubs and would know that she was only doing what a mother fox had to do.

For days I kept my cold sad vigil by the loch. The cob was sheltering the cygnets now, my silver swan sleeping near by, her head tucked under her wing. She scarcely ever moved.

I wasn't there, but I knew the precise moment she died. I knew it because she sang it. It's quite true what they say about swans singing only when they die. I was at home. I had been sent out to fetch logs for the fire before I went up to bed. The world about me was crisp and bright under the moon. The song was clearer and sweeter than any human voice, than any birdsong, I had ever heard before. So sang my silver swan and died.

I expected to see her lying dead on the island the next morning. But she was not there. The cob was sitting still as a statue on his nest, his five cygnets around him.

I went looking for her. I picked up the trail of feathers and blood at the lochside, and followed where I knew it must lead, up through the woods. I approached silently.

The fox cubs were frolicking fat and furry in the sunshine, their mother close by intent on her grooming. There was a terrible wreath of white feathers near by, and telltale feathers too on her snout. She was trying to shake them off. How I hated her.

I ran at her. I picked up stones. I hurled them. I screamed at her. The foxes vanished into the undergrowth and left me alone in the woods. I picked up a silver feather, and cried tears of such raw grief, such fierce anger.

Spring came at long last the next day, and melted the ice. The cob and his five cygnets were safe. After that I came less and less to the loch. It wasn't quite the same without my silver swan. I went there only now and again, just to see how he was doing, how they were all doing.

At first, to my great relief, it seemed as if he was managing well enough on his own. Then one day I noticed there were only four cygnets swimming alongside him, the four bigger ones. I don't know what happened to the smaller one. He just wasn't there. Not so lucky, after all.

The cob would sometimes bring his cygnets to the lochside to see me. I would feed them when he came, but then after a while he just stopped coming.

The weeks passed and the months passed, and the cygnets grew and flew. The cob scarcely left his island now. He stayed on the very spot I had last seen my silver swan. He did not swim; he did not feed; he did not preen himself. Day by day it became clear that he was pining for her, dying for her.

Now my vigil at the lochside was almost constant again. I had to be with him; I had to see him through. It was what my silver swan would have wanted, I thought.

So I was there when it happened. A swan flew in from nowhere one day, down onto the glassy stillness of the loch. She landed right in front of him. He walked down into the loch, settled into the water and swam out to meet her. I watched them look each other over for just a few minutes. When they drank, they dipped their necks together, as one. When they flew, their wings beat together, as one.

Five years on and they're still together. Five years on and I still have the feather from my silver swan. I take it with me wherever I go. I always will.

Snow

**

Edward Thomas

In the gloom of whiteness,
In the great silence of snow,
A child was sighing
And bitterly saying: 'Oh,
They have killed a white bird up there on her
    nest,
The down is fluttering from her breast!'
And still it fell through the dusky brightness
On the child crying for the bird of the snow.

Wolf

White Fang

★★

EXTRACT FROM PART II, CHAPTER II

Jack London

(approximate reading time 17 minutes)

White Fang is the story of an animal who is three quarters wolf and one quarter dog. His parents are a she-wolf and One Eye. In this extract we hear about his birth in the wild where there is only one law: eat or be eaten.

The she-wolf's need to find the thing for which she searched had now become imperative. She was getting very heavy, and could run but slowly. Once, in the pursuit of a rabbit, which she ordinarily would have caught with ease, she gave over and lay down and rested. One Eye came to her; but when he touched her neck gently with his muzzle she snapped at him with such quick fierceness that he tumbled over backward and cut a ridiculous figure in his effort to escape her teeth. Her temper was now shorter than ever; but he had become more patient than ever and more solicitous.

And then she found the thing for which she sought. It was a few miles up a small stream that was frozen over and frozen down to its rocky bottom – a dead stream of solid white from source to mouth. The she-wolf was trotting wearily along, her mate well in advance, when she came upon the overhanging, high clay-bank. The wear and tear of spring storms and melting snows had underwashed the bank and in one place had made a small cave out of a narrow fissure.

She paused and entered its narrow mouth. For a short three feet she was compelled to crouch, then the walls widened and rose higher in a little round chamber nearly six feet in diameter. The roof barely cleared her head. It was dry and cosy. She inspected it with painstaking care, while One Eye, who had returned, stood in the entrance and patiently watched her. She dropped her head, with her nose to the ground and directed toward a point near to her closely bunched feet, and around this point she circled several times; then, with a tired sigh that was almost a grunt, she curled her body in, relaxed her legs, and dropped down, her head toward the entrance. One Eye, with pointed, interested ears, laughed at her, and beyond, outlined against the white light, she could see the brush of his tail waving good-naturedly. Her own ears, with a snuggling movement, laid their sharp points backward and down against the head for a moment, while her mouth opened and her tongue lolled peaceably out, and in this way she expressed that she was pleased and satisfied.

One Eye was hungry. Though he lay down in the entrance and slept, his sleep was fitful. He kept awaking and cocking his ears at the bright world without, where the April sun was blazing across the snow. When he dozed, upon his ears would steal the faint whispers of hidden trickles of running water, and he would rouse and listen intently. The sun had come back, and all the awakening Northland world was calling to him. Life was stirring. The feel of spring was in the air, the feel of growing life under the snow, of sap ascending in the trees, of buds bursting the shackles of the frost.

He cast anxious glances at his mate, but she showed no desire to get up. He could resist the call of the world no longer. Besides, he was hungry.

He crawled over to his mate and tried to persuade her to get up. But she only snarled at him, and he walked out alone into the bright sunshine to find the snow-surface soft underfoot and the travelling difficult. He went up the frozen bed of the stream, where the snow, shaded by the trees, was yet hard and crystalline. He was gone eight hours, and he came back through the darkness hungrier than when he had started. He had found game, but he had not caught it.

He paused at the mouth of the cave with a sudden shock of suspicion. Faint, strange sounds came from within. They were sounds not made by his mate, and yet they were remotely familiar. He bellied cautiously inside and was met by a warning snarl from the she-wolf. This he received without perturbation, though he obeyed it by keeping his distance; but he remained interested in the other sounds – faint, muffled sobbings and slubberings.

His mate warned him irritably away, and he curled up and slept in the entrance. When morning came and a dim light pervaded the lair, he again sought after the source of the remotely familiar sounds. There was a new note in his mate's warning snarl. It was a jealous note, and he was very careful in keeping a respectful distance. Nevertheless, he made out, sheltering between her legs against the length of her body, five strange little bundles of life, very feeble, very helpless, making tiny whimpering noises, with eyes that did not open to the light. He was surprised. It was not the first time in his long and successful life that this thing had happened. It had happened many times, yet each time it was as fresh a surprise as ever to him.

His mate looked at him anxiously. Every little while she emitted a low growl, and at times, when it seemed to her he approached too near, the growl shot up in her throat to a sharp snarl. Of her own experience she had no memory of the thing happening; but in her instinct, which was the experience of all the mothers of wolves, there lurked a memory of fathers that had eaten their new-born and helpless progeny. It manifested itself as a fear strong within her, that made her prevent One Eye from more closely inspecting the cubs he had fathered.

But there was no danger. Old One Eye was feeling the urge of an impulse, that was, in turn, an instinct that had come down to him from all the fathers of wolves. He did not question it, nor puzzle over it. It was there, in the fibre of his being; and it was the most natural thing in the world that he should obey it by turning his back on his new-born family and by trotting out and away on the meat-trail whereby he lived.

Five or six miles from the lair, the stream divided, its forks going off among the mountains at a right angle. Here, leading up the left fork, he came upon a fresh track. The footprint was much larger than the one his own feet made, and he knew that in the wake of such a trail there was little meat for him.

Half a mile up the right fork, his quick ears caught the sound of gnawing teeth. He stalked the quarry and found it to be a porcupine, standing upright against a tree and trying his teeth on the bark. One Eye approached carefully but hopelessly. He knew the breed, though he had never met it so far north before; and never in his long life had porcupine served him for a meal. But he had long since learned that there was such a thing as Chance, or Opportunity, and he continued to draw near. There was never any telling what might happen, for with live things events were somehow always happening differently.

The porcupine rolled itself into a ball, radiating long, sharp needles in all directions that defied attack. In his youth One Eye had once sniffed too near a similar, apparently inert ball of quills, and had the tail flick out suddenly in his face. One quill he had carried away in his muzzle, where it had remained for weeks, a rankling flame, until it finally worked out. So he lay down, in a comfortable crouching position, his nose fully a foot away, and out of the line of the tail. Thus he waited, keeping perfectly quiet. There was no telling. Something might happen. The porcupine might unroll. There might be opportunity for a deft and ripping thrust of paw into the tender, unguarded belly.

But at the end of half an hour he arose, growled wrathfully at the motionless ball, and trotted on. The day wore along, and nothing rewarded his hunt.

The urge of his awakened instinct of fatherhood was strong upon him. He must find meat. In the afternoon he blundered upon a ptarmigan. He came out of a thicket and found himself face to face with the slow-witted bird. It was sitting on a log, not a foot beyond the end of his nose. Each saw the other. The bird made a startled rise, but he struck it with his paw, and smashed it down to earth, then pounced upon it, and caught it in his teeth as it scuttled across the snow trying to rise in the air again. As his teeth crunched through the tender flesh and fragile bones, he began naturally to eat. Then he remembered, and, turning on the back-track, started for home, carrying the ptarmigan in his mouth.

A mile above the forks he came upon later imprints of the large tracks he had discovered in the early morning. He followed, prepared to meet the maker of it at every turn of the stream.

He slid his head around a corner of rock, where began an unusually large bend in the stream, and his quick eyes made out something that sent him crouching swiftly down. It was the maker of the track, a large female lynx. She was crouching as he had crouched once that day, in front of her the tight-rolled ball of quills. He now became a shadow, as he crept and circled around, and came up well to leeward of the silent, motionless pair.

He lay down in the snow, depositing the ptarmigan beside him, and with eyes peering through the needles of a low-growing spruce he watched the play of life before him – the waiting lynx and the waiting porcupine, each intent on life; and, such was the curiousness of the game, the way of life for one lay in the eating of the other, and the way of life for the other lay in being not eaten. While old One Eye, the wolf crouching in the covert, played his part, too, in the game, waiting for some strange freak of Chance, that might help him on the meat-trail which was his way of life.

Half an hour passed, an hour; and nothing happened.

One Eye moved slightly and peered forth with increased eagerness. Something was happening. The porcupine had at last decided that its enemy had gone away. Slowly, cautiously, it was unrolling its ball of impregnable armour. Slowly, slowly, the bristling ball straightened out and lengthened. One Eye, watching, felt a sudden moistness in his mouth and a drooling of saliva, involuntary, excited by the living meat that was spreading itself like a repast before him.

Not quite entirely had the porcupine unrolled when it discovered its enemy. In that instant the lynx struck. The blow was like a flash of light. The paw, with rigid claws curving like talons, shot under the tender belly and came back with a swift ripping movement. Had the porcupine been entirely unrolled, or had it not discovered its enemy a fraction of a second before the blow was struck, the paw would have escaped unscathed; but a side-flick of the tail sank sharp quills into it as it was withdrawn.

Everything had happened at once – the blow, the counter-blow, the squeal of agony from the porcupine, the big cat's squall of sudden hurt and astonishment. One Eye half arose in his excitement, his ears up, his tail straight out and quivering behind him. The lynx's bad temper got the best of her. She sprang savagely at the thing that had hurt her. But the porcupine, squealing and grunting, with dis-rupted anatomy trying feebly to roll up into its ball-protection, flicked out its tail again, and again the big cat squalled with hurt and astonishment. Then she fell to backing away and sneezing, her nose bristling with quills like a monstrous pin-cushion. She brushed her nose with her paws, trying to dislodge the fiery darts, thrust it into the snow, and rubbed it against twigs and branches, all the time leaping about, ahead, sidewise, up and down, in a frenzy of pain and fright.

She sneezed continually, and her stub of a tail was doing its best toward lashing about by giving quick, violent jerks. She quit her antics, and quieted down for a long minute. One Eye watched. And even he could not repress a start and an involuntary bristling of hair along his back when she suddenly leaped, without warning, straight up in the air, at the same time emitting a long and most terrible squall. Then she sprang away, up the trail, squall-ing with every leap she made.

It was not until her racket had faded away in the

distance and died out that One Eye ventured forth. He walked as delicately as though all the snow were carpeted with porcupine quills, erect and ready to pierce the soft pads of his feet. The porcupine met his approach with a furious squealing and a clashing of its long teeth. It had managed to roll up in a ball again, but it was not quite the old compact ball; its muscles were too much torn for that. It had been ripped almost in half, and was still bleeding profusely.

One Eye scooped out mouthfuls of the blood-soaked snow, and chewed and tasted and swallowed. This served as a relish, and his hunger increased mightily; but he was too old in the world to forget his caution. He waited. He lay down and waited, while the porcupine grated its teeth and uttered grunts and sobs and occasional sharp little squeals. In a little while, One Eye noticed that the quills were drooping and that a great quivering had set up. The quivering came to an end suddenly. There was a final defiant clash of the long teeth. Then all the quills drooped quite down, and the body relaxed and moved no more.

With a nervous, shrinking paw, One Eye stretched out the porcupine to its full length and turned it over on its back. Nothing had happened. It was surely dead. He studied it intently for a moment, then took a careful grip with his teeth and started off down the stream, partly carrying, partly dragging the porcupine, with head turned to the side so as to avoid stepping on the prickly mass. He recollected something, dropped the burden, and trotted back to where he had left the ptarmigan. He did not hesitate a moment. He knew clearly what was to be done, and this he did by promptly eating the ptarmigan. Then he returned and took up his burden.

When he dragged the result of his day's hunt into the cave, the she-wolf inspected it, turned her muzzle to him, and lightly licked him on the neck. But the next instant she was warning him away from the cubs with a snarl that was less harsh than usual and that was more apologetic than menacing. Her instinctive fear of the father of her progeny was toning down. He was behaving as a wolf father should, and manifesting no unholy desire to devour the young lives she had brought into the world.

Amulet

★★

Ted Hughes

Inside the wolf's fang, the mountain of heather.
Inside the mountain of heather, the wolf's fur.
Inside the wolf's fur, the ragged forest.
Inside the ragged forest, the wolf's foot.
Inside the wolf's foot, the stony horizon.
Inside the stony horizon, the wolf's tongue.
Inside the wolf's tongue, the doe's tears.
Inside the doe's tears, the frozen swamp.
Inside the frozen swamp, the wolf's blood.
Inside the wolf's blood, the snow wind.
Inside the snow wind, the wolf's eye.
Inside the wolf's eye, the North star.
Inside the North star, the wolf's fang.

Snake

The Siege of White Deer Park

★★

EXTRACT FROM CHAPTERS FOUR AND SIX

Colin Dann

(approximate reading time 10 minutes)

The animals of White Deer Park are in dreadful danger, for there is a savage killer at large in their nature reserve. No one has ever seen 'The Beast', but every day another animal goes missing.

Adder had returned to his home area after quitting the pondside, using the secluded route that was habitual to him. He liked to enjoy as much of the spring sunshine as he could, and he lay amongst the bracken very often, sleepily absorbing the sun's rays. The first new fern shoots were just pushing their heads above the surface and the pale green tightly-curled heads carried a promise of the fragrance that was to come in the summer. One day Adder was lying in this way, his red eyes glinting in the sunlight. He was thinking about his next meal but he was in no hurry to look for it. His reptilian stomach did not require to be filled with the mechanical regularity of a bird's or a mammal's. Because of his proximity to the stream that ran through the Park, he happened to be the first recipient of news brought by a very flustered Whistler.

It was early morning and the heron had been standing in the shallows in his usual sentry-like posture. As he watched for the rippling movement of a fish, out of the corner of his eye he saw an animal move slowly along the bank away from him. It was some twenty metres away and appeared to be looking for the best spot to descend for a drink. Whistler's immobility had kept him unobserved. He noted the animal was large, with sleek brown and black fur in blotches of colour which merged into stripes on its back. Its body had a powerful but streamlined appearance, with a long, thin, furry tail. It got down to the water's edge and, leaning on its front legs, lapped thirstily. As it drank, it maintained a watchful eye on its surroundings. It paused two or three times to look about. When it was satisfied it raised itself, shook one front paw in a kind of fastidiousness, and moved away with an unhurried, loose and undulating motion. Whistler was impressed by the creature's graceful movement. It looked round once more and he caught just a glimpse of a round whiskered face with two green eyes, and small ears and nose.

Whistler had held himself quite still during this entire episode. But now he hastened to fly off. He flapped his long wings and, with his stilt-like legs trailing beneath, he gained height and turned in the direction of his friends. A few seconds later he spied Adder sunbathing. He dropped down briefly to tell him what he had seen.

'What do you think it was?' he asked the snake.

'Oh, the creature we've all been looking for,' Adder answered nonchalantly, without even shifting his position. 'No question about it.'

'I wondered the same myself,' Whistler replied. 'I must go and spread the word.' He gave a farewell 'krornk' and flew away.

Adder's feigned lack of interest turned into action as soon as the heron was gone. He slid furtively from his couch in the bracken and made for the stream side. There would be footprints by the water and he wanted to compare them. He went along the bank and his eyes soon picked out the place where the animal had drunk. Yes, there were the marks! He examined them for a while to make quite sure.

'Just as I thought,' he lisped to himself. 'Identical.'

Now his curiosity was aroused. He wanted to see the creature for himself. He debated whether it was safe to follow in its wake along the bank. There was very little cover at that spot and he wanted to remain undetected. Only in that way could he hope to have a chance ofsurprising the stranger. He slithered hastily into the nearest patch of vegetation. As he lay hidden his mind began to concentrate itself on a grand scheme.

Some seasons ago, Adder had been the chief victor in a battle that the Farthing Wood animals had fought against some foxes. These had resented the animals establishing a new home for themselves in the Reserve. The snake had a weapon more telling than any of his friends possessed – the weapon of poison. He had used it before to rid them of a dangerous enemy. Now he began to entertain thoughts of doing so again – and with much more purpose. For the stranger who had come to dominate their lives was more powerful and dangerous than any fox. And, as long as it lived amongst them, it was a potential enemy of every animal in the Park. Adder had no way of knowing if his poison was sufficiently potent to immobilize such a big hunter. So there was only one way of finding out.

The snake glided through the plant stems, intent on his secret pursuit. Surprise was everything. There was a patch of bare ground between the clumps of vegetation he needed to cross. But, once across it, the cover was thick and tangled again. He slid into the open. All was quiet. His head was about to enter the next mass of growth when the breath was driven from his body. A heavy weight came down in the centre of his back along his vertebrae. He was pressed against the hard ground so tightly that he was unable even to wriggle his tail. Adder was securely pinioned . . .

Adder could see nothing of his attacker. He was unable to turn to look behind, and the pressure was so great on his body that he thought his bones might break. There were no animals in the Park who ate snake and so Adder was in no doubt that he was trapped either by a human foot, or, more likely, by the very creature he had intended himself to surprise. There was a momentary easing of the pressure and Adder at once tried to turn. As soon as he moved, a huge paw swung round and patted at his head. Luckily for him the claws were retracted.

For the first time in his life Adder was really scared. He was scared in a way that he would not have been if the beast who was attacking him had been one he understood – such as a fox or a hawk. Fear of the unknown coursed through his sluggish blood. He felt he had no hope of escape. Then, abruptly, the great weight bearing down on his back was removed.

For a moment Adder's fear kept him frozen into

immobility. He awaited the great blow that would crush the life out of him. But his paralysis lasted only a moment. Then he squirmed away painfully, in a desperate bid to reach the patch of vegetation. He was not permitted to. The paw descended again and knocked him back. The Beast was toying with him.

Adder kept moving – first this way, then that. Each time he was knocked back into place. Once a blow lifted him up into the air. He landed awkwardly. Pain racked his body but still he strove to get away. The Beast prodded him, tapped him and, finally, he felt its claws sear through his skin. He imagined he was going to be killed slowly in a form of torture, just as a cat will torment a bird or a mouse before the final kill. He wriggled in vain, like a creature in its death throes. Then a particularly heavy blow hooked him up high above the ground, over the vegetation, and suddenly Adder's scaly coils landed with a plop in the shallow part of the stream.

Like all snakes he was a good swimmer and, before he quite knew where he was, he instinctively rippled away into the deeper water. Only his head protruded above the surface. He looked back towards the bank and saw his assailant for the first time quite clearly. The Beast was staring out at the stream in an attempt to discover where its plaything had gone. Adder kept himself well hidden. After a while the Beast got bored and slowly padded away.

For a long time the snake dared not approach dry land, although the water felt as cold as ice. He had to keep moving to avoid sinking to the bottom, but he merely swam through a cluster of weeds and then back again, until he was convinced the Beast would not return.

He made his way to the bank and slowly, painfully, drew his battered body into a cluster of rushes and reed mace. Here he rested and nursed his wounds. He was scratched, bruised and some of his scales were torn, but his bones were sound and for that Adder was profoundly grateful. All his grandiose ideas of performing the heroic act of ridding White Deer Park of this menace, seemed now to him piffling and nonsensical. A paltry creature like him trying to meddle with this great hunter from an unknown world! Why, he was no more than a worm who afforded a minute or two's distraction as a toy for such a powerful beast. Any animals who had made their homes in the Park had about as much chance of diverting it from its intentions as of learning how to walk on two legs. Adder would have chuckled at the absurdity of such a notion if he had been capable of it.

When he had recovered a little he moved carefully away from the stream, always keeping himself well screened, and slid with the utmost caution towards that quarter of the Reserve where his friends maintained their community. He had to make them understand about this Beast in no uncertain manner.

The Ssssnake Hotel

★★

Brian Moses

An Indian python will welcome you
to the Ssssnake hotel.
As he finds you your keys he'll maybe enquire
if you're feeling well.
And he'll say that he hopes
you survive the night,
that you sleep without screaming
and don't die of fright
at the Ssssnake hotel.

There's an anaconda that likes to wander
the corridors at night,
and a boa that will lower itself onto guests
as they reach, reach out for the light.
And if, by chance, you lie awake
and nearby something hisses,
I warn you now, you're about to be covered
in tiny vipery kisses,
at the Sssnake hotel, at the Sssnake hotel.

And should you hear a chorus of groans
coming from the room next door,
and the python cracking someone's bones,
don't go out and explore.
Just ignore all the screams
and the strangled yells
when you spend your weekend
At the Ssssnake hotel.

Nests

The Wild Duck's Nest

★★

Michael McLaverty

(approximate reading time 10 minutes)

The sun was setting, spilling gold light on the low western hills of Rathlin Island. A small boy walked jauntily along a hoof-printed path that wriggled between the folds of these hills and opened out into a crater-like valley on the cliff-top. Presently he stopped as if remembering something, then suddenly he left the path, and began running up one of the hills. When he reached the top he was out of breath and stood watching streaks of light radiating from golden-edged clouds, the scene reminding him of a picture he had seen of the Transfiguration. A short distance below him was the cow standing at the edge of a reedy lake. Colm ran down to meet her waving his stick in the air, and the wind rumbling in his ears made him give an exultant whoop which splashed upon the hills in a shower of echoed sound. A flock of gulls lying on the short grass near the lake rose up languidly, drifting like blown snowflakes over the rim of the cliff.

The lake faced west and was fed by a stream, the

drainings of the semi-circling hills. One side was open to the winds from the sea and in winter a little outlet trickled over the cliffs making a black vein in their grey sides. The boy lifted stones and began throwing them into the lake, weaving web after web on its calm surface. Then he skimmed the water with flat stones, some of them jumping the surface and coming to rest on the other side. He was delighted with himself and after listening to his echoing shouts of delight he ran to fetch his cow. Gently he tapped her on the side and reluctantly she went towards the brown-mudded path that led out of the valley. The boy was about to throw a final stone into the lake when a bird flew low over his head, its neck a-strain, and its orange-coloured legs clear in the soft light. It was a wild duck. It circled the lake twice, thrice, coming lower each time and then with a nervous flapping of wings it skidded along the surface, its legs breaking the water into a series of silvery arcs. Its wings closed, it lit silently, gave a slight shiver, and began pecking indifferently at the water.

Colm with dilated eyes eagerly watched it making for the further end of the lake. It meandered between tall bulrushes, its body black and solid as stone against the greying water. Then as if it had sunk it was gone. The boy ran stealthily along the bank looking away from the lake, pretending indifference. When he came opposite to where he had last seen the bird he stopped and peered through the sighing reeds whose shadows streaked the water in a maze of black strokes. In front of him was a soddy islet guarded by the spears of sedge and separated from the bank by a narrow channel of water. The water wasn't too deep – he could wade across with care.

Rolling up his short trousers he began to wade, his arms outstretched, and his legs brown and stunted in the mountain water. As he drew near the islet, his feet sank in the cold mud and bubbles winked up at him. He went more carefully and nervously. Then one trouser fell and dipped into the water; the boy dropped his hands to roll it up, he unbalanced, made a splashing sound, and the bird arose with a squawk and whirred away over the cliffs. For a moment the boy stood frightened. Then he clambered on to the wet-soaked sod of land, which was spattered with seagulls' feathers and bits of wind-blown rushes.

Into each hummock he looked, pulling back the long grass. At last he came on the nest, facing seawards. Two flat rocks dimpled the face of the water and between them was a neck of land matted with coarse grass containing the nest. It was untidily built of dried rushes, straw and feathers, and in it lay one solitary egg. Colm was delighted. He looked around and saw no one. The nest was his. He lifted the egg, smooth and green as the sky, with a faint tinge of yellow like the reflected light from a buttercup; and then he felt he had done wrong. He put it back. He knew he shouldn't have touched it and he wondered would the bird forsake the nest. A vague sadness stole over him and he felt in his heart he had sinned. Carefully smoothing out his footprints he hurriedly left the islet and ran after his cow. The sun had now set and the cold shiver of evening enveloped him, chilling his body and saddening his mind.

In the morning he was up and away to school. He took the grass rut that edged the road for it was softer on the bare feet. His house was the last on the western headland and after a mile or so he was joined by Paddy McFall; both boys dressed in similar hand-knitted blue jerseys and grey trousers carried home-made school bags. Colm was full of the nest and as soon as he joined his companion he said eagerly: 'Paddy, I've a nest – a wild duck's with one egg.'

'And how do you know it's a wild duck's?' asked Paddy slightly jealous.

'Sure I saw her with my own two eyes, her brown speckled back with a crow's patch on it, and her yellow legs . . .'

'Where is it?' interrupted Paddy in a challenging tone.

'I'm not going to tell you, for you'd rob it!'

'Ach! I suppose it's a tame duck's you have or maybe an old gull's.'

Colm put out his tongue at him. 'A lot you know!' he said, 'for a gull's egg has spots and this one is greenish-white, for I had it in my hand.'

And then the words he didn't want to hear rushed from Paddy in a mocking chant, 'You had it in your hand! . . . She'll forsake it! She'll forsake it! She'll forsake it!' he said, skipping along the road before him.

Colm felt as if he would choke or cry with vexation.

His mind told him that Paddy was right, but somehow he couldn't give in to it and he replied: 'She'll not forsake it! She'll not! I know she'll not!'

But in school his faith wavered. Through the windows he could see moving sheets of rain – rain that dribbled down the panes filling his mind with thoughts of the lake creased and chilled by wind; the nest sodden and black with wetness; and the egg cold as a cave stone. He shivered from the thoughts and fidgeted with the inkwell cover, sliding it backwards and forwards mechanically. The mischievous look had gone from his eyes and the school day dragged on interminably. But at last they were out in the rain, Colm rushing home as fast as he could.

He was no time at all at his dinner of potatoes and salted fish until he was out in the valley now smoky with drifts of slanting rain. Opposite the islet he entered the water. The wind was blowing into his face, rustling noisily the rushes heavy with the dust of rain. A moss-cheeper, swaying on a reed like a mouse, filled the air with light cries of loneliness.

The boy reached the islet, his heart thumping with excitement, wondering did the bird forsake. He went slowly, quietly, on to the strip of land that led to the nest. He rose on his toes, looking over the ledge to see if he could see her. And then every muscle tautened. She was on, her shoulders hunched up, and her bill lying on her breast as if she were asleep. Colm's heart hammered wildly in his ears. She hadn't forsaken. He was about to turn stealthily away. Something happened. The bird moved, her neck straightened, twitching nervously from side to side. The boy's head swam with lightness. He stood trans-fixed. The wild duck with a panicky flapping, rose heavily, and flew off towards the sea . . . A guilty silence chilled the boy . . . He turned to go away, hesitated, and glanced back at the dark nest; it'd be no harm to have a look. Timidly he approached it, standing straight, and gazing over the edge. There in the nest lay two eggs. He drew in his breath with delight, splashed quickly from the island, and ran off whistling in the rain.

Hen's Nest

★★

John Clare

Among the orchard weeds, from every search,
Snugly and sure, the old hen's nest is made,
Who cackles every morning from her perch
To tell the servant girl new eggs are laid;
Who lays her washing by, and far and near
Goes seeking all about from day to day,
And stung with nettles tramples everywhere;
But still the cackling pullet lays away.
The boy on Sundays goes the stack to pull
In hopes to find her there, but naught is seen,
And takes his hat and thinks to find it full,
She's laid so long so many might have been.
But naught is found and all is given o'er
Till the young brood come chirping to the door.

If Trees Could Talk

Guess

★★

Philippa Pearce

(approximate reading time 13 minutes)

That last day of October a freak storm hit the suburb of Woodley Park. Slates rattled off roofs, dustbins chased dustbin lids along the streets, hoardings were slammed down, and at midnight there was a huge sound like a giant breaking his kindling wood, and then an almighty crash, and then briefly the sound of the same giant crunching his toast.

Then only the wind, which died surprisingly soon.

In the morning everyone could see that the last forest tree of Grove Road – of the whole suburb – had fallen, crashing down on to Grove Road Primary School. No lives had been lost, since the caretaker did not live on the premises; but the school hamster had later to be treated for shock. The school buildings were wrecked.

Everyone went to stare, especially, of course, the children of the school. They included Netty and Sid Barr.

The fallen tree was an awesome sight, partly because of its size and partly because of its evident great age. Someone in the crowd said that the acorn that grew into *that* must have been planted centuries ago.

As well as the confusion of fallen timber on the road and on the school premises, there was an extraordinary spatter of school everywhere: slates off the roof, bricks from the broken walls, glass from the windows, and the contents of classrooms, cloakrooms and storerooms – books and collages and clay and paints and Nature tables and a queer mixture of clothing, both dingy and weird, which meant that the contents of the Lost Property cupboard and the dressing-up cupboard had been whirled together and tossed outside. Any passer-by could have taken his pick, free of charge. Netty Barr, who had been meaning to claim her gym-shoes from Lost Property, decided that they had gone for good now. This was like the end of the world – a school world.

Council workmen arrived with gear to cut, saw, and haul timber. Fat old Mr Brown from the end of the Barrs' road told the foreman that they ought to have taken the tree down long ago. Perhaps he was right. In spite of last season's leaves and next year's buds, the trunk of the tree was quite hollow: a cross-section revealed a rim of wood the width of a man's hand, encircling a space large enough for a child or a smallish adult. As soon as the workmen's backs were turned, Sid Barr crept in. He then managed to get stuck and had to be pulled out by Netty. An untidy young woman near by was convulsed with silent laughter at the incident.

'You didn't stay inside for a hundred years,' she said to Sid.

'That smelt funny,' said Sid. 'Rotty.' Netty banged his clothes for him: the smell clung.

'Remember that day last summer, Net? After the picnic? When I got stuck inside that great old tree in Epping Forest?' Sid liked to recall near-disasters.

'Epping Forest?' said the young woman, sharply interested. But no one else was.

Meanwhile the headmaster had arrived, and that meant all fun was over. School would go on, after all, even if not in these school-buildings for the time being. The pupils of Grove Road were marshalled and then sent off in groups to various other schools in the neighbourhood. Netty and Sid Barr, with others, went to Stokeside School: Netty in the top class, Sid in a lower one.

There was a good deal of upheaval in Netty's new classroom before everyone had somewhere to sit. Netty was the next-to-last to find a place; the last was a thin, pale girl who chose to sit next to Netty. Netty assumed that she was a Stokesider; yet there was something familiar about her, too. Perhaps she'd just seen her about. The girl had dark, lank hair gathered into a pony-tail of sorts, and a pale pointed face with greyish-green eyes. She wore a dingy green dress that looked ready for a jumble sale, and gym-shoes.

Netty studied her sideways. At last, 'You been at Stokeside long?' Netty asked.

The other girl shook her head and glanced at the teacher, who was talking. She didn't seem to want to talk; but Netty did.

'A tree fell on our school,' whispered Netty. The other girl laughed silently, although Netty could see nothing to laugh about. She did see something, however: this girl bore a striking resemblance to the young woman who had watched Sid being pulled from the hollow tree-trunk. The silent laughter clinched the resemblance.

Of course, this girl was much, much younger. Of course.

'How old are you?' whispered Netty.

The girl said a monosyllable, still looking amused.

'What did you say?'

Clearly now: 'Guess.'

Netty was furious: 'I'm just eleven,' she said coldly.

'So am I,' said the other girl.

Netty felt tempted to say 'Liar'; but instead she asked, 'Have you an elder sister?'

'No.'

'What's your name?'

Again that irritating monosyllable. Netty refused to acknowledge it. 'Did you say Jess?' she asked.

'Yes. Jess.'

In spite of what she felt, Netty decided not to argue about that Jess, but went on: 'Jess what?'

The girl looked blank.

'I'm Netty Barr; you're Jess Something – Jess what?'

This time they were getting somewhere: after a tiny hesitation, the girl said, 'Oakes.'

'Jess Oakes. Jessy Oakes.' But whichever way you said it, Netty decided, it didn't sound quite right; and that was because Jess Oakes herself didn't seem quite right. Netty wished now that she weren't sitting next to her.

At playtime Netty went out into the playground; Jess Oakes followed her closely. Netty didn't like that. Unmistakably, Jess Oakes wanted to stick with her. Why? She hadn't wanted to answer Netty's questions; she hadn't been really friendly. But she clung to Netty. Netty didn't like it – didn't like *her*.

Netty managed to shake Jess Oakes off, but then saw her talking with Sid on the other side of the playground. That made her uneasy. But Jess Oakes did not reappear in the classroom after playtime: Netty felt relieved, although she wondered. The teacher made no remark.

Netty went cheerfully home to tea, a little after Sid.

And there was Jess Oakes sitting with Sid in front of the television set. Netty went into the kitchen, to her mother.

'Here you are,' said Mrs Barr. 'You can take all the teas in.' She was loading a tray.

'When did *she* come?' asked Netty.

'With Sid. Sid said she was your friend.' Netty said nothing. 'She's a lot older than you are, Netty.'

'She's exactly my age. So she says.'

'Well, I suppose with that face and that figure – or that no-figure – she could be any age. Any age.'

'Yes.'

Mrs Barr looked thoughtfully at Netty, put down the breadknife she still held, and with decision set her hands on her hips: 'Netty!'

'Yes?'

'I don't care what age she is, I like your friends better washed than that.'

Netty gaped at her mother.

'She smells,' said Mrs Barr. 'I don't say it's unwashed body, I don't say it's unwashed clothes – although I don't think much of hers. All I know is she smells nasty.'

'Rotty,' said Netty under her breath.

'Don't bring her again,' said Mrs Barr crisply.

Netty took the tea-tray in to the other two. In the semi-dark they all munched and sipped while they watched the TV serial. But Netty was watching Jess Oakes: the girl only seemed to munch and sip; she ate nothing, drank nothing.

A friend called for Sid, and he went out. Mrs Barr looked in to ask if the girls wanted more tea; Netty said no. When her mother had gone, Netty turned off the television and switched on the light. She faced Jess Oakes: 'What do you want?'

The girl's green glance slid away from Netty. 'No harm. To know something.'

'What?'

'The way home.'

Netty did not ask where she had been living, or why she was lost, or any other commonsense questions. They weren't the right questions, she knew. She just said savagely: 'I wish I knew what was going on inside your head, Jess Oakes.'

Jess Oakes laughed almost aloud, as though Netty had said something really amusing. She reached out her hand and touched Netty, for the first time: her touch was cool, damp. 'You shall,' she said. 'You shall.'

And where was Netty now? If she were asleep and dreaming, the falling asleep had been very sudden, at the merest touch of a cool, damp hand. But certainly Netty must be dreaming . . .

She dreamt that she was in a strange room filled with a greenish light that seemed partly to come in through two windows, of curious shape, set together rather low down at one side. The walls and ceilings of this chamber were continuous, as in a dome; all curved. There was nothing inside the dome-shaped chamber except the greenish light, of a curious intensity; and Netty. For some reason Netty wanted to look out of the two windows, but she knew that before she could do that, something was required of her. In her dreaming state, she was not at first sure what this was, except that it was tall – very tall – and green. Of course, green: green in spring and summer, and softly singing to itself with leaves; in autumn, yellow and brown and red, and its leaves falling. In winter, leafless. A tree, a forest tree, a tree of the Forest, a tree of Epping Forest. A tree – a hundred trees – a thousand trees – a choice of all the trees of Epping Forest. She had been to the Forest; she was older than Sid, and therefore she knew the direction in which the Forest lay, the direction in which one would have to go to reach the Forest. Her knowledge of the Forest and its whereabouts was in the green-glowing room, and it passed from her in that room, and became someone else's knowledge too . . .

Now Netty knew that she was free to look out of the windows of the room. Their frames were curiously curved;

there was not glass in them, but some other greenish-grey substance. She approached the windows; she looked through them; and she saw into the Barrs' sitting-room, and she saw Netty Barr sitting in her chair by the television set, huddled in sudden sleep.

She saw herself apart from herself, and she cried out in terror, so that she woke, and she was sitting in her chair, and the girl who called herself Jess Oakes was staring at her with her grey-green eyes, smiling.

'Thank you,' said Jess Oakes. 'Now I know all I need to know.' She got up, unmistakably to go. 'Good-bye.'

She went out of the sitting-room, leaving the door open; Netty heard her go out of the front door, leaving that open too. The doors began to bang in a wind that had risen. The front gate banged as well.

Mrs Barr came crossly out of the kitchen to complain. She saw that Netty was alone in the sitting-room. 'Has she gone, then?'

Netty nodded, dumb.

They went into the hall together. Scattered along the hall were pieces of clothing: one gym-shoe by the sitting-room door, another by the coat-hooks; a dingy green dress, looking like something out of a dressing-up box, by the open front door . . .

Mrs Barr ran to the front gate and looked up and down the road. No one; just old Mr Brown on the lookout, as usual. Mrs Barr called to him: 'Have you seen anyone?'

'No. Who should I have seen?'

Mrs Barr came back, shaken. 'She can't have gone stark

naked,' she said. Then, as an afterthought, 'She can't have gone, anyway.' Then, again, 'But she has gone.'

Netty was looking at the gym-shoes in the hall. She could see inside one of them; and she could see a name printed there. It would not be JESS OAKES; it would be some other name. Now she would find out the true identity of the girl with the greenish eyes. She stooped, picked up the shoe, read the name: NETTY BARR.

'Those are the gym-shoes you lost at the school,' said Mrs Barr. 'How did she get hold of them? Why was she wearing them? What kind of a girl or a woman was she, with that smell on her? Where did she come from? And where's she gone? Netty, you bad girl, what kind of a friend was she?'

'She wasn't my friend,' said Netty.

'What was she then? And where's she gone – *where's she gone?*'

'I don't know,' said Netty. 'But guess.'

The Trees

★★

Philip Larkin

The trees are coming into leaf
Like something almost being said;
The recent buds relax and spread,
Their greenness is a kind of grief.

Is it that they are born again
And we grow old? No, they die too.
Their yearly trick of looking new
Is written down in rings of grain.

Yet still the unresting castles thresh
In fullgrown thickness every May.
Last year is dead, they seem to say,
Begin afresh, afresh, afresh.

Waking at Midnight

Moonfleet

★★

EXTRACT FROM CHAPTER THREE
J. Meade Falkner

(approximate reading time 16 minutes)

Moonfleet is the story of fifteen-year-old John Trenchard, who lives with his aunt in the small village of Moonfleet in Dorset. In this extract we learn how his life is changed for ever when he accidentally becomes mixed up in the dangerous business of smuggling.

It came about that on a certain afternoon in the beginning of February, in the year 1758, I was sitting on the flat top of a raised stone tomb in the churchyard, looking out to sea. Ever since the floods, the weather had been open, but with high winds, and little or no rain. Thus as the land dried there began to open cracks in the heavy clay soil on which Moonfleet is built. There were cracks in the churchyard itself, and one running right up to this very tomb.

It must have been past four o'clock in the afternoon, and I was for returning to tea at my aunt's, when underneath the stone on which I sat I heard a rumbling and crumbling, and on jumping off saw that the crack in the ground had still further widened, just where it came up to the tomb, and that there was a hole in the ground a foot or more across. Now this hole reached under the big stone that formed one side of the tomb, and falling on my hands and knees and looking down it, I perceived that there was under the monument a larger cavity, into which the hole opened. I slipped myself in feet foremost, dropped down on to a heap of fallen mould, and found that I could stand upright under the monument itself.

As soon as my eyes were used to the dimmer light, I saw that the hole into which I had crept was only the mouth of a passage, which sloped gently down in the direction of the church. My heart fell to thumping with eagerness and surprise, for I thought I had made a wonderful discovery, and that this hidden way would certainly lead to great things, perhaps even to Blackbeard's hoard; for ever since Mr Glennie's tale I had constantly before my eyes a vision of the diamond and the wealth it was to bring me. The passage was two paces broad, as high as a tall man, and cut through the soil, without bricks or any other lining.

So I set out down the passage, reaching out my hand before me lest I should run against anything in the dark. But before I had gone half a dozen paces, the darkness grew so black that I was frightened, and so far from going on was glad to turn sharp about, and see the glimmer of light that came in through the hole under the tomb. Then a horror of the darkness seized me, and before I well knew what I was about I found myself wriggling my body up under the tombstone on to the churchyard grass, and was once more in the low evening sunlight and the soft sweet air.

Home I ran to my aunt's, for it was past tea-time, and beside that I knew I must fetch a candle if I were ever to search out the passage. My aunt gave me but a sorry greeting when I came into the kitchen, for I was late and hot. She never said much when displeased, but had a way of saying nothing, which was much worse; and would only reply yes or no. So the meal was silent enough.

You may guess that I said nothing of what I had seen, but made up my mind that as soon as my aunt's back was turned I would get a candle and tinder-box, and return to the churchyard. The sun was down before Aunt Jane said in a cold and measured voice:

'John, I will not have you out again this evening, no, nor any other evening, after dusk. Bed is the place for youth when night falls, but if this seem to you too early you can sit with me for an hour in the parlour, and I will read you a discourse of Doctor Sherlock that will banish vain thoughts, and leave you in a fit frame for quiet sleep.'

So she led the way into the parlour and took the book from the shelf. It was dull enough, though all the time my aunt read of spiritualities and saving grace, I had my mind on diamonds, for I never doubted that Blackbeard's treasure would be found at the end of that secret passage. The sermon finished at last, and my aunt closed the book with a stiff 'good night' for me. I was for giving her my formal kiss, but she made as if she did not see me and turned away; so we went upstairs each to our own room, and I never kissed Aunt Jane again.

There was a moon three-quarters full, already in the sky, and on moonlight nights I was allowed no candle to show me to bed. But on that night I needed none, for I never took off my clothes, having resolved to wait till my aunt was asleep, and then, ghosts or no ghosts, to make my way back to the churchyard.

Thus I lay wide awake on my bed. At last, I heard my aunt snoring in her room, and knew that I was free. Yet I waited a few minutes and then took off my boots, and in stockinged feet slipped past her room and down the stairs. How stair, handrail, and landing creaked that night, but the snoring never ceased, and the sleeper woke not, though her waking then might have changed all my life. So I came safely to the kitchen, and there put in my pocket one of the best winter candles and the tinder-box.

Out in the street I kept in the shadow of the houses. Everyone was fast asleep in Moonfleet and there was no light in any window. At the churchyard wall my courage had waned somewhat: it seemed a shameless thing to come to rifle Blackbeard's treasure. I half-expected that a tall figure, hairy and evil-eyed, would spring out from the shadow on the north side of the church. But nothing stirred.

When I got round the yews, there was the tomb standing out white against them, and at the foot of the tomb was the hole like a patch of black velvet spread upon the ground. I took one last look round, and down into the hole forthwith, the same way as I had got down earlier in the day. So on that February night John Trenchard found himself standing in the heap of loose fallen mould at the bottom of the hole, with a mixture of courage and cowardice in his heart, but overruling all a great desire to get at Blackbeard's diamond.

Out came tinder-box and candle, and I was glad indeed when the light burned up bright enough to show that no one, at any rate, was standing by my side. But then there was the passage, and who could say what might be lurking there? Yet I did not falter, but set out on this adventurous journey, walking very slowly indeed – but that was from fear of pitfalls – and nerving myself with the thought of the great diamond which surely would be found at the end of the passage; and then I came upon a stone wall which was now broken through so as to make a ragged doorway into a chamber beyond. There I stood on the rough sill of the door, holding my breath and reaching out my candle arm's-length into the darkness, to see what sort of a place this was before I put foot into it. And before the light had well time to fall on things, I knew that I was underneath the church, and that this chamber was none other than the Mohune Vault.

It was a large room. I satisfied myself that there was nothing evil lurking in the dark corners, or nothing visible at least, and then began to look round and note what was to be seen. Walls and roof were stone, and at one end was a staircase closed by a great flat stone at top – that same stone which I had often seen, with a ring in it, in the floor of the church above. All round the sides were stone shelves, with divisions between them like great bookcases, but instead of books there were the coffins of the Mohunes. Yet these lay only at the sides, and in the middle of the room was something very different, for here were stacked scores of casks and kegs. They were marked all of them in white paint on the end with figures and letters, that doubtless set forth the quality to those that understood. Here indeed was a discovery, and instead of picking up at the end of the passage a little brass or silver casket, which had only to be opened to show Blackbeard's diamond gleaming inside, I had stumbled on the Mohunes' vault, and found it to be nothing but a cellar of gentlemen of the contraband, for surely good liquor would never be stored in so shy a place if it ever had paid the excise.

It was plain enough that the whole place had been under water: the floor was still muddy, and the green and sweating walls showed the flood-mark within two feet of the roof, yet the coffins were but little disturbed. They lay on the shelves in rows, one above the other, and numbered twenty-three in all: most were in lead, and so could never float, but of those in wood some were turned slantways in their niches, and one had floated right away and been left on the floor upside down in a corner when the waters went back.

First I fell to wondering as to whose cellar this was, and how so much liquor could have been brought in with secrecy. These reflections gave me more courage, for I considered that the tales of Blackbeard walking or digging among the graves had been set afloat to keep those that were not wanted from the place, and guessed now that when I saw the light moving in the churchyard that night I went to fetch Dr Hawkins, it was no corpse-candle, but a lantern of smugglers running a cargo.

Soon I wished I had not come at all, considering that the diamond had vanished into air, and it was a sad thing to be cabined with so many dead men. I was resolved to give up further inquiry and foot it home, when the clock in the tower struck midnight. Surely never was ghostly hour sounded in more ghostly place. Bim-bom it went, bim-bom, twelve heavy thuds that shook the walls, twelve resonant echoes that followed, and then a purring and vibration of the air, so that the ear could not tell when it ended.

I was wrought up, perhaps, by the strangeness of the hour and place, and my hearing quicker than at other times, but before the tremor of the bell was quite passed away I knew there was some other sound in the air, and that the awful stillness of the vault was broken. At first I could not tell what this new sound was, nor whence it came, and now it seemed a little noise close by, and now a great noise in the distance. And then it grew nearer and more defined, and in a moment I knew it was the sound of voices talking. They must have been a long way off at first, and for a minute, that seemed as an age, they came no nearer. What a minute was that to me! Even now, so many years after, I can recall the anguish of it, and how I stood with ears pricked up, eyes starting, and a clammy sweat upon my face, waiting for those speakers to come. It was the anguish of the rabbit at the end of his burrow, with the ferret's eyes gleaming in the dark, and gun and lurcher waiting at the mouth of the hole. I was caught in a trap, and knew beside that contraband-men had a way of sealing prying eyes and stilling babbling tongues; and I remembered poor Cracky Jones found dead in the churchyard, and how men *said* he had met Blackbeard in the night.

These were but the thoughts of a second, but the voices were nearer, and I heard a dull thud far up the passage, and knew that a man had jumped down from the churchyard into the hole. So I took a last stare round, agonizing to see if there was any way of escape; but the stone walls and roof were solid enough to crush me, and the stack of casks too closely packed to hide more than a rat. There was a man speaking now from the bottom of the hole to others in the churchyard, and then my eyes were led as by a loadstone to a great wooden coffin that lay by itself on the top shelf, a full six feet from the ground. When I saw the coffin I knew that I was respited, for, as I judged, there was space between it and the wall behind enough to contain my little carcass; and in a second I had put out the candle, scrambled up the shelves, half-stunned my senses with dashing my head against the roof, and squeezed my body betwixt wall and coffin. There I lay on one side with a thin and rotten plank between the dead man and me, dazed with the blow to my head, and breathing hard; while the glow of torches as they came down the passage reddened and flickered on the roof above.

A Smuggler's Song

★★

Rudyard Kipling

If you wake at midnight, and hear a horse's feet,
Don't go drawing back the blind, or looking in the
    street,
Them that asks no questions isn't told a lie,
Watch the wall, my darling, while the Gentlemen go by!
    Five and twenty ponies
    Trotting through the dark –
    Brandy for the Parson,
    'Baccy for the Clerk;
    Laces for a lady, letters for a spy,
And watch the wall, my darling, while the Gentlemen
    go by!

Running round the woodlump if you chance to find
Little barrels, roped and tarred, all full of brandy-wine,
Don't you shout to come and look, nor use 'em for
    your play.
Put the brushwood back again – and they'll be gone
    next day!

If you see the stable-door setting open wide;
If you see a tired horse lying down inside;
If your mother mends a coat cut about and tore;
If the lining's wet and warm – don't you ask no more!

If you meet King George's men, dressed in blue and red,
You be careful what you say, and mindful what is said.
If they call you 'pretty maid', and chuck you 'neath the
    chin,
Don't you tell where no-one is, nor yet where no-one's
    been!

Knocks and footsteps round the house – whistles after
    dark –
You've no call for running out till the house-dogs bark.
Trusty's here, and *Pincher*'s here, and see how dumb they
    lie –
They don't fret to follow when the Gentlemen go by!

If you do as you've been told, likely there's a chance,
You'll be give a dainty doll, all the way from France,
With a cap of Valenciennes, and a velvet hood –
A present from the Gentlemen, along o' being good!
    Five and twenty ponies,
    Trotting through the dark –
    Brandy for the Parson,
    'Baccy for the Clerk,
Them that asks no questions isn't told a lie –
Watch the wall, my darling, while the Gentlemen go by!

Monsters of the Deep

A Battle of Monsters

★★

FROM *JOURNEY TO THE CENTRE OF THE EARTH* (CHAPTER THIRTY-TWO)

Jules Verne
Translated by Joyce Gard

(approximate reading time 9 minutes)

Professor Lidenbrock has decoded an old manuscript, and he and his nervous nephew, Axel, journey across Iceland in search of the way to the centre of the earth. They enlist the help of Hans as a guide, and the three of them descend into a deep crater and, after a series of adventures, discover a subterranean ocean. The explorers build a raft out of trees and set sail.

The story was originally written in French. Some translations of this book are old fashioned and difficult to read nowadays, so if you decide to read the rest of the book, make sure you look for this lovely modern translation.

S*unday, 16th August.* Nothing new. The weather was the same, the wind slightly stronger. The light was as bright as ever. The sea seemed to be infinite — as big as the Mediterranean, or even the Atlantic. And why not, indeed?

My uncle tried to take soundings. He tied one of the heaviest picks to the end of a rope four hundred yards long. It did not touch bottom and we had difficulty in hauling in our line. When at last we recovered the pick, Hans pointed out a row of deep dents, as if the iron had been gripped in a rough vice. I looked at Hans.

'*Tander!*' he said. I did not understand, and looked towards my uncle. But he was in a brown study and I did not want to disturb him. I turned to Hans again. He opened and closed his jaws, and I understood.

'Teeth!' I cried, looking at the iron bar again. Yes, the dents were certainly teeth-marks, but what prodigious beast could have made them? Some ancient monster, fiercer than a shark, more formidable than a killer-whale! I could not take my eyes from the gnawed iron. Was my dream about to become reality? These thoughts weighed on my mind and troubled my sleep.

Monday, 17th August. I started thinking about prehistoric reptiles, trying to recall what I knew about their individual characteristics. They had been in complete command of the seas; they were gigantic and terribly powerful. Our modern alligators and crocodiles, however nasty to meet, would be child's play compared with their ancestors.

I shuddered. I had seen the skeleton of one of these saurians in the Hamburg Museum; it was at least thirty feet long. Was it to be our fate to meet one of these creatures in the living flesh? It seemed impossible; but then

I had another look at the iron bar, and there were the terrible marks plain to be seen.

I looked in terror at the sea. My uncle must have shared my thoughts, if not my fears, for he too, after examining the pick, was gazing out over the water.

'What could have possessed him to take soundings?' I thought. 'He's wakened one of these monsters from its age-long sleep, and now it'll be on the warpath!' I took a look at the guns; they were loaded and ready, my uncle saw what I was doing and nodded his approval.

I was right! I could see an eddying on the surface; something was moving not far away.

Tuesday, 18th August. Evening came, or rather the time to sleep, for there was no night in this ocean, and the cruel light was a weariness to the eyes. Hans was at the tiller: during his watch I fell asleep.

I was wakened by a violent shock; the raft was lifted bodily from the sea and hurled to a great distance; by extraordinary good fortune it was not upset.

'What is it?' said my uncle, still half asleep. 'Have we run aground?'

Hans was pointing with his finger; we saw a dark mass rising and falling in the sea, about five hundred yards away.

'An enormous porpoise!' I cried.

'Yes,' my uncle shouted, 'and now I can see an uncommonly large lizard!'

'And over there – see – a monstrous crocodile! Look at its great jaws filled with rows of teeth! It's diving!'

'A whale!' cried the professor. 'Look at its flippers – and now it's blowing!'

Two great water-jets rose high into the air. We were paralysed with fear. All these sea-monsters at once! – and the smallest of them could shatter the raft with one snap of its jaws or lash of its mighty tail. Hans came to his senses and started to put the tiller hard over, when we saw yet more enemies on the other beam – a turtle forty feet across, and a serpent thirty feet long, darting its huge head here and there above the waves.

We were cut off. They were drawing near, sweeping round the raft faster than the fastest convoy, making huge rings in the water. I took my gun. But what impression could a bullet make against these armour-plated brutes?

We were dumb with terror. They were coming near, to starboard the crocodile, to port the serpent. The other creatures seemed to have vanished. I was about to fire, when Hans stopped me. The two monsters passed us, a hundred yards away, hurling themselves against one another with such frenzy that they did not notice the raft.

Then began an epic fight; we had a ringside seat.

It seemed to me that the other beasts were now taking part in the fight, the porpoise, the whale, the lizard, the turtle – I kept on seeing parts of all of them. I pointed them out to the Icelander, but he only shook his head.

'*Tva*,' he said.

'Only two! He thinks there are only two!'

'He's right,' cried my uncle, 'he's been looking through the telescope all the time.'

'Are there really only two?'

'Yes! The first has the snout of a porpoise, the head of a lizard, and the teeth of a crocodile – that's why we were bewildered. It's the most alarming of the antediluvian reptiles – the Ichthyosaurus!'

'What about the other?'

'That's the serpent with the shell of a turtle – the Plesiosaurus!'

Now I could see that there were indeed only two monsters. I saw the bloodshot eye of the Ichthyosaurus, as big as a man's head. The whole creature was at least a hundred feet long, as I could judge when its vertical tail-fins came up out of the water. Its huge jaws had at least a hundred and eighty-two teeth, according to the naturalists.

The Plesiosaurus was a sort of sea-serpent with a short tail and legs sticking out like oars. Its body was covered with a shell, and its neck swayed about like a swan's, towering thirty feet above the waves.

These beasts were now locked in a life-and-death struggle; the violent contortions of their bodies caused mountainous seas which tossed the raft about like a cork. Twenty times we were on the point of overturning. Violent hissing like steam-whistles pierced our ears.

For an hour we watched the furious fight, and still another hour passed without a decision. The battle swayed towards the raft, then away again. We clung on as best we could, our guns loaded, unable to tear ourselves away from the scene of this stupendous struggle.

Suddenly both monsters disappeared below the waves, down the gulf of a mighty whirlpool they had made in their rage. I wondered whether the fight would go on under water.

Then all at once a huge head was thrust up from the sea, the head of the Plesiosaurus. The monster was mortally wounded, only its head and long neck were visible above the waves. The neck twisted this way and that in violent contortions, lashing the foaming water like a giant whip, wriggling like a severed worm. Water dashed upwards, blinding us, but it was almost the end of the death-agony. The reptile's convulsions slackened, and soon its long serpent's body lay still on the calmed waves.

We wondered whether the Ichthyosaurus had gone to lick its wounds in its submarine cavern, or whether it was about to emerge again and turn its fury against us poor humans on our defenceless raft.

The Kraken

★★

Alfred, Lord Tennyson

Below the thunders of the upper deep;
Far far beneath in the abysmal sea,
His ancient, dreamless, uninvaded sleep
The Kraken sleepeth: faintest sunlights flee
About his shadowy sides: above him swell
Huge sponges of millennial growth and height;
And far away into the sickly light,
From many a wondrous grot and secret cell

Unnumber'd and enormous polypi
Winnow with giant fins the slumbering green.
There hath he lain for ages and will lie
Battening upon huge seaworms in his sleep,
Until the latter fire shall heat the deep;
Then once by man and angels to be seen,
In roaring he shall rise and on the surface die.

When No One Seems
to Care

The Invisible Child

★★

FROM *TALES FROM MOOMIN VALLEY*

Tove Jansson

(approximate reading time 19 minutes)

One dark and rainy evening the Moomin family sat around the verandah table picking over the day's mushroom harvest. The big table was covered with newspapers, and in the centre of it stood the lighted kerosene lamp. But the corners of the verandah were dark.

'My has been picking pepper spunk again,' Moominpappa said. 'Last year she collected flybane.'

'Let's hope she takes to chanterelles next autumn,' said Moominmamma. 'Or at least to something not directly poisonous.'

'Hope for the best and prepare for the worst,' Little My observed with a chuckle.

They continued their work in peaceful silence.

Suddenly there were a few light taps on the glass pane in the door, and without waiting for an answer Too-ticky came in and shook the rain off her oilskin jacket. Then she held the door open and called out in the dark: 'Well, come along!'

'Whom are you bringing?' Moomintroll asked.

'It's Ninny,' Too-ticky said. 'Yes, her name's Ninny.'

She still held the door open, waiting. No one came.

'Oh, well,' Too-ticky said and shrugged her shoulders. 'If she's too shy she'd better stay there for a while.'

'She'll be drenched through,' said Moominmamma.

'Perhaps that won't matter much when one's invisible,' Too-ticky said and sat down by the table. The family stopped working and waited for an explanation.

'You all know, don't you, that if people are frightened very often, they sometimes become invisible,' Too-ticky said and swallowed a small egg mushroom that looked like a little snowball. 'Well. This Ninny was frightened the wrong way by a lady who had taken care of her without really liking her. I've met this lady, and she was horrid. Not the angry sort, you know, which would have been understandable. No, she was the icily ironical kind.'

'What's ironical,' Moomintroll asked.

'Well, imagine that you slip on a rotten mushroom and sit down on the basket of newly picked ones,' Too-ticky said. 'The natural thing for your mother would be to be angry. But no, she isn't. Instead she says, very coldly: "I understand that's your idea of a graceful dance, but I'd thank you not to do it in people's food." Something like that.'

'How unpleasant,' Moomintroll said.

'Yes, isn't it,' replied Too-ticky. 'This was the way this lady used to talk. She was ironic all day long every day, and finally the kid started to turn pale and fade around the edges, and less and less was seen of her. Last Friday one couldn't catch sight of her at all. The lady gave her away to me and said she really couldn't take care of relatives she couldn't even see.'

'And what did you do to the lady?' My asked with bulging eyes. 'Did you bash her head?'

'That's of no use with the ironic sort,' Too-ticky said. 'I took Ninny home with me, of course. And now I've brought her here for you to make her visible again.'

There was a slight pause. Only the rain was heard, rustling along over the verandah roof. Everybody stared at Too-ticky and thought for a while.

'Does she talk?' Moominpappa asked.

'No. But the lady has hung a small silver bell around her neck so that one can hear where she is.'

Too-ticky arose and opened the door again. 'Ninny!' she called out in the dark.

The cool smell of autumn crept in from the garden, and a square of light threw itself on the wet grass. After a while there was a slight tinkle outside, rather hesitantly. The sound came up the steps and stopped. A bit above the floor a small silver bell was seen hanging in the air on a black ribbon. Ninny seemed to have a very thin neck.

'All right,' Too-ticky said. 'Now, here's your new family. They're a bit silly at times, but rather decent, largely speaking.'

'Give the kid a chair,' Moominpappa said. 'Does she know how to pick mushrooms?'

'I really know nothing at all about Ninny,' Too-ticky

said. 'I've only brought her here and told you what I know. Now I have a few other things to attend to. Please look in some day, won't you, and let me know how you get along. Cheerio.'

When Too-ticky had gone the family sat quite silent, looking at the empty chair and the silver bell. After a while one of the chanterelles slowly rose from the heap on the table. Invisible paws picked it clean from needles and earth. Then it was cut to pieces, and the pieces drifted away and laid themselves in the basin. Another mushroom sailed up from the table.

'Thrilling!' My said with awe. 'Try to give her something to eat. I'd like to know if you can see the food when she swallows it.'

'How on earth does one make her visible again,' Moominpappa said worriedly. 'Should we take her to a doctor?'

'I don't think so,' said Moominmamma. 'I believe she wants to be invisible for a while. Too-ticky said she's shy. Better leave the kid alone until something turns up.'

And so it was decided.

The eastern attic room happened to be unoccupied, so Moominmamma made Ninny a bed there. The silver bell tinkled along after her upstairs and reminded Moominmamma of the cat that once had lived with them. At the bedside she laid out the apple, the glass of juice and the three striped pieces of candy everybody in the house was given at bedtime.

Then she lighted a candle and said:

'Now have a good sleep, Ninny. Sleep as late as you can. There'll be tea for you in the morning any time you want. And if you happen to get a funny feeling or if you want anything, just come downstairs and tinkle.'

Moominmamma saw the quilt raise itself to form a very small mound. A dent appeared in the pillow. She went downstairs again to her own room and started looking through her granny's old notes about Infallible Household Remedies. Evil Eye. Melancholy. Colds. No. There didn't seem to be anything suitable. Yes, there was. Towards the end of the notebook she found a few lines written down at the time when Granny's hand was already rather shaky. 'If people start getting misty and difficult to see.' Good. Moominmamma read the recipe, which was rather complicated, and started at once to mix the medicine for little Ninny.

The bell came tinkling downstairs, one step at a time, with a small pause between each step. Moomintroll had waited for it all morning. But the silver bell wasn't the exciting thing. That was the paws. Ninny's paws were coming down the steps. They were very small, with anxiously bunched toes. Nothing else of Ninny was visible. It was very odd.

Moomintroll drew back behind the porcelain stove and stared bewitchedly at the paws that passed him on their way to the verandah. Now she served herself some tea. The cup was raised in the air and sank back again. She ate some bread and butter and marmalade. Then the cup and saucer drifted away to the kitchen, were washed and put away in the closet. You see, Ninny was a very orderly little child.

Moomintroll rushed out in the garden and shouted: 'Mamma! She's got paws! You can see her paws!'

I thought as much, Moominmamma was thinking where she sat high in the apple tree. Granny knew a thing or two. Now when the medicine starts to work we'll be on the right way.

'Splendid,' said Moominpappa. 'And better still when she shows her snout one day. It makes me feel sad to talk with people who are invisible. And who never answer me.'

'Hush, dear,' Moominmamma said warningly. Ninny's paws were standing in the grass among the fallen apples.

'Hello Ninny,' shouted My. 'You've slept like a hog. When are you going to show your snout? You must look a fright if you've wanted to be invisible.'

'Shut up,' Moomintroll whispered, 'she'll be hurt.' He went running up to Ninny and said:

'Never mind My. She's hardboiled. You're really safe here among us. Don't even think about that horrid lady. She can't come here and take you away . . .'

In a moment Ninny's paws had faded away and become nearly indistinguishable from the grass.

'Darling, you're an ass,' said Moominmamma. 'You can't go about reminding the kid about those things. Now pick apples and don't talk rubbish.'

They all picked apples.

After a while Ninny's paws became clearer again and climbed one of the trees.

It was a beautiful autumn morning. The shadows made one's snout a little chilly but the sunshine felt nearly like summer. Everything was wet from the night's rain, and all colours were strong and clear. When all the apples were picked or shaken down Moominpappa carried the biggest apple mincer out in the garden, and they started making apple-cheese.

Moomintroll turned the handle, Moominmamma fed the mincer with apples and Moominpappa carried the filled jars to the verandah. Little My sat in a tree singing the Big Apple Song.

Suddenly there was a crash.

On the garden path appeared a large heap of apple-cheese, all prickly with glass splinters. Beside the heap one could see Ninny's paws, rapidly fading away.

'Oh,' said Moominmamma. 'That was the jar we use to give to the bumble-bees. Now we needn't carry it down to the field. And Granny always said that if you want the earth to grow something for you, then you have to give it a present in the autumn.'

Ninny's paws appeared back again, and above them a pair of spindly legs came to view. Above the legs one could see the faint outline of a brown dress hem.

'I can see her legs!' cried Moomintroll.

'Congrats,' said Little My, looking down out of her tree. 'Not bad. But the Groke knows why you must wear snuff-brown.'

Moominmamma nodded to herself and sent a thought to her Granny and the medicine.

Ninny padded along after them all day. They became used to the tinkle and no longer thought Ninny very remarkable.

By evening they had nearly forgotten about her. But when everybody was in bed Moominmamma took out a rose-pink shawl of hers and made it into a little dress. When it was ready she carried it upstairs to the eastern attic room and cautiously laid it out on a chair. Then she made a broad hair ribbon out of the material left over.

Moominmamma was enjoying herself tremendously. It was exactly like sewing doll's clothes again. And the funny thing was that one didn't know if the doll had yellow or black hair.

The following day Ninny had her dress on. She was visible up to her neck, and when she came down to morning tea she bobbed and piped:

'Thank you all ever so much.'

The family felt very embarrassed, and no one found anything to say. Also it was hard to know where to look when one talked to Ninny. Of course one tried to look a bit above the bell where Ninny was supposed to have her eyes. But then very easily one found oneself staring at some of the visible things further down instead, and it gave one an impolite feeling.

Moominpappa cleared his throat. 'We're happy to see,' he started, 'that we see more of Ninny today. The more we see the happier we are . . .'

My gave a laugh and banged the table with her spoon.

'Fine that you've started talking,' she said. 'Hope you have anything to say. Do you know any good games?'

'No,' Ninny piped. 'But I've heard about games.'

Moomintroll was delighted. He decided to teach Ninny all the games he knew.

After coffee all three of them went down to the river to play. Only Ninny turned out to be quite impossible. She bobbed and nodded and very seriously replied, quite, and how funny, and of course, but it was clear to all that she played only from politeness and not to have fun.

'Run, run, can't you!' My cried. 'Or can't you even jump?'

Ninny's thin legs dutifully ran and jumped. Then she stood still again with arms dangling. The empty dress neck over the bell was looking strangely helpless.

'D'you think anybody likes that?' My cried. 'Haven't you any life in you? D'you want a biff on the nose?'

'Rather not,' Ninny piped humbly.

'She can't play,' mumbled Moomintroll.

'She can't get angry,' Little My said. 'That's what's wrong with her. Listen, you,' My continued and went close to Ninny with a menacing look. 'You'll never have a face of your own until you've learned to fight. Believe me.'

'Yes, of course,' Ninny replied, cautiously backing away.

There was no further turn for the better.

At last they stopped trying to teach Ninny to play. She didn't like funny stories either. She never laughed at the right places. She never laughed at all, in fact. This had a depressing effect on the person who told the story. And she was left alone to herself.

Days went by, and Ninny was still without a face. They became accustomed to seeing her pink dress marching along behind Moominmamma. As soon as Moominmamma stopped, the silver bell also stopped, and when she continued her way the bell began tinkling again. A bit above the dress a big rose-pink bow was bobbing in thin air.

Moominmamma continued to treat Ninny with Granny's medicine, but nothing further happened. So after some time she stopped the treatment, thinking that many people had managed all right before without a head, and besides perhaps Ninny wasn't very good looking.

Now everyone could imagine for himself what she looked like, and this can often brighten up a relationship.

One day the family went off through the wood down to the beach. They were going to pull the boat up for winter. Ninny came tinkling behind as usual, but when they came in view of the sea she suddenly stopped. Then she lay down on her stomach in the sand and started to whine.

'What's come over Ninny? Is she frightened?' asked Moominpappa.

'Perhaps she hasn't seen the sea before,' Moominmamma said. She stooped and exchanged a few whispering words with Ninny. Then she straightened up again and said:

'No, it's the first time. Ninny thinks the sea's too big.'

'Of all the silly kids,' Little My started, but Moomin-mamma gave her a severe look and said: 'Don't be a silly kid yourself. Now let's pull the boat ashore.'

They went out on the landing-stage to the bathing hut where Too-ticky lived, and knocked at the door.

'Hullo,' Too-ticky said, 'how's the invisible child?'

'There's only her snout left,' Moominpappa replied. 'At the moment she's a bit startled but it'll pass over. Can you lend us a hand with the boat?'

'Certainly,' Too-ticky said.

While the boat was pulled ashore and turned keel upwards Ninny had padded down to the water's edge and was standing immobile on the wet sand. They left her alone.

Moominmamma sat down on the landing-stage and looked down into the water. 'Dear me, how cold it looks,' she said. And then she yawned a bit and added that nothing exciting had happened for weeks.

Moominpappa gave Moomintroll a wink, pulled a horrible face and started to steal up to Moominmamma from behind.

Of course he didn't really think of pushing her in the water as he had done many times when she was young. Perhaps he didn't even want to startle her, but just to amuse the kids a little.

But before he reached her a sharp cry was heard, a pink streak of lightning shot over the landing-stage and Moominpappa let out a scream and dropped his hat into the water. Ninny had sunk her small invisible teeth in Moominpappa's tail, and they were sharp.

'Good work!' cried My. 'I couldn't have done it better myself!'

Ninny was standing on the landing-stage. She had a small, snub-nosed, angry face below a red tangle of hair. She was hissing at Moominpappa like a cat.

'Don't you *dare* push her into the big horrible sea!' she cried.

'I see her, I see her!' shouted Moomintroll. 'She's sweet!'

'Sweet my eye,' said Moominpappa, inspecting his bitten tail. 'She's the silliest, nastiest, badly-brought-uppest child I've ever seen, with or without a head.'

He knelt down on the landing-stage and tried to fish for his hat with a stick. And in some mysterious way he managed to tip himself over, and tumbled in on his head.

He came up at once, standing safely on the bottom, with his snout above water and his ears filled with mud.

'Oh dear!' Ninny was shouting. 'Oh, how great! Oh, how funny!'

The landing-stage shook with her laughter.

'I believe she's never laughed before,' Too-ticky said wonderingly. 'You seem to have changed her, she's even worse than Little My. But the main thing is that one can see her, of course.'

'It's all thanks to Granny,' Moominmamma said.

There's Someone

★★

Benjamin Zephaniah

It may not be the one you're with
They may not have much love to give,
It may not be the girl next door
Or that nice boy on the first floor,
It may not be the friend you taught
Who helps you out when you're distraught,
You may not know this one that well
But there's someone who loves you.

It may not be the one you kissed
It may not be the one you've missed,
You may think someone is your friend
But then you find that they pretend,
When you are down and you are out
When you're in tears, sad, and in doubt,
Life may feel like a living hell
But there's someone who loves you.

Invisible Men

The Invisible Man

★★

CHAPTER TWENTY-ONE: IN OXFORD STREET

H. G. Wells

(approximate reading time 11 minutes)

The scientist Griffin has spent his whole career trying to discover how to make himself invisible. At last he has found the answer and decides to test his discovery on himself. Now, as the Invisible Man, he ventures out into London's Oxford Street. Of course he has to go naked, and what seems at first to be high adventure soon turns into nightmare . . .

In going downstairs the first time I found an unexpected difficulty because I could not see my feet; indeed I stumbled twice, and there was an unaccustomed clumsiness in gripping the bolt. By not looking down, however, I managed to walk on the level passably well.

My mood, I say, was one of exaltation. I felt as a seeing man might do, with padded feet and noiseless clothes, in a city of the blind. I experienced a wild impulse to jest, to startle people, to clap men on the back, fling people's hats astray, and generally revel in my extraordinary advantage.

But hardly had I emerged upon Great Portland Street, however (my lodging was close to the big draper's shop there), when I heard a clashing concussion and was hit violently behind, and turning saw a man carrying a basket of soda-water syphons, and looking in amazement at his burden. Although the blow had really hurt me, I found something so irresistible in his astonishment that I laughed aloud. 'The devil's in the basket,' I said, and suddenly twisted it out of his hand. He let go incontinently, and I swung the whole weight into the air.

But a fool of a cabman, standing outside a public house, made a sudden rush for this, and his extending fingers took me with excruciating violence under the ear. I let the whole down with a smash on the cabman, and then, with shouts and the clatter of feet about me, people coming out of shops, vehicles pulling up, I realised what I had done for myself, and cursing my folly, backed against a shop window and prepared to dodge out of the confusion. In a moment I should be wedged into a crowd and inevitably discovered. I pushed by a butcher boy, who luckily did not turn to see the nothingness that shoved him aside, and dodged behind the cabman's four-wheeler. I do not know how they settled the business. I hurried straight across the road, which was happily clear, and hardly heeding which way I went, in the fright of detection the incident had given me, plunged into the afternoon throng of Oxford Street.

I tried to get into the stream of people, but they were too thick for me, and in a moment my heels were being trodden upon. I took to the gutter, the roughness of which I found painful to my feet, and forthwith the shaft of a crawling hansom dug me forcibly under the shoulder blade, reminding me that I was already bruised severely. I staggered out of the way of the cab, avoided a per-ambulator by a convulsive movement, and found myself behind the hansom. A happy thought saved me, and as this drove slowly along I followed in its immediate wake, trembling and astonished at the turn of my adventure. And not only trembling, but shivering. It was a bright day in January and I was stark naked and the thin slime of mud that covered the road was freezing. Foolish as it seems to me now, I had not reckoned that, transparent or not, I was still amenable to the weather and all its consequences.

Then suddenly a bright idea came into my head. I ran round and got into the cab. And so, shivering, scared, and snifling with the first intimations of a cold, and with the bruises in the small of my back growing upon my attention, I drove slowly along Oxford Street and past Tottenham Court Road. My mood was as different from that in which I had sallied forth ten minutes ago as it is possible to imagine. *This* invisibility indeed! The one thought that possessed me was – how was I to get out of the scrape I was in.

We crawled past Mudie's, and there a tall woman with five or six yellow-labelled books hailed my cab, and I sprang out just in time to escape her, shaving a railway van narrowly in my flight. I made off up the roadway to Bloomsbury Square, intending to strike north past the

Museum and so get into the quiet district. I was now cruelly chilled, and the strangeness of my situation so unnerved me that I whimpered as I ran. At the northward corner of the Square a little white dog ran out of the Pharmaceutical Society's offices, and incontinently made for me, nose down.

I had never realised it before, but the nose is to the mind of a dog what the eye is to the mind of a seeing man. Dogs perceive the scent of a man moving as men perceive his vision. This brute began barking and leaping, showing, as it seemed to me, only too plainly that he was aware of me. I crossed Great Russell Street, glancing over my shoulder as I did so, and went some way along Montague Street before I realised what I was running towards.

Then I became aware of a blare of music, and looking along the street saw a number of people advancing out of Russell Square, red shirts, and the banner of the Salvation Army to the fore. Such a crowd, chanting in the roadway and scoffing on the pavement, I could not hope to penetrate, and dreading to go back and farther from home again, and deciding on the spur of the moment, I ran up the white steps of a house facing the museum railings and stood there until the crowd should have passed. Happily the dog stopped at the noise of the band too, hesitated, and turned tail, running back to Bloomsbury Square again.

On came the band, bawling with unconscious irony some hymn about 'When shall we see his Face?' and it seemed an interminable time to me before the tide of the crowd washed along the pavement by me. Thud, thud, thud, came the drum with a vibrating resonance, and for the moment I did not notice two urchins stopping at the railings by me. 'See 'em,' said one. 'See what?' said the other. 'Why – them footmarks – *bare*. Like what you makes in mud.'

I looked down and saw the youngsters had stopped and were gaping at the muddy footmarks I had left behind me up the newly whitened steps. The passing people elbowed and jostled them, but their confounded intelligence was arrested. 'Thud, thud, thud, When, thud, shall we see, thud, his Face, thud, thud.' 'There's a barefoot man gone up them steps, or I don't know nothing,' said one. 'And he ain't never come down again. And his foot was a-bleeding.'

The thick of the crowd had already passed. 'Looky there, Ted,' quoth the younger of the detectives, with the sharpness of surprise in his voice, and pointed straight to my feet. I looked down and saw at once the dim suggestion of their outline sketched in splashes of mud. For a moment I was paralysed.

'Why, that's rum,' said the elder. 'Dashed rum! It's just like the ghost of a foot, ain't it?' He hesitated and advanced with outstretched hand. A man pulled up short to see what he was catching, and then a girl. In another moment he would have touched me. Then I saw what to do. I made a step, the boy started back with an exclama-tion, and with a rapid movement I swung myself over into the portico of the next house. But the smaller boy was sharp-eyed enough to follow the movement, and before I was well down the steps and upon the pavement, he had recovered from his momentary astonishment and was shouting out that the feet had gone over the wall.

They rushed round and saw my new footmarks flash into being on the lower step and upon the pavement. 'What's up?' asked someone. 'Feet! Look! Feet running!' Everybody in the road, except my three pursuers, was pouring along after the Salvation Army, and this blow not only impeded me but them. There was an eddy of surprise and interrogation. At the cost of bowling over one young fellow I got through, and in another moment I was rushing headlong round the circuit of Russell Square, with six or seven astonished people following my footmarks. There was no time for explanation, or else the whole host would have been after me.

Twice I doubled round corners, thrice I crossed the road and came back upon my tracks, and then, as my feet grew hot and dry, the damp impressions began to fade. At last I had a breathing space and rubbed my feet clean with my hands, and so got away altogether. The last I saw of the chase was a little group of a dozen people perhaps, studying with infinite perplexity a slowly drying footprint that had resulted from a puddle in Tavistock Square – a footprint as isolated and incomprehensible to them as Crusoe's solitary discovery.

This running warmed me to a certain extent, and I went on with a better courage through the maze of less frequented roads that runs hereabouts. My back had now become very stiff and sore, my tonsils were painful from the cabman's fingers, and the skin of my neck had been scratched by his nails; my feet hurt exceedingly and I was lame from a little cut on one foot. I saw in time a blind man approaching me, and fled limping, for I feared his subtle intuitions. Once or twice accidental collisions occurred and I left people amazed, with unaccountable curses ringing in their ears. Then came something silent and quiet against my face, and across the Square fell a thin veil of slowly, falling flakes of snow. I had caught a cold, and do as I would I could not avoid an occasional sneeze. And every dog that came in sight, with its pointing nose and curious sniffing, was a terror to me.

Then came men and boys running, first one and then others, and shouting as they ran. It was a fire. They ran in the direction of my lodging, and looking back down the street I saw a mass of black smoke streaming up above the roofs and telephone wires. It was my lodging burning; my clothes, my apparatus, all my resources indeed, except my cheque-book and the three volumes of memoranda that awaited me in Great Portland Street, were there. Burning! I had burnt my boats – if ever a man did! The place was blazing.

The Little Man Who Wasn't There

★★

Hughes Mearns

Yesterday, upon the stair,
I met a man who wasn't there
He wasn't there again today
I wish, I wish he'd go away . . .

When I came home last night at three
The man was waiting there for me
But when I looked around the hall
I couldn't see him there at all!
Go away, go away, don't you come back
    any more!
Go away, go away, and please don't slam
    the door . . . (slam!)

Last night I saw upon the stair
A little man who wasn't there
He wasn't there again today
Oh, how I wish he'd go away.

Other Worlds

The Amber Spyglass

★★

EXTRACT FROM CHAPTER SEVEN

Philip Pullman

(approximate reading time 16 minutes)

Dr Mary Malone is a scientist. She has discovered a window-like opening into a parallel world and has climbed through.

Mary awoke with the early sun full in her face. The air was cool, and the dew had settled in tiny beads on her hair and on the sleeping-bag. She lay for a few minutes lapped in freshness, feeling as if she were the first human being who had ever lived.

She sat up, yawned, stretched, shivered, and washed in the chilly spring before eating a couple of dried figs and taking stock of the place.

Behind the little rise she had found herself on, the land sloped gradually down and then up again; the fullest view lay in front, across that immense prairie. The long shadows of the trees lay towards her now, and she could see flocks of birds wheeling in front of them, so small against the towering green canopy that they looked like motes of dust.

Loading her rucksack again, she made her way down on to the coarse rich grass of the prairie, aiming for the nearest stand of trees, four or five miles away.

The grass was knee-high, and growing among it there were low-lying bushes, no higher than her ankles, of something like juniper; and there were flowers like poppies, like buttercups, like cornflowers, giving a haze of different tints to the landscape; and then she saw a large bee, the size of the top joint of her thumb, visiting a blue flower-head and making it bend and sway. But as it backed out of the petals and took to the air again, she saw that it was no insect, for a moment later it made for her hand and perched on her finger, dipping a long needle-like beak against her skin with the utmost delicacy and then taking flight again when it found no nectar. It was a minute humming-bird, its bronze-feathered wings moving too fast for her to see.

How every biologist on earth would envy her, if they could see what she was seeing!

She moved on, and found herself getting closer to a herd of those grazing creatures she had seen the previous evening, and whose movement had puzzled her without her knowing why. They were about the size of deer or antelopes, and similarly coloured, but what made her stop still and rub her eyes was the arrangement of their legs. They grew in a diamond formation: two in the centre, one at the front, and one under the tail, so that the animals moved with a curious rocking motion. Mary longed to examine a skeleton and see how the structure worked.

For their part, the grazing creatures regarded her with

mild incurious eyes, showing no alarm. She would have loved to go closer and take time to look at them, but it was getting hot, and the shade of the great trees looked inviting; and there was plenty of time, after all.

Before long she found herself stepping out of the grass on to one of those rivers of stone she'd seen from the hill: something else to wonder at.

It might once have been some kind of lava-flow. The underlying colour was dark, almost black, but the surface was paler, as if it had been ground down or worn by crushing. It was as smooth as a stretch of well-laid road in Mary's own world, and certainly easier to walk on than the grass.

She followed the one she was on, which flowed in a wide curve towards the trees. The closer she got, the more astounded she was by the enormous size of the trunks, as wide, she estimated, as the house she lived in, and as tall – as tall as . . . She couldn't even make a guess.

When she came to the first trunk she rested her hands on the deeply-ridged red-gold bark. The ground was covered ankle-deep in brown leaf-skeletons as long as her foot, soft and fragrant to walk on. She was soon surrounded by a cloud of midge-like flying things, as well as a little flock of the tiny humming-birds, a yellow butterfly with a wingspread as broad as her hand, and too many crawling things for comfort. The air was full of humming and buzzing and scraping.

She walked along the floor of the grove feeling much as if she were in a cathedral: there was the same stillness, the same sense of upwardness in the structures, the same awe in herself.

It had taken her longer than she thought to walk here. It was getting on for midday, for the shafts of light coming down through the canopy were almost vertical. Drowsily, Mary wondered why the grazing creatures didn't move under the shade of the trees during this hottest part of the day.

She soon found out.

Feeling too hot to move any further, she lay down to rest between the roots of one of the giant trees, with her head on her rucksack, and fell into a doze.

Her eyes were closed for twenty minutes or so, and she was not quite asleep, when suddenly, from very close by, there came a resounding crash that shook the ground.

Then came another. Alarmed, Mary sat up and gathered her wits, and saw a movement which resolved itself into a round object, about a yard across, rolling along the ground, coming to a halt, and falling on its side.

And then another fell, further off; she saw the massive thing descend, and watched it crash into the buttress-like root of the nearest trunk and roll away.

The thought of one of those things falling on her was enough to make her take her rucksack and run out of the grove altogether. What were they? Seed-pods?

Watching carefully upwards, she ventured under the canopy again to look at the nearest of the fallen objects. She pulled it upright and rolled it out of the grove, and then laid it on the grass to look at it more closely.

It was perfectly circular, and as thick as the width of her palm. There was a depression in the centre, where it had been attached to the tree. It wasn't heavy, but it was immensely hard, and covered in fibrous hairs that lay along the circumference so that she could run her hand around it easily one way but not the other. She tried her knife on the surface: it made no impression at all.

Her fingers seemed smoother. She smelt them: there was a faint fragrance there, under the smell of dust. She looked at the seed-pod again. In the centre there was a slight glistening, and as she touched it again she felt it slide easily under her fingers. It was exuding a kind of oil.

Mary laid the thing down and thought about the way this world had evolved.

If her guess about these universes was right, and they were the multiple worlds predicted by quantum theory, then some of them would have split off from her own much earlier than others. And clearly in this world evolution had favoured enormous trees and large creatures with a diamond-framed skeleton.

She was beginning to see how narrow her scientific horizons were. No botany, no geology, no biology of any sort – she was as ignorant as a baby.

And then she heard a low thunder-like rumble, which was hard to locate until she saw a cloud of dust moving along one of the roads – towards the stand of trees, and towards her. It was about a mile away, but it wasn't moving slowly, and all of a sudden she felt afraid.

She darted back into the grove. She found a narrow

space between two great roots and crammed herself into it, peering over the great buttress beside her and out towards the approaching dust-cloud.

What she saw made her head spin. At first it looked like a motorcycle gang. Then she thought it was a herd of *wheeled* animals. But that was impossible. No animal could have wheels. She wasn't seeing it. But she was.

There were a dozen or so. They were roughly the same size as the grazing creatures, but leaner and grey-coloured, with horned heads and short trunks like elephants'. They had the same diamond-shaped structure as the grazers, but somehow they had evolved, on their fore and rear single legs, a wheel.

But wheels did not exist in nature, her mind insisted; they couldn't; you needed an axle with a bearing that was completely separate from the rotating part, it couldn't happen, it was impossible –

Then, as they came to a halt not fifty yards away, and the dust settled, she suddenly made the connection, and she couldn't help laughing out loud with a little cough of delight.

The wheels were seed-pods. Perfectly round, immensely hard and light – they couldn't have been designed better. The creatures hooked a claw through the centre of the pods with their front and rear legs, and used their two lateral legs to push against the ground and move along. While she marvelled at this, she was also a little anxious, for their horns looked formidably sharp, and even at this distance she could see intelligence and curiosity in their gaze.

And they were looking for her.

One of them had spotted the seed-pod she had taken out of the grove, and he trundled off the road towards it. When he reached it, he lifted it on to an edge with his trunk and rolled it over to his companions.

They gathered around the pod and touched it delicately with those powerful, flexible trunks, and she found herself interpreting the soft chirrups and clicks and hoots they were making as expressions of disapproval. Someone had tampered with this: it was wrong.

Then she thought: I came here for a purpose, although I don't understand it yet, Be bold. Take the initiative.

So she stood up and called, very self-consciously:

'Over here. This is where I am. I looked at your seed-pod. I'm sorry. Please don't harm me.'

Instantly their heads snapped round to look at her, trunks held out, glittering eyes facing forward. Their ears had all flicked upright.

She stepped out of the shelter of the roots and faced them directly. She held out her hands, realizing that such a gesture might mean nothing to creatures with no hands themselves. Still, it was all she could do. Picking up her rucksack, she walked across the grass and stepped on to the road.

Close up – not five steps away – she could see much more about their appearance, but her attention was held by something lively and aware in their gaze, by an intelligence. These creatures were as different from the grazing animals nearby as a human was from a cow.

Mary pointed to herself and said, 'Mary.'

The nearest creature reached forward with its trunk. She moved closer, and it touched her on the breast, where she had pointed, and she heard her voice coming back to her from the creature's throat: 'Merry.'

'What are you?' she said, and, 'Watahyu?' the creature responded.

All she could do was respond. 'I am a human,' she said.

'Ayama yuman,' said the creature, and then something even odder happened: the creatures laughed.

Their eyes wrinkled, their trunks waved, they tossed their heads – and from their throats came the unmistakable sound of merriment. She couldn't help it: she laughed too.

Then another creature moved forward and touched her hand with its trunk. Mary offered her other hand as well to its soft, bristled, questing touch.

'Ah,' she said, 'you're smelling the oil from the seed-pod . . .'

'Seepot,' said the creature.

'If you can make the sounds of my language, we might be able to communicate, one day. God knows how. *Mary,*' she said, pointing to herself again.

Nothing. They watched. She did it again: 'Mary.'

The nearest creature touched its own breast with its trunk and spoke. Was it three syllables, or two? The creature spoke again, and this time Mary tried hard to make the same sounds: 'Mulefa,' she said tentatively.

Others repeated 'Mulefa' in her voice, laughing, and

even seemed to be teasing the creature who had spoken. 'Mulefa!' they said again, as if it was a fine joke.

'Well, if you can laugh, I don't suppose you'll eat me,' Mary said. And from that moment, there was an ease and friendliness between her and them, and she felt nervous no more.

And the group itself relaxed: they had things to do, they weren't roaming at random. Mary saw that one of them had a saddle or pack on its back, and two others lifted the seed-pod on to it, making secure by tying straps around it, with deft and intricate movements of their trunks. When they stood still, they balanced with their lateral legs, and when they moved, they turned both front and back legs to steer. Their movements were full of grace and power.

One of them wheeled to the edge of the road and raised its trunk to utter a trumpeting call. The herd of grazers all looked up as one and began to trot towards them. When they arrived they stood patiently at the verge and let the wheeled creatures move slowly through them, checking, touching, counting.

Then Mary saw one reach beneath a grazer and milk it with her trunk; and then the wheeled one rolled over to her, and raised her trunk delicately to Mary's mouth.

At first she flinched, but there was an expectation in the creature's eye, so she came forward again and opened her lips. The creature expressed a little of the sweet thin milk into her mouth, watched her swallow, and gave her some more, again and again. The gesture was so clever and kindly that Mary impulsively put her arms around the creature's head and kissed her, smelling the hot dusty hide and feeling the hard bones underneath and the muscular power of the trunk.

Presently, the leader trumpeted softly and the grazers moved away. The *mulefa* were preparing to leave. She felt joy that they had welcomed her, and sadness that they were leaving; but then she felt surprise as well.

One of the creatures was lowering itself, kneeling down on the road, and gesturing with its trunk, and the others were beckoning and inviting her . . . No doubt about it: they were offering to carry her, to take her with them.

Another took her rucksack and fastened it to the saddle of a third, and awkwardly Mary climbed on the back of the kneeling one, wondering where to put her legs – in front of the creature's, or behind? And what could she hold on to?

But before she could work it out, the creature had risen, and the group began to move away along the highway, with Mary riding among them.

Jabberwocky

★★

Lewis Carroll

'Twas brillig, and the slithy toves
　　Did gyre and gimble in the wabe;
All mimsy were the borogoves,
　　And the mome raths outgrabe.

'Beware the Jabberwock, my son!
　　The jaws that bite, the claws that catch!
Beware the Jubjub bird, and shun
　　The frumious Bandersnatch!'

He took his vorpal sword in hand:
　　Long time the manxome foe he sought –
So rested he by the Tumtum tree,
　　And stood awhile in thought.

And as in uffish thought he stood,
　　The Jabberwock, with eyes of flame,
Came whiffling through the tulgey wood,
　　And burbled as it came!

One, two! One, two! And through and
    through
    The vorpal blade went snicker-snack!
He left it dead, and with its head
    He went galumphing back.

'And hast thou slain the Jabberwock?
    Come to my arms, my beamish boy!
O frabjous day! Callooh! Callay!'
    He chortled in his joy.

'Twas brillig, and the slithy toves
    Did gyre and gimble in the wabe;
All mimsy were the borogoves,
    And the mome raths outgrabe.

Fear

Under Plum Lake

★★

CHAPTERS FIFTEEN AND SIXTEEN
Lionel Davidson

(approximate reading time 16 minutes)

While on holiday, thirteen-year-old Barry Gordon nearly drowns off the Cornish cliffs. When he goes back to the place, he meets the strange white-haired boy, Dido (pronounced Deedo), who leads him into an astonishing and fantastic kingdom under the sea called Egon. In this extract, Dido takes Barry to the power slopes at Plum Lake but does not tell him that power skiing is the most dangerous sport in the world.

You wear ski clothes up there. You wear snow goggles. It's the top of Mount Julas, and the light is blinding. We went up on the fast cable, and he gave me a ski practice. They have a practice slope for beginners. I'd never done any skiing. He put my skis on and attached the sticks, and I fell over right away.

It's power skiing. The controls are in the sticks. There's a switch in each handle, with three positions.

With the switch up, the power is off, which means you ski normally, on the ground.

In the middle position, power is on the skis, and they lift off the ground. They lift about four inches off.

In the bottom position power is in your suit as well as your skis, which means you can't touch ground, either.

It's very tricky. You can't hit ground, but you can over-balance and go tumbling in the air with your skis flying.

He gave me a practice with everything switched on, so I could get my balance. I toppled a few times, but I got it.

Then we did a few with just the skis switched on. It's dangerous, because you can go downhill fast – faster than on snow – so if you fall you're dragged fast. I didn't manage that so well.

With everything switched off, I couldn't manage at all. I just went sliding and falling.

He got impatient and said we'd skip it, because he had to do a run. He said, 'We'll do one together later. I'll help you. You can watch for now.'

We went to the starting point, and when I saw the run I nearly fainted.

A girl was just doing it.

I saw her flying through the air.

The run is seven miles long. It starts at Mount Julas, goes steeply downhill for a mile, then you fly over a dip, hit the opposite side, ski about half a mile, do a sharp turn, and race down the long last slope. There are red flags all the way to show the route.

The idea is to race against time. It's faster with skis off the ground because there's no friction with the snow. You can do a hundred miles an hour that way. But when you've got up speed, the idea is to get on the ground. It's more dangerous. You get points for it. You fly as fast as possible in the air, and stay as long as you dare on the ground.

All the way down, instruments show when the skis are touching the ground. By the time you reach the end, they have the result.

Just before he took off he gave me a wink and said, 'See you soon.' And when he was half-way down the slope someone told me he was a champion.

They didn't have to tell me.

He went like a jet.

He took off normally, and then seemed to vanish. He didn't so much fly the dip as jump it. He hit the other side at colossal speed, and after that I couldn't see him. All I saw was a spray of snow. It did a sharp wiggle at the bend, and then there was something like a vapour trail on the last long slope, and it stopped.

I heard them yelling and jumping all round me.

He returned on the fast cable, and they all started thumping his back, and he was grinning himself. 'Not bad,' he said, 'but not my best. Want to have a try now?' he said to me.

'I don't know,' I said.

'We'll do it slowly,' he said.

I didn't want to do it any way. I couldn't stop trembling. We had to wait some time, and then he had an argument with the starter. The starter said I didn't have enough experience. I thought he was dead right, and I told him I didn't have any. But Dido said he'd hold me and that

I was keen to do it, so the starter said okay and we did it.

'If you wobble, hang on,' Dido said.

'Okay,' I said.

'You'll manage easily. Switch everything on.' He saw that I did. 'And remember what I told you. A nice slow start. Bend forward a bit. Everybody's watching. Are you all right?'

'I don't know. I don't think so,' I said.

'Yes you are. You're fine. Bend *forward*.' He caught me just as I was wobbling back.

Somehow we got off. He was on the ground, and I was up off it. I started leaning against him, which seemed a good idea, except it unbalanced him, and he had to work hard with his sticks. Also we started going too fast.

'Get on the *ground*,' he said. 'Put your switches up!'

I was so terrified I couldn't even feel the switches.

'Up!' he said. '*Up!* Like this.' He managed to work the switch nearest him.

This brought one ski down and left the other in the air. It also left me hanging round his neck.

'Switch the other one up!' he said. 'Get it *up!*'

I found the other switch and got it up, and both skis were on the ground, and I went wobbling there and back, hanging onto him, and we were still going downhill, quite fast.

I could see he was mainly afraid of making a fool of himself, so I tried hard and listened to everything he yelled, and somehow we got down the slope. I was hanging on to him all the time.

Before we got to the dip, he put me in the air, and we went gently over it.

Just then I started enjoying it. It was frightening, but it was fun. I'd got the idea, too. You had to crouch forward with your legs bent.

At the other side of the dip he got on the ground himself, but he kept me in the air. He put his arm round me as we rounded the corner flag, and we went into the long last lap. He kept me in the air all the way down it, slowing us by turning his skis in. Somehow we managed it, but right at the end, where there were people waiting, he took his arm away, and I ended up in a heap, with my skis in the air. I couldn't touch ground, and went bobbing about upside down with my skis crossed, and everyone almost collapsed with laughter.

He didn't mind. He was quite proud of me. I hadn't tripped him. I hadn't made a fool of him. He said he'd like to see anyone else try after just half an hour's practice. He said they'd been doing it for forty years. I was beginning to feel pretty good myself then, when he said we could try the real slopes now.

I'd thought these were the real slopes.

He said no, the *real* slopes were at the other side of the mountain. They had the mountain switched on there. They had to, to stop you falling off it.

It was when we got there, and I saw how easy it was to fall off anyway, that I had that feeling I couldn't bear it.

I was beginning to understand him. He was best at everything. It was why he'd gone round and made the speeches. It wasn't because his father was president. He *had* to be best; and he liked danger. Everything he did was dangerous.

I'll say what he did.

He did two runs, very carefully, without trying anything. He pointed out every detail to me. It's power tobogganing. The power comes from the mountain. The toboggan just has the controls. You sit one behind the other, tightly strapped in. You toboggan up the mountain as well as down it. There's an up-track and a down-track. You go up quite slowly. The toboggan grips the track like a magnet. Coming down, it still grips it tightly, but you're going faster. If you switch off, you're going much faster.

That's the trick. You go as fast as you dare before switching on again. They have the same procedure, a starter on top and a judge below. But this way, it's pure speed. You get from top to bottom as fast as you can, in any way you can.

He didn't tell me the various ways you could do it. He just did the first two runs nice and steadily.

He showed me how you worked the toboggan. The front person worked the controls. The back person helped steer, leaning out sideways or backwards when the toboggan rounded a bend or leaped a hump.

He gave me good warning when I had to do it. He'd yell 'Right!' or 'Left!' and I'd lean out to right or left, and we'd swish round the bend without the rear end wobbling. Or if a hump was coming, he'd yell, 'Back!' and I'd lean out backwards and we'd sail over and land flat without the nose scooping. (The toboggan is heavier at the front because of the controls.)

At the sharper bends there was a red sign, to give advance warning. But at some of them I saw a yellow sign, with an arrow pointing outwards from the mountain, and I asked why.

He pointed over the side. 'Lower track,' he said. 'You can take a short cut.'

Below, I could see the track zig-zagging down the mountain.

Second time round, he showed me the short cut.

Turning sideways at the yellow arrow, you could leave the track, grip tightly to the mountain with power on, and descend to join the next stretch of track below. You could save seconds that way.

He told me when we were going to do it. He yelled, 'Back!' and I stretched back as far as I could and we took a slow dive vertically down the mountain.

My head swam.

I was standing upright.

We were stuck like flies to the side of the mountain. I felt my eyes glazing, my body rigid. Yet the moment we hit the lower track and he switched power off and we were whizzing away again, it felt like colossal fun. We did it four or five times, and by the end I was yelling, 'Whee!' and laughing as gleefully as he did.

His eyes were shining behind his goggles as we went up for the third run, and he said something to the starter.

'We'll do a timing now,' he told me.

I'd forgotten about the timing. He hadn't asked for a timing before.

He started off fast right away, and he didn't even bother putting power on at the first wide bend, just yelled, 'Right!' and I swung out and we lurched round the bend at speed.

I felt my heart beginning to thud. I could see the red sign ahead for a hairpin bend. It came rushing up in a sickening blur, and he still didn't put power on. He began yelling, '*Left! Left!*' without slackening speed for an instant. I saw, without believing it, that he didn't mean to put power on at all. We were going racing into the hairpin bend. He was leaning out to left himself. I leaned out as far as I could. I leaned so far my head brushed the snow on the banking as we swished in a jack-knife curve round it, and levelled out into a wild dangerous wobble, racing from side to side of the icy track as we hurtled down it, not losing speed for an instant.

I could hear him cackling in front. I could see another red sign coming up, with a yellow one.

'Dido!' I yelled. 'Slow down!'

He couldn't hear me. The wind snatched my words away. I could hear him, though. He was yelling, '*Back!*'

Back? He meant left. I had to bend *left* again. Another tight hairpin was coming. It was almost here.

'*Back!*' he yelled. '*Back!*' and started straining back himself, so I did, too.

He didn't turn into the bend. He followed the yellow arrow. He went full speed off the mountain.

I thought my heart had stopped.

We were in the air, off the mountain.

Just as we lost contact, he snapped power on. I felt the magnet clamp tight. We fell and hit the lower track hard, and the instant we did so, he let power off, and we were still going at terrific speed.

I couldn't bear it. I wanted to get out. I wanted to get off.

He was cackling like a lunatic in front.

I followed blindly whatever he said. '*Left!*' '*Right!*' '*Back!*' We skated madly round the banking. We flew through the air over humps.

We came to another arrow.

'*Back!*'

Again we flew off the mountain. I wanted to close my eyes, but daren't. I was straining back, waiting for the thud of power to come on. It came on, and I clenched my toes, waiting for the thump. There was no thump. Almost immediately, he let power off again. The lower track sailed past us, and we were still dropping. He let one track, two tracks, flash past, before bringing on power, and we landed on the third. He switched power off just as we landed, but we did it with such a thud we leaped clear in the air, a good five feet, still scudding down at breakneck pace.

I'd practically given up now. I wasn't even sure when it ended. We were stopped. People were jumping and yelling. The judge was checking the figures. He was checking them again. I hadn't even got out of the toboggan. I was still strapped in.

'Well. Not bad,' Dido said. He'd shoved his goggles up,

and was grinning. 'Second best time for eighty years. What do you say to that?'

I didn't say anything.

'Barry?' he said. He seemed to be looking at me closely.

Then I was in a hut, and he was giving me tigra.

'Are you all right?' he said.

I still couldn't speak.

'Barry?'

I sipped the tigra. I felt better every second.

'Didn't you like it?' he said.

'I hated it,' I said. 'Don't do it again. Never do *anything* like that with me again.'

He just blinked at me.

'Have a nap,' he said. 'It's time for one now.'

I asked him about it later. I asked about the danger. I asked if it wasn't possible to be killed in Egon.

He said of course you could be killed. If you smashed yourself badly, you were killed.

So he knew. He knew what could happen.

All of Us

★★

Kit Wright

All of us are afraid
More often than we tell.

There are times we cling like mussels to
    the sea-wall,
And pray that the pounding waves
Won't smash our shell.

Times we hear nothing but the sound
Of our loneliness, like a cracked bell
From fields far away where the trees are in
    icy shade.

O many a time in the night-time and in
    the day,
More often than we say,
We are afraid.

If people say they are never frightened,
I don't believe them.

If people say they are frightened,
I want to retrieve them
From that dark shivering haunt
Where they don't want to be,
Nor I.

Let's make of ourselves, therefore,
   an enormous sky
Over whatever
We hold most dear.

And we'll comfort each other,
Comfort each other's
Fear.

The Undead

Dracula

★★

EXTRACT FROM CHAPTER TWO
Bram Stoker

(approximate reading time 16 minutes)

Jonathan Harker is a young lawyer, engaged to Mina. He has been summoned on business to the castle of Count Dracula in Transylvania. He has had a long and fearful journey by coach and now the driver has just left him in front of a huge door, old and studded with iron nails. This is an excerpt from his journal.

I stood in silence where I was, for I did not know what to do. Of bell or knocker there was no sign; through these frowning walls and dark window openings it was not likely that my voice could penetrate. The time I waited seemed endless, and I felt doubts and fears crowding upon me. What sort of place had I come to, and among what kind of people? What sort of grim adventure was it on which I had embarked? Was this a customary incident in the life of a solicitor's clerk sent out to explain the purchase of a London estate to a foreigner? Solicitor's clerk! Mina would not like that.

Solicitor – for just before leaving London I got word that my examination was successful; and I am now a full-blown solicitor! I began to rub my eyes and pinch myself to see if I were awake. It all seemed like a horrible nightmare to me, and I expected that I should suddenly awake, and find myself at home, with the dawn struggling in through the windows. But my flesh answered the pinching test, and my eyes were not to be deceived. I was indeed awake. All I could do now was to be patient, and to wait the coming of the morning.

Just as I had come to this conclusion I heard a heavy step approaching behind the great door, and saw through the chinks the gleam of a coming light. Then there was the sound of rattling chains and the clanking of massive bolts drawn back. A key was turned with the loud grating noise of long disuse, and the great door swung back.

Within, stood a tall old man, clean-shaven save for a long white moustache, and clad in black from head to foot, without a single speck of colour about him anywhere. He held in his hand an antique silver lamp, in which the flame burned without chimney or globe of any kind, throwing long, quivering shadows as it flickered in the draught of the open door. The old man motioned me in with his right hand with a courtly gesture, saying in excellent English, but with a strange intonation:

'Welcome to my house! Enter freely and of your own will!' He made no motion of stepping to meet me, but stood like a statue, as though his gesture of welcome had fixed him into stone. The instant, however, that I had stepped over the threshold, he moved impulsively forward, and holding out his hand grasped mine with a strength which made me wince, an effect which was not lessened by the fact that it seemed as cold as ice – more like the hand of a dead than a living man.

'I am Dracula. And I bid you welcome, Mr Harker, to my house. Come in; the night air is chill, and you must need to eat and rest.' As he was speaking he put the lamp on a bracket on the wall, and stepping out, took my luggage; he had carried it in before I could forestall him. I protested, but he insisted:

'Nay, sir, you are my guest. It is late, and my people are not available. Let me see to your comfort myself.' He insisted on carrying my traps along the passage, and then up a great winding stair, and along another great passage, on whose stone floor our steps rang heavily. At the end of this he threw open a heavy door, and I rejoiced to see within a well-lit room in which a table was spread for supper, and on whose mighty hearth a great fire of logs flamed and flared.

The Count halted, putting down my bags, closed the door, and crossing the room, opened another door, which led into a small octagonal room lit by a single lamp, and seemingly without a window of any sort. Passing through this, he opened another door, and motioned me to enter. It was a welcome sight; for here was a great bedroom well lighted and warmed with another log fire, which sent a hollow roar up the wide chimney. The Count himself left my luggage inside and withdrew, saying, before he closed the door:

'You will need, after your journey, to refresh yourself
by making your toilet. I trust you will find all you wish.
When you are ready come into the other room, where you
will find your supper prepared.'

The light and warmth and the Count's courteous welcome seemed to have dissipated all my doubts and fears.
Having then reached my normal state, I discovered that I
was half-famished with hunger; so making a hasty toilet,
I went into the other room.

I found supper already laid out. My host, who stood
on one side of the great fireplace, leaning against the stone-
work, made a graceful wave of his hand to the table, and
said:

'I pray you, be seated and sup how you please. You will,
I trust, excuse me that I do not join you; but I have dined
already, and I do not sup.'

The Count himself came forward and took off the
cover of a dish, and I fell to at once on an excellent roast
chicken. This, with some cheese and a salad and a bottle of
old Tokay, of which I had two glasses, was my supper.
During the time I was eating it the Count asked me many
questions as to my journey, and I told him by degrees all
I had experienced.

By this time I had finished my supper, and by my host's
desire had drawn up a chair by the fire and begun to smoke
a cigar which he offered me, at the same time excusing
himself that he did not smoke. I had now an opportunity
of observing him.

His face was a strong – a very strong – aquiline, with high bridge of the thin nose and peculiarly arched nostrils; with lofty domed forehead, and hair growing scantily round the temples, but profusely elsewhere. His eyebrows were very massive, almost meeting over the nose, and with bushy hair that seemed to curl in its own profusion. The mouth, so far as I could see it under the heavy moustache, was fixed and rather cruel-looking, with peculiarly sharp white teeth; these protruded over the lips, whose remark-able ruddiness showed astonishing vitality in a man of his years. For the rest, his ears were pale and at the tops extremely pointed; the chin was broad and strong, and the cheeks firm though thin. The general effect was one of extraordinary pallor.

Hitherto I had noticed the backs of his hands as they lay on his knees in the firelight, and they had seemed rather white and fine; but seeing them now close to me, I could not but notice that they were rather coarse – broad, with squat fingers. Strange to say, there were hairs in the centre of the palm. The nails were long and fine, and cut to a sharp point. As the Count leaned over me and his hands touched me, I could not repress a shudder. It may have been that his breath was rank, but a horrible feeling of nausea came over me, which, do what I would, I could not conceal. The Count, evidently noticing it, drew back; and with a grim sort of smile, which showed more than he had yet done his protuberant teeth, sat himself down again on his own side of the fireplace. We were both silent for a while; and as I looked towards the window I saw the first dim streak of the coming dawn. There seemed a strange stillness over everything; but as I listened I heard, as if from down below in the valley, the howling of many wolves. The Count's eyes gleamed, and he said:

'Listen to them – the children of the night. What music they make!' Seeing, I suppose, some expression in my face strange to him, he added:

'Ah, sir, you dwellers in the city cannot enter into the feelings of the hunter.' Then he rose and said:

'But you must be tired. Your bedroom is all ready, and tomorrow you shall sleep as late as you will. I have to be away till the afternoon; so sleep well and dream well!' and, with a courteous bow, he opened for me himself the door to the octagonal room, and I entered my bedroom . . .

I am all in a sea of wonders. I doubt; I fear; I think strange things which I dare not confess to my own soul. God keep me, if only for the sake of those dear to me!

7 May. – It is again early morning, but I have rested and enjoyed the last twenty-four hours. I slept till late in the day, and awoke of my own accord. When I had dressed myself I went into the room where we had supped, and found a cold breakfast laid out, with coffee kept hot by the pot being placed on the hearth. There was a card on the table, on which was written:

'I have to be absent for a while. Do not wait for me. – D.' So I set to and enjoyed a hearty meal. When I had done, I looked for a bell, so that I might let the servants know I had finished; but I could not find one. There are certainly odd deficiencies in the house, considering the extraordinary evidences of wealth which are round me. The table service is of gold, and so beautifully wrought that it must be of immense value. The curtains and uphol-stery of the chairs and sofas and the hangings of my bed are of the costliest and most beautiful fabrics. But still in none of the rooms is there a mirror. There is not even a toilet glass on my table, and I had to get the little shaving-glass from my bag before I could either shave or brush my hair. I have not yet seen a servant anywhere, or heard a sound near the castle except for the howling of wolves.

8 May. – There is something so strange about this place and all in it that I cannot but feel uneasy. I wish I were safe out of it, or that I had never come. If there were anyone to talk to I could bear it, but there is no one. I have only the Count to speak with, and he! – I fear I am myself the only living soul within the place.

I only slept a few hours when I went to bed, and feel-ing that I could not sleep any more, got up. I had hung my shaving-glass by the window, and was just beginning to shave. Suddenly I felt a hand on my shoulder, and heard the Count's voice saying to me, 'Good morning.' I started, for it amazed me that I had not seen him, since the reflec-tion of the glass covered the whole room behind me. In starting I had cut myself slightly, but did not notice it at the moment. Having answered the Count's salutation, I turned to the glass again to see how I had been mistaken. This time there could be no error, for the man was close to me, and I could see him over my shoulder. But there was no reflection of him in the mirror! The whole room behind me was displayed; but there was no sign of a man in it, except myself. This was startling, and, coming on the top of so many strange things, was beginning to increase that vague feeling of uneasiness which I always have when the Count is near; but at that instant I saw that the cut had bled a little, and the blood was trickling over my chin. I laid down the razor, turning as I did so half-round to look for some sticking-plaster. When the Count saw my face, his eyes blazed with a sort of demoniac fury, and he suddenly made a grab at my throat. I drew away and his hand touched the string of beads which held the crucifix. It made an instant change in him, for the fury passed so quickly that I could hardly believe that it was ever there.

'Take care,' he said, 'take care how you cut yourself. It is more dangerous than you think in this country.' Then seizing the shaving-glass, he went on: 'And this is the wretched thing that has done the mischief. It is a foul bauble of man's vanity. Away with it!' and opening the window with one wrench of his terrible hand, he flung out the glass, which was shattered into a thousand pieces on the stones of the courtyard far below. Then he withdrew without a word. It is very annoying, for I do not see how I am to shave, unless in my watch-case or the bottom of the shaving-pot, which is fortunately of metal.

When I went into the dining-room, breakfast was prepared; but I could not find the Count anywhere. So I breakfasted alone. It is strange that as yet I have not seen the Count eat or drink. He must be a very peculiar man! After breakfast I did a little exploring in the castle. I went out on the stairs and found a room looking towards the south. The view was magnificent, and from where I stood there was every opportunity of seeing it. The castle is on the very edge of a terrible precipice. A stone falling from the window would fall a thousand feet without touching anything! As far as the eye can reach is a sea of green tree-tops, with occasionally a deep rift where there is a chasm. Here and there are silver threads where the rivers wind in deep gorges through the forests.

But I am not in heart to describe beauty, for when I had seen the view I explored further; doors, doors, doors everywhere, and all locked and bolted. In no place save from the windows in the castle walls is there an available exit. The castle is a veritable prison, and I am a prisoner!

In the Stump of the Old Tree . . .

★★

Hugh Sykes-Davies

In the stump of the old tree, where the heart has rotted out,/ there is a hole the length of a man's arm, and a dank pool at the/ bottom of it where the rain gathers, and the old leaves turn into/ lacy skeletons. But do not put your hand down to see, because

in the stumps of old trees, where the hearts have rotted out,/ there are holes the length of a man's arm, and dank pools at the/ bottom where the rain gathers and old leaves turn to lace, and the/ beak of a dead bird gapes like a trap. But do not put your/ hand down to see, because

in the stumps of old trees with rotten hearts, where the rain/ gathers and the laced leaves and the dead bird like a trap, there/ are holes the length of a man's arm, and in every crevice of the/ rotten wood grow weasels' eyes like molluscs, their lids open and shut with the tide. But do not put your hand down to see, because

in the stumps of old trees where the rain gathers and the/ trapped leaves and the beak, and the laced weasel's eyes, there are/ holes the length of a man's arm, and at the bottom a sodden bible/ written in the language of rooks. But do not put your hand down/ to see, because

in the stumps of old trees where the hearts have rotted out there are holes the length of a man's arm where the weasels are/ trapped and the letters of the rook language are laced on the/ sodden leaves, and at the bottom there is a man's arm. But do/ not put your hand down to see, because

in the stumps of old trees where the hearts have rotted out/ there are deep holes and dank pools where the rain gathers, and/ if you ever put your hand down to see, you can wipe it in the/ sharp grass till it bleeds, but you'll never want to eat with/ it again.

Silver

The Girl of Silver Lake

★★

Berlie Doherty

(approximate reading time 12 minutes)

This is the story of a girl who fell in love with a fish. But it wasn't an ordinary fish. And she wasn't an ordinary girl. She was a girl who didn't want to grow up.

She lived by a lake in a beautiful valley. Sometimes the lake was busy with boats; yachts with butterfly sails, speedboats with water-skiers towed along behind in white wings of spray, launches full of waving tourists. But at other times the lake was so quiet that she could hear the water breathing, and that was when she loved it best.

When she was very young she used to play on the shores of the lake, paddling and swimming, skimming pebbles to make them bounce across its surface. When her father had finished his work in the hotel kitchens he would take her out in his old rowing boat. What she loved was to be right out in the very middle of the lake. Then her father would paddle with just one oar so the boat turned slowly round in a circle.

Now she could see how the lake, too, was like a circle. Like a round mirror. The trees and mountains seemed to turn themselves upside down into it.

'The world is under the water!' she laughed.

'No,' her father said. 'What you can see is a reflection of our world.'

She understood what he was saying and yet she understood something else too. Deep inside herself she felt that the mirror world of the lake *was* the real world. But she said nothing of this to her father. She didn't tell him how happy she felt when she looked down over the side of the lake and saw her own face reflected there. Her long hair draped down from her shoulders and floated like strands of reeds on the surface. She let her fingertips sip the water, and when she lifted her hand out the water drops slipped away as if they were threads breaking. At times like this she knew that she was part of the water and that the water was part of herself.

'I want to see the world under the water,' she said dreamily.

Her father laughed. She thought how strange it was that grown-ups didn't understand these things. That was why she didn't want to grow up.

And then, one day, she saw the fish and fell in love with it. Of course, she had seen many fish before. She had seen them leaping for flies on summer evenings. She'd seen them in little silvery shoals, clustered together and flowing through the water in the way that flocks of birds drift through the sky. She had seen the shimmering catch her father brought home sometimes in the bottom of his boat.

One day she went out in the boat on her own. If her

mother and father had known, they wouldn't have let her go; she knew that. The lake was deep and dangerous. It was so wide that a boat would be lost from sight before it reached the other side. And sometimes, because it was sur-rounded by mountains, it harboured thunderstorms. She knew all that, and yet when her parents were busy one day in the hotel she took the boat out and rowed as far into the middle of the lake as she dared. She shipped her oars and waited, letting the lake's silence sing to her.

A fish leapt from the water. It flashed with such bril-liance that she cried out for it to leap again, but the water was calm except for the ring of ripples the fish had made. They spread out into wider and wider circles until they lapped against the side of the boat, making it rock gently. At last the water settled and lay perfectly still. Yet she could see that there was a glittering circle on the surface of the water where the fish had risen and sunk.

She dipped her oars in and paddled slowly towards the circle, careful not to break it. Now she could see that the circle was made of small bright iridescent flakes like float-ing stars. And every one of them reflected her face.

Without thinking twice about it, she scooped up as many of them as she could and tipped them into the bottom of the boat. There they lay like the tiny pieces of a broken mirror, smiling up at her as she smiled down at them. She wanted to wait and see the fish again, but it was growing dusk, and a pink light stole over the water. She must go home.

She moored the boat on the lake shore and gathered up

the glittering fragments in her hands. She ran into the cottage near the hotel.

'I've found something wonderful!' she shouted. 'Come and see! I think they might be stars that have fallen out of the sky.' She opened her hand to show her mother, but the jewel flakes had turned dull and brown in her palm.

'Fish scales!' her mother said. 'What's wonderful about fish scales? Throw them away, child.'

The girl couldn't believe what had happened. But she didn't throw them away. She took them up to her room and threaded them on to a piece of cotton and wore them round her neck all night. But in the morning she hid her necklace inside her dress so no one would see it and make her throw it away. All she could think about was the beautiful fish, and she longed to row out on to the lake and look for it again, but the chance didn't come. She stood by her window, watching the lake, hoping for a sign of the fish. For three days the lake lay like a sheet of white glass.

And then her mother noticed a strange thing. The girl had shiny flakes like the scales of fish on her arms.

'What have you been doing?' she shouted. She bathed her daughter and scrubbed her skin, but nothing she did could remove the scales. She found the necklace, which the girl had hidden under her pillow, and threw it into the lake.

'Keep away from that water,' she warned her.

But the girl couldn't get the leaping, brilliant fish of Silver Lake out of her mind. Next day, when her parents were busy she went out in the boat again. As she rowed, the scales on her arms gleamed and flashed in the sun, and she smiled to see them because they were beautiful. She rowed right to the middle of the lake again, where the mountains formed a perfect circle round her and plunged their green arms into the water. She shipped the oars inside the boat and waited. The sun grew cold, clouds gathered in the sky, and still she waited.

She saw many fish leaping for flies, and heard the *plash!* as they sank into the water again. But there was no sign of her mirror fish or the ring of jewels. The light began to grow dim and soft like pearls, and she knew that she should leave. And then, just as the first stars bloomed in the sky, a fish leapt out of the water in a gleaming arc. Everything was reflected in it: the silver speck in the purple sky, the deep blue of the mountain tops, the watery glow of the rising moon. And then the fish sank into the water, leaving a ring of ripples which grew wider and slighter until all that was left was a circle of floating jewels.

Quickly the girl dipped her oars down and rowed into the circle. She leaned out and saw her face reflected in a hundred different ways in the mirror scales. This time she left them in the water. She knew them for what they were, and she didn't want to drain away their light and their life. But as she looked down at them she could hear the ripple of water all around her, and it was as if it was washing over her, as if she was inside the lake instead of peering into it.

During the night there was a thunderstorm. The girl stood at her open window and looked out at the black sky and the lightning forking through it as if it was trying to rip it apart, and she thought of the beautiful mirror fish. She closed her eyes and felt the swish of chopped water around her. She heard the rain drumming above her on the lid of the lake.

'What are you doing, child? You should be in bed.' Her mother led her away from the window and pulled back the covers of her bed. Just as the girl climbed in, there was a mighty flash of lightning that lit up the room, and in the white light the mother saw what her daughter had tried to hide from her. Her body gleamed with the scales of a fish.

'You must never, never go on the lake again. Do you hear me?' her mother demanded.

But how could the girl say yes, when every bone in her body ached to be swimming under the black water with her mirror fish?

As soon as her parents were asleep the girl crept out of the house and ran to the lakeside. Her father had filled the boat with rocks, but she had no need of it now. She waded into the lake, up to her ankles, up to her thighs, and when the water lapped against her breasts she knew that she was no longer a child. Joyously she plunged down and down. Reeds stroked her. Little fishes swarmed around her. She turned over and over in her element. The water was like silk streaming across her flesh. In the moonlight she saw how her body gleamed, and how beautiful it was. Her mirror fish swam with her, twisting this way and that, leaping with her into the soft rain.

When morning came, her father and mother stood on the shore of the lake, looking for their daughter. They were frantic with worry. Rain sliced round them like silver arrows. The mountains breathed white mist, and Silver Lake was as grey as ice.

'Our child has gone,' the mother cried, and a hush fell across the lake. The mist cleared, the rain stopped. Grey drained away from the sky like smoke and the blue of day poured through. The colours of the mountains reflected green, dun, amber, purple into their own perfect images. There was a holy silence on the water.

The man and woman gazed around them in wonder. They had never known the lake to be so still, or to take the colours of the world into itself so perfectly. Even in their grief for their lost child they wondered at its beauty.

Then they saw the fish leaping into the air. They saw the colours of the mountains and the trees and the sky reflected in it. 'How beautiful!' they gasped. The fish made a perfect shimmering arc. As it dipped towards the water the jewel scales fell away from it and there stood their daughter, a young woman in all her beauty. She waded towards them and stood watching with them. The circle of mirror scales spread out around the mother and father and their daughter in a perfect ring, and sank down into the dark, quiet mystery of Silver Lake.

The Song of Wandering Aengus*

★★

W. B. Yeats

I went out to the hazel wood,
Because a fire was in my head,
And cut and peeled a hazel wand,
And hooked a berry to a thread;
And when white moths were on the wing,
And moth-like stars were flickering out,
I dropped the berry in a stream
And caught a little silver trout.

When I had laid it on the floor
I went to blow the fire aflame,
But something rustled on the floor,
And some one called me by my name:
It had become a glimmering girl
With apple blossom in her hair
Who called me by my name and ran
And faded through the brightening air.

*pronounced Eengus

Though I am old with wandering
Through hollow lands and hilly lands,
I will find out where she has gone,
And kiss her lips and take her hands;
And walk among long dappled grass,
And pluck till time and times are done
The silver apples of the moon,
The golden apples of the sun.

Convicts Bound
In Chains

Great Expectations

★★

CHAPTER ONE

Charles Dickens

(approximate reading time 11 minutes)

In this opening chapter Pip is visiting the graves of his parents. He lives with his elder sister and her husband, Joe, the village blacksmith. In those days many men and women convicted of crimes were sentenced to be transported to Australia in convict ships.

My father's family name being Pirrip, and my christian name Philip, my infant tongue could make of both names nothing longer or more explicit than Pip. So, I called myself Pip, and came to be called Pip.

I give Pirrip as my father's family name, on the authority of his tombstone and my sister – Mrs Joe Gargery, who married the blacksmith. As I never saw my father or my mother, and never saw any likeness of either of them (for their days were long before the days of photographs), my first fancies regarding what they were like, were unreasonably derived from their tombstones. The shape of the letters on my father's, gave me an odd idea that he was a square, stout, dark man, with curly black hair. From the character and turn of the inscription, '*Also Georgiana Wife of the Above*', I drew a childish conclusion that my mother was freckled and sickly. To five little stone lozenges, each about a foot and a half long, which were arranged in a neat row beside their grave, and were sacred to the memory of five little brothers of mine – who gave up trying to get a living, exceedingly early in that universal struggle – I am indebted for a belief I religiously entertained that they had all been born on their backs with their hands in their trousers-pockets, and had never taken them out in this state of existence.

Ours was the marsh country, down by the river, within, as the river wound, twenty miles of the sea. My first most vivid and broad impression of the identity of things, seems to me to have been gained on a memorable raw afternoon towards evening. At such a time I found out for certain, that this bleak place overgrown with nettles was the churchyard; and that Philip Pirrip, late of this parish, and also Georgiana wife of the above, were dead and buried; and that Alexander, Bartholomew, Abraham, Tobias, and Roger, infant children of the aforesaid, were also dead and buried; and that the dark flat wilderness beyond the churchyard, intersected with dykes and mounds and gates, with scattered cattle feeding on it, was the marshes; and that the low leaden line beyond, was the river; and that the distant savage lair from which the wind was rushing, was the sea; and that the small bundle of shivers growing afraid of it all and beginning to cry, was Pip.

'Hold your noise!' cried a terrible voice, as a man started up from among the graves at the side of the church porch. 'Keep still, you little devil, or I'll cut your throat!'

A fearful man, all in coarse grey, with a great iron on his leg. A man with no hat, and with broken shoes, and with an old rag tied round his head. A man who had been soaked in water, and smothered in mud, and lamed by stones, and cut by flints, and stung by nettles, and torn by briars; who limped, and shivered, and glared and growled; and whose teeth chattered in his head as he seized me by the chin.

'O! Don't cut my throat, sir,' I pleaded in terror. 'Pray don't do it, sir.'

'Tell us your name!' said the man. 'Quick!'

'Pip, sir.'

'Once more,' said the man, staring at me. 'Give it mouth!'

'Pip. Pip, sir.'

'Show us where you live,' said the man. 'Pint out the place!'

I pointed to where our village lay, on the flat in-shore among the alder-trees and pollards, a mile or more from the church.

The man, after looking at me for a moment, turned me upside down, and emptied my pockets. There was nothing in them but a piece of bread. When the church came to itself – for he was so sudden and strong that he made it go head over heels before me, and I saw the steeple under my feet – when the church came to itself, I say, I was seated on a high tombstone, trembling, while he ate the bread ravenously.

'You young dog,' said the man, licking his lips, 'what fat cheeks you ha' got.'

I believe they were fat, though I was at that time undersized for my years, and not strong.

'Darn Me if I couldn't eat 'em,' said the man, with a threatening shake of his head, 'and if I han't half a mind to't!'

I earnestly expressed my hope that he wouldn't, and held tighter to the tombstone on which he had put me; partly, to keep myself upon it; partly, to keep myself from crying.

'Now lookee here!' said the man. 'Where's your mother?'

'There, sir!' said I.

He started, made a short run, and stopped and looked over his shoulder.

'There, sir!' I timidly explained. 'Also Georgiana. That's my mother.'

'Oh!' said he, coming back. 'And is that your father alonger your mother?'

'Yes, sir,' said I; 'him too; late of this parish.'

'Ha!' he muttered then, considering. 'Who d'ye live with – supposin' you're kindly let to live, which I han't made up my mind about?'

'My sister, sir – Mrs Joe Gargery – wife of Joe Gargery, the blacksmith, sir.'

'Blacksmith, eh?' said he. And looked down at his leg.

After darkly looking at his leg and me several times, he came closer to my tombstone, took me by both arms, and tilted me back as far as he could hold me; so that his eyes looked most powerfully down into mine, and mine looked most helplessly up into his.

'Now lookee here,' he said, 'the question being whether you're to be let to live. You know what a file is?'

'Yes, sir.'

'And you know what wittles is?'

'Yes, sir.'

After each question he tilted me over a little more, so as to give me a greater sense of helplessness and danger.

'You get me a file.' He tilted me again. 'And you get me wittles.' He tilted me again. 'You bring 'em both to me.' He tilted me again. 'Or I'll have your heart and liver out.' He tilted me again.

I was dreadfully frightened, and so giddy that I clung to him with both hands, and said, 'If you would kindly please to let me keep upright, sir, perhaps I shouldn't be sick, and perhaps I could attend more.'

He gave me a most tremendous dip and roll, so that the church jumped over its own weather-cock. Then, he held me by the arms, in an upright position on the top of the stone, and went on in these fearful terms:

'You bring me, to-morrow morning early, that file and them wittles. You bring the lot to me, at that old Battery over yonder. You do it, and you never dare to say a word or dare to make a sign concerning your having seen such a person as me, or any person sumever, and you shall be let to live. You fail, or you go from my words in any partick-ler, no matter how small it is, and your heart and your liver shall be tore out, roasted and ate. Now, I ain't alone, as you may think I am. There's a young man hid with me, in comparison with which young man I am a Angel. That young man hears the words I speak. That young man has a secret way pecooliar to himself, of getting at a boy, and at his heart, and at his liver. It is in wain for a boy to attempt to hide himself from that young man. A boy may lock his door, may be warm in bed, may tuck himself up, may draw the clothes over his head, may think himself comfortable and safe, but that young man will softly creep and creep his way to him and tear him open. I am a keep-ing that young man from harming of you at the present moment, with great difficulty. I find it wery hard to hold that young man off of your inside. Now, what do you say?'

I said that I would get him the file, and I would get him what broken bits of food I could, and I would come to him at the Battery, early in the morning.

'Say Lord strike you dead if you don't!' said the man.

I said so, and he took me down.

'Now,' he pursued, 'you remember what you've under-took, and you remember that young man, and you get home!'

'Goo-good night, sir,' I faltered.

'Much of that!' said he, glancing about him over the cold wet flat. 'I wish I was a frog. Or a eel!'

At the same time, he hugged his shuddering body in both his arms – clasping himself, as if to hold himself together – and limped towards the low church wall. As I saw him go, picking his way among the nettles, and among the brambles that bound the green mounds, he looked in my young eyes as if he were eluding the hands of the dead people, stretching up cautiously out of their graves, to get a twist upon his ankle and pull him in.

When he came to the low church wall, he got over it, like a man whose legs were numbed and stiff, and then turned round to look for me. When I saw him turning, I set my face towards home, and made the best use of my legs. But presently I looked over my shoulder, and saw him going on again towards the river, still hugging himself in both arms, and picking his way with his sore feet among the great stones dropped into the marshes here and there, for stepping-places when the rains were heavy, or the tide was in.

The marshes were just a long black horizontal line then, as I stopped to look after him; and the river was just another horizontal line, not nearly so broad nor yet so black; and the sky was just a row of long angry red lines and dense black lines intermixed. On the edge of the river I could faintly make out the only two black things in all the prospect that seemed to be standing upright; one of these was the beacon by which the sailors steered – like an unhooped cask upon a pole – an ugly thing when you were near it; the other a gibbet, with some chains hanging to it which had once held a pirate. The man was limping on towards this latter, as if he were the pirate come to life, and come down, and going back to hook himself up again. It gave me a terrible turn when I thought so; and as I saw the cattle lifting their heads to gaze after him, I wondered whether they thought so too. I looked all round for the horrible young man, and could see no signs of him. But, now I was frightened again, and ran home without stopping.

Transported to Australia

★★

Clive Webster

Transported to Australia,
A convict bound in chains,
Transported to Australia,
Through winds and storms and rains.

Raging sea, raging sea,
I know you'll be the death of me.

Transported to Australia –
I stole a loaf of bread,
Tired, hungry, racked with pain,
And more than halfway dead.

Raging sea, raging sea,
I know you'll be the death of me.

Transported to Australia
In eighteen twenty five,
Crying for my England home,
And only just alive.

Raging sea, raging sea,
I know you'll be the death of me.

Transported to Australia
With countless other men,
Thinking of the family
I'll never see again.

Raging sea, raging sea,
I know you'll be the death of me.

Raging sea, raging sea,
Oh take me now and set me free.

White Faces in
the Gloom

Skellig

★★

CHAPTERS ONE TO FOUR
David Almond

(approximate reading time 13 minutes)

I found him in the garage on a Sunday afternoon. It was the day after we moved into Falconer Road. The winter was ending. Mum had said we'd be moving just in time for the spring. Nobody else was there. Just me. The others were inside the house with Doctor Death, worrying about the baby.

He was lying there in the darkness behind the tea chests, in the dust and dirt. It was as if he'd been there forever. He was filthy and pale and dried out and I thought he was dead. I couldn't have been more wrong. I'd soon begin to see the truth about him, that there'd never been another creature like him in the world.

We called it the garage because that's what the estate agent, Mr Stone, called it. It was more like a demolition site or a rubbish dump or like one of those ancient warehouses they keep pulling down at the quay. Stone led us down the garden, tugged the door open and shone his little torch into the gloom. We shoved our heads in at the doorway with him.

'You have to see it with your mind's eye,' he said. 'See it cleaned, with new doors and the roof repaired. See it as a wonderful two-car garage.'

He looked at me with a stupid grin on his face.

'Or something for you, lad – a hideaway for you and your mates. What about that, eh?'

I looked away. I didn't want anything to do with him. All the way round the house it had been the same. Just see it in your mind's eye. Just imagine what could be done. All the way round I kept thinking of the old man, Ernie Myers, that had lived here on his own for years. He'd been dead nearly a week before they found him under the table in the kitchen. That's what I saw when Stone told us about seeing with the mind's eye. He even said it when we got to the dining room and there was an old cracked toilet sitting there in the corner behind a plywood screen. I just wanted him to shut up, but he whispered that towards the end Ernie couldn't manage the stairs. His bed was brought in here and a toilet was put in so everything was easy for him. Stone looked at me like he didn't think I should know about such things. I wanted to get out, to get back to our old house again, but Mum and Dad took it all in. They went on like it was going to be some big adventure. They bought the house. They started cleaning it and scrubbing it and painting it. Then the baby came too early. And here we were.

I nearly got into the garage that Sunday morning. I took my own torch and shone it in. The outside doors to the back lane must have fallen off years ago and there were dozens of massive planks nailed across the entrance. The timbers holding the roof were rotten and the roof was sagging in. The bits of the floor you could see between the rubbish were full of cracks and holes. The people that took the rubbish out of the house were supposed to take it out of the garage as well, but they took one look at the place and said they wouldn't go in it even for danger money. There were old chests of drawers and broken washbasins and bags of cement, ancient doors leaning against the walls, deck chairs with the cloth seats rotted away. Great rolls of rope and cable hung from nails. Heaps of water pipes and great boxes of rusty nails were scattered on the floor. Everything was covered in dust and spiders' webs. There was mortar that had fallen from the walls. There was a little window in one of the walls but it was filthy and there were rolls of cracked lino standing in front of it. The place stank of rot and dust. Even the bricks were crumbling like they couldn't bear the weight any more. It was like the whole thing was sick of itself and would collapse in a heap and have to get bulldozed away.

I heard something scratching in one of the corners, and something scuttling about, then it all stopped and it was just dead quiet in there.

I stood daring myself to go in.

I was just going to slip inside when I heard Mum shouting at me.

'Michael! What you doing?'

She was at the back door.

'Didn't we tell you to wait till we're sure it's safe?'

I stepped back and looked at her.

'Well, didn't we?' she shouted.

'Yes,' I said.

'So keep out! All right?'

I shoved the door and it lurched half-shut on its single hinge.

'All right?' she yelled.

'All right,' I said. 'Yes. All right. All right.'

'Do you not think we've got more to worry about than stupid you getting crushed in a stupid garage?'

'Yes.'

'You just keep out, then! Right?'

'Right. Right, right, right.'

Then I went back into the wilderness we called a garden and she went back to the flaming baby.

The garden was another place that was supposed to be wonderful. There were going to be benches and a table and a swing. There were going to be goalposts painted on one of the walls by the house. There was going to be a pond with fish and frogs in it. But there was none of that. There were just nettles and thistles and weeds and half-bricks and lumps of stone. I stood there kicking the heads off a million dandelions.

After a while, Mum shouted was I coming in for lunch and I said no, I was staying out in the garden. She brought me a sandwich and a can of Coke.

'Sorry it's all so rotten and we're all in such rotten moods,' she said.

She touched my arm.

'You understand, though. Don't you, Michael? Don't you?'

I shrugged.

'Yes,' I said.

She touched me again and sighed.

'It'll be great again when everything's sorted out,' she said.

I sat on a pile of bricks against the house wall. I ate the sandwich and drank the Coke. I thought of Random Road where we'd come from, and all my old mates like Leakey and Coot. They'd be up on the top field now, playing a match that'd last all day.

Then I heard the doorbell ringing, and heard Doctor Death coming in. I called him Doctor Death because his face was grey and there were black spots on his hands and he didn't know how to smile. I'd seen him lighting up a fag in his car one day as he drove away from our door. They told me to call him Doctor Dan, and I did when I had to speak to him, but inside he was Doctor Death to me, and it fitted him much better.

I finished the Coke, waited a minute, then I went down to the garage again. I didn't have time to dare myself or to stand there listening to the scratching. I switched the torch on, took a deep breath, and tiptoed straight inside.

Something little and black scuttled across the floor. The door creaked and cracked for a moment before it was still. Dust poured through the torch beam. Something scratched and scratched in a corner. I tiptoed further in and felt spider webs breaking on my brow. Everything was packed in tight – ancient furniture, kitchen units, rolled-up carpets, pipes and crates and planks. I kept ducking down under the hosepipes and ropes and kitbags that hung from the roof. More cobwebs snapped on my clothes and skin. The floor was broken and crumbly. I opened a cupboard an inch, shone the torch in and saw a million woodlice scattering away. I peered down into a great stone jar and saw the bones of some little animal that had died in there. Dead bluebottles were everywhere. There were ancient newspapers and magazines. I shone the torch on to one and saw that it came from nearly fifty years ago. I moved so carefully. I was scared every moment that the whole thing was going to collapse. There was dust clogging my throat and nose. I knew they'd be yelling for me soon and I knew I'd better get out. I leaned across a heap of tea chests and shone the torch into the space behind and that's when I saw him.

I thought he was dead. He was sitting with his legs stretched out, and his head tipped back against the wall. He was covered in dust and webs like everything else and his face was thin and pale. Dead bluebottles were scattered on his hair and shoulders. I shone the torch on his white face and his black suit.

'What do you want?' he said.

He opened his eyes and looked up at me.

His voice squeaked like he hadn't used it in years.

'What do you want?'

My heart thudded and thundered.

'I said, what do you want?'

Then I heard them yelling for me from the house.

'Michael! Michael! Michael!'

I shuffled out again. I backed out through the door.

It was Dad. He came down the path to me.

'Didn't we tell you—' he started.

'Yes,' I said. 'Yes. Yes.'

I started to brush the dust off myself. A spider dropped away from my chin on a long string.

He put his arm around me.

'It's for your own good,' he said.

He picked a dead bluebottle out of my hair.

He thumped the side of the garage and the whole thing shuddered.

'See?' he said. 'Imagine what might happen.'

I grabbed his arm to stop him thumping it again.

'Don't,' I said. 'It's all right. I understand.'

He squeezed my shoulder and said everything would be better soon.

He laughed.

'Get all that dust off before your mother sees, eh?'

I hardly slept that night. Every time I did drop off I saw him coming out of the garage door and coming through the wilderness to the house. I saw him in my bedroom. I saw him come right to the bed. He stood there all dusty and white with the dead bluebottles all over him.

'What do you want?' he whispered. 'I said, what do you want?'

I told myself I was stupid. I'd never seen him at all. That had all been part of a dream as well. I lay there in the dark. I heard Dad snoring and when I listened hard I could hear the baby breathing. Her breathing was cracked and hissy. In the middle of the night when it was pitch black I dropped off again but she started bawling. I heard Mum getting up to feed her. I heard Mum's voice cooing and comforting. Then there was just silence again, and Dad snoring again. I listened hard for the baby again and I couldn't hear her.

It was already getting light when I got up and tiptoed into their room. Her cot was beside their bed. They were lying fast asleep with their arms around each other. I looked down at the baby. I slipped my hand under the covers and touched her. I could feel her heart beating fast. I could feel the thin rattle of her breath, and her chest rising and falling. I felt how hot it was in there, how soft her bones were, how tiny she was. There was a dribble of spit and milk on her neck. I wondered if she was going to die. They'd been scared about that in the hospital. Before they let her come home she'd been in a glass case with tubes and wires sticking in her and we'd stood around staring in like she was in a fish tank.

I took my hand away and tucked the covers around her again. Her face was dead white and her hair was dead black. They'd told me I had to keep praying for her but I didn't know what to pray.

'Hurry up and get strong if you're going to,' I whispered.

Mum half woke up and saw me there.

'What d'you want, love?' she whispered.

She stretched her hand out of the bed towards me.

'Nothing,' I whispered, and tiptoed back to my room.

I looked down into the wilderness. There was a blackbird singing away on the garage roof. I thought of him lying behind the tea chests with the cobwebs in his hair. What was he doing there?

John Mouldy

★★

Walter de la Mare

I spied John Mouldy in his cellar,
Deep down twenty steps of stone;
In the dusk he sat a-smiling,
   Smiling there alone.

He read no book, he snuffed no candle;
The rats ran in, the rats ran out;
And far and near, the drip of water
   Went whisp'ring about.

The dusk was still, with dew a-falling,
I saw the Dog-star bleak and grim,
I saw a slim brown rat of Norway
   Creep over him.

I spied John Mouldy in his cellar,
Deep down twenty steps of stone;
In the dusk he sat a-smiling,
   Smiling there alone.

Angels

Angel to Angel

★★

Annie Dalton

(approximate reading time 13 minutes)

When the call came, my old teacher, Miss Rowntree, was giving me an ear-bashing. 'There's more to life than makeovers, Melanie,' she nagged. I tried to tell her dying had totally improved my attitude; that the Agency was so impressed, they were sending me on a trouble-shooting mission! But dreams never work out the way you want them to, and an irritating bell had started to ring.

I woke up and answered the phone.

'We need you right away,' said Michael's voice. 'We've got a hiccup in seventh-century Ireland.'

I peered outside. An Agency limo was waiting, its lights blinking in the dark. 'Omigod!' I squeaked. 'They really are letting me go solo!'

Down at Headquarters, one of the night staff gave my skirt a disbelieving stare. 'Are you sure they didn't confuse her with another agent?' he muttered. I'd thrown on the first clothes I could find. It wasn't my fault they were short and sparkly.

'Sorry for the short notice,' said Michael, whizzing me

through Departures. Mike's a sweetie, but totally terrifying like all archangels. He started up about how the Agency wanted me to rescue a valuable saint, from bloodthirsty pagans presumably. But I was in such a flap, I didn't take in the details.

'All our experienced agents are tied up in the late 1990s,' Michael sighed. 'That period is such a drain on our resources.'

Tell me about it. I'm still sore about being permanently removed from history by a speeding joyrider, the day after my thirteenth birthday. Sometimes I worry that they won't ever sort my favourite century out. But Michael's dead confident.

I know what you're thinking, Melanie Beeby, training to be an angel! This is a joke, right? That's what *I* thought. But Orlando (he's another trainee and totally gorgeous!) set me straight. 'The Agency's been going quite a few millennia, Mel. They know angel material when they see it.'

Of course, strictly speaking I'm not Mel any more. Angels travel in time as well as space, you see. And like Michael says, 'You can't have the angel Melanie popping up in ancient Egypt. It confuses people.' So my angel name is Helix. Dignified or what!

Still, it was a hairy moment when the door on my time-portal slid shut. Weird stuff flitted through my head. Like, if Miss Rowntree could only see me now. And what was that sweet-faced boy Orlando up to these days? I hadn't seen him for months. We're not encouraged to discuss each other's comings and goings. The tutors just say,

'He moves in mysterious ways,' which basically means MYOB.

'Erm, what have I got to do in that century again?' I yelled through the glass.

Michael's eyebrows shot up. 'You did memorise your manual?'

Luckily, just then my portal lit up like the Blackpool illuminations, and I was catapulted into a seventh-century sunrise.

What a trip! I tried to act like Helix, all calm and dignified, but a few Melanie-style squeals *might* have leaked out. Anyway, first I got this like, *huge* overview of the entire British Isles. Wow, was the place empty! Then as I got closer I saw all these brilliant details. Whales coming up for air. Fishermen mending nets. Even a musician on the shore, trying out a cool song on his weird little harp.

Then, next thing, I was tumbling to earth, nose to nose with some tiny violets. Hello, world, I'm back. It's me, Melanie!

I was just admiring the scenery (a hill with bouncy little lambs, plus stream and fluffy pussy-willows) when a chariot thundered past. The driver had the dirtiest hair I've ever seen and more tattoos than the average biker. He hurtled into the distance, his outsized wheels churning up the mud.

Well, can't stand about all day, I thought. Better rescue this wrinkly old saint or whatever.

I headed for a village at the top of the hill. I say 'village', but it was more like a bunch of giant bee-hives really.

People were up and about already. Feeding horses, lighting fires; dirty little kids racing round scattering chickens. The usual Robin Hood stuff. This was the place, no question. True, there wasn't a saint in sight. But he was probably tied up nearby. Agency timing is dead reliable like that.

Outside one of the huts, youths were taking turns firing arrows at a straw target, jeering when someone missed. I think they were trying to impress these two girls, but the girls went on eating their dried plums, completely ignoring them.

'King, warrior, shepherd, saint,' chanted the red-headed girl. She counted again but it still came out 'saint'. 'Give me yours, Brigid,' she demanded. 'Or I'll never find a king to buy me a gold chain. A big one I want, mind. Thick enough to choke a donkey!'

'Throw one stone away, Niamh, and marry the shep-herd,' teased Brigid.

Niamh laughed. 'And spend my days stinking of damp wool, like Mother!'

'Niamh! Get in here!' yelled a woman's voice.

The girl rolled her eyes. 'We're to clean the wall hang-ings today.' She scrambled to her feet and I followed her indoors.

You've probably heard angels can read people's thoughts? The truth is, we can't *not* do it; human thoughts just jump out at us like radio signals. So I found out about Niamh's life with no trouble at all.

For instance, her people *weren't* pagans. So it was highly unlikely they'd got my saint under lock and key somewhere. I found out other things too. Like when Niamh was little, she sang all day long for sheer enjoyment. Until her Mum remarked that no-one in their right mind would marry a girl who cawed like a crow. After that, Niamh gave up on life and took up daydreaming full-time, deciding her only hope was to find a king to marry.

Then a few months ago, walking in the hazel woods, she stumbled across an incredibly beautiful young man, delirious with fever.

Naturally Niamh was primed to recognise royal blood when she saw it. So she came back every day to spoon nettle soup into him, until he was well enough to remember his name, which turned out to be Colum. Of course, Niamh was thrilled when Colum finally confessed his father was the king of Kinvara. Her dream was coming true!

You see, the king wanted his son to be a great warrior but Colum hated violence. That's why he was hiding out in the woods, eating nuts and berries. Niamh promised not to tell a soul she'd seen him.

Colum was nothing like the tough biker-types in Niamh's village. He was so pure and gentle, shy forest creatures came up to lick his hands. Niamh thought this was pretty weird. But he'd probably grow out of it, once he'd resumed his royal responsibilities. So all winter she'd been smuggling him food and clothing, convinced he'd soon forget his silly quarrel and take her home to Kinvara with him.

I found out something else about Niamh as I watched

her dreamily doing her chores. When no-one was around, she sang to herself, in a voice which made my whole spine tingle.

Miss Rowntree says TV soaps rot your brains. But I learned heaps from watching them. For instance, I knew right off Niamh didn't love Colum. He was just her most convenient career option. Unfortunately there was one tiny drawback. Me.

You see, by now I'd figured out that Colum was the saint the Agency'd sent me to rescue. Not from blood-thirsty pagans. But from Niamh.

I don't know how clued up you are about the Dark Ages? Well, during that period, it was only a bunch of wild and wonderful Irish saints who kept the divine light burning in Europe. Some of these saints were so holy that natural laws were suspended in their vicinity. Which basically means miracles became, like, normal. And hopefully this balanced out the really gross stuff going on elsewhere. So you can see why the Agency couldn't afford to lose a saint. It'd be like England losing a striker during the World Cup.

But what about Niamh? Okay, she was no saint. But didn't she count for anything? Wasn't there any way I could do this without hurting her feelings?

Anyway, when Niamh sneaked away to the woods that night, I followed. But when we got there, there was a bunch of total strangers in Colum's grove, listening to him explaining about Time being like a honeycomb with many chambers. (I think that was it.)

'Who are these people?' demanded Niamh.

'My friends,' said Colum serenely.

'But you love *me*,' yelled Niamh, her nostrils going pinched and white, which I'm afraid did absolutely nothing for her.

'Colum loves all creation,' said a girl. 'Birds, stones, dew.'

So of course Niamh went crashing off into the woods, furious about wasting her time on some bloke who loved dew. At the same moment Colum moved near the fire. And for the first time I saw his sweet familiar face.

'*Orlando?*' I whispered.

He didn't seem surprised to see me. 'I'm at my wits' end, Mel,' he sighed. 'Niamh's a great kid. But I can't marry her. It would ruin the Agency's strategy.'

'I didn't know angels could be saints,' I said.

'They were one short,' he explained casually. 'I'm helping out.' A baby deer nuzzled his hand. And in the branches over our heads, a couple of owls looked down adoringly. Orlando really made an excellent saint.

'But she'll tell the King you're here,' I said. 'He'll have you killed and Ireland will *still* be a saint short of a full set.'

No-one could hear us, by the way. It was strictly angel to angel.

'That's why I asked the Agency to send you,' said Orlando.

'You're kidding! You actually *asked* for me?'

'Yes. Because you'll know how to help her,' he said simply.

And for a dizzy second I was falling through the sunrise again. And as I fell, I registered once again that young musician practising his song on a lonely beach. Orlando was right. I knew exactly what to do.

Look, the next bit is dead technical, okay, unless you're into angel science. All you need to know is that with a helpful cosmic nudge or three, they finally met up; Niamh and her travelling musician. (His name was Marvan by the way.) And it turned out they were made for each other. So, mission accomplished, I'd say!

Back at the Agency, Michael gave me a tape of the whole experience, for future reference. But I keep rewinding to the bit where they're on the beach, at sunset, and Marvan finally says the words I'd been whispering to him. 'So Niamh, won't you sing for me?'

And Niamh tosses her head like Scarlett O'Hara in *Gone with the Wind* and says, 'I will not. My mother says I sound like a crow.'

But you'll never guess what Marvan says next, with no help whatsoever.

'Are you telling me there is no song locked inside that lovely swan's throat of yours?'

Romantic or what!! So Niamh sings and Marvan's totally blown away by her beautiful voice, like I knew he would be. Then he tells her how the two of them will travel the wide world, and perform before the High King of Ireland himself. And off they go, hand in hand. And at that exact moment some wild geese fly overhead. It makes me cry every time. And I just know that Miss Rowntree would totally approve.

So that's all really. Except to say, don't worry, next time I get a midnight call, I'll be properly prepared. It took ages but I've finally come up with the perfect outfit; cropped top, combats and some cool boots. To me this look says committed, it says *now*, it says ready for action.

I mean, I'm an angel, so I should look *divine*, right?

Angels

★★

Jan Dean

We are made from light.
Called into being we burn
Brighter than the silver white
of hot magnesium.
More sudden than yellow phosphorus.
We are the fire of heaven;
Blue flames and golden ether.

We are from stars.
Spinning beyond the farthest galaxy
In an instant gathered to this point
We shine, speak our messages and go,
Back to brilliance.
We are not separate, not individual,
We are what we are made of. Only
Shaped sometimes into tall-winged
    warriors,
Our faces solemn as swords,
Our voices joy.

The skies are cold;
Suns do not warm us;
Fire does not burn itself.
Only once we touched you
And felt a human heat.
Once, in the brightness of the frost.
Above the hills, in glittering starlight,
Once, we sang.

The Emperor's
New Clothes

★★

Roald Dahl

The Royal Tailor, Mister Ho,
Had premises on Savile Row,
And thence the King would make his way
At least a dozen times a day.
His passion was for gorgeous suits
And sumptuous cloaks and fur-lined boots
And brilliant waistcoats lined in red,
Hand-sewn with gold and silver thread.
Within the Palace things were grand,
With valets everywhere on hand
To hang the clothes and clean and press
And help the crazy King to dress.
But clothes are very dangerous things,
Especially for wealthy kings.
This King had gone to pot so fast,
His clothes came first, his people last.
One valet who was seen to leave
A spot of gravy on a sleeve

Was hung from rafters by his hair
And left forever dangling there.
Another who had failed to note
A fleck of dust upon a coat
Was ordered to be boiled alive,
A fate not easy to survive.
And one who left a pinch of snuff
Upon a pale-blue velvet cuff
Was minced inside a large machine
And reappeared as margarine.
Oh, what a beastly horrid King!
The people longed to do him in!
And so a dozen brainy men
Met secretly inside a den
To formulate a subtle plot
To polish off this royal clot.
Up spake the very brainiest man
Who cried, 'I've got a wizard plan.
Please come with me. We all must go
To see the royal tailor, Ho.
We'll tell him very strong and true
Exactly what he's got to do.'
So thus the secret plans were laid
And all arrangements quickly made.
T'was winter-time with lots of snow
And every day the King would go
To ski a bit before he dined
In ski-suits specially designed.
But even on these trips he'd stop

To go into the tailor's shop.
'O Majesty!' cried Mister Ho,
'I cannot wait to let you know
That I've contrived at last to get
From secret weavers in Tibet
A cloth so magical and fine,
So unbelievably divine,
You've never seen its like before
And never will do any more!'
The King yelled out, 'I'll buy the lot!
I'll purchase every yard you've got!'
The tailor smiled and bowed his head.
'O honoured sire,' he softly said,
'This marvellous magic cloth has got
Amazing ways to keep you hot,
And even when it's icy cold
You still feel warm as molten gold.
However hard the north wind blows
You still won't need your underclothes.'
The King said, 'If it's all that warm,
I'll have a ski-ing uniform!
I want ski-trousers and a jacket!
I don't care if it costs a packet!
Produce the cloth. I want to see
This marvellous stuff you're selling me.'
The tailor, feigning great surprise,
Said, 'Sire, it's here before your eyes.'
The King said, 'Where? Just tell me where.'
'It's in my hands, O King, right here!'

The King yelled, tearing at his hair,
'Don't be an ass! There's nothing there!'
The tailor cried, 'Hold on, I pray!
There's something I forgot to say!
This cloth's invisible to fools
And nincompoops and other ghouls.
For brainless men who're round the twist
This cloth does simply not exist!
But seeing how you're wise and bright,
I'm sure it glistens in your sight.'
Now right on cue, exactly then,
In burst the dozen brainy men.
They shouted, 'Oh, what lovely stuff!
We want some too! D'you have enough?'
Extremely calm, the tailor stands,
With nothing in his empty hands,
And says, 'No, no! this gorgeous thing
Is only for my lord, the King.'
The King, not wanting to admit
To being a proper royal twit
Cried out, 'Oh, isn't it divine!
I want it all! It's mine! It's mine!
I want a ski-ing outfit most
So I can keep as warm as toast!'
The brainy men all cried, 'Egad!
Oh, Majesty, you lucky lad!
You'll feel so cosy in the snow
With temps at zero and below!'
Next day the tailor came to fit

The costume on the royal twit.

The brainy men all went along

To see that nothing should go wrong.

The tailor said, 'Strip naked, sire.

This suit's so warm you won't require

Your underclothes or pants or vest

Or even hair upon your chest.'

And now the clever Mister Ho

Put on the most terrific show

Of dressing up the naked King

In nothing – not a single thing.

'That's right sir, slip your arm in there,

And now I'll zip you up right here.

Do you feel comfy? Does it fit?

Or should I take this in a bit?'

Now during this absurd charade,

And while the King was off his guard,

The brainy men, so shrewd and sly,

Had turned the central heating high.

The King, although completely bare,

With not a stitch of underwear,

Began to sweat and mop his brow,

And cried, 'I do believe you now!

I feel as though I'm going to roast!

This suit will keep me warm as toast!'

The Queen, just then, came strolling through

With ladies of her retinue.

They stopped. They gasped. There stood

   the King

As naked as a piece of string,
As naked as a popinjay,
With not a fig-leaf in the way.
He shouted, striking up a pose,
'Behold my marvellous ski-ing clothes!
These clothes will keep me toasty-warm
In hail or sleet or snow or storm!'
Some ladies blushed and hid their eyes
And uttered little plaintive cries.
But some, it seemed, enjoyed the pleasures
Of looking at the royal treasures.
A brazen wench cried, 'Oh my hat!
Hey girls, just take a look at that!'
The Queen, who'd seen it all before,
Made swiftly for the nearest door.
The King cried, 'Now I'm off to ski!
You ladies want to come with me?'
They shook their heads, so off he went,
A madman off on pleasure bent.
The crazy King put on his skis,
And now, oblivious to the freeze
He shot outdoors and ski'd away,
Still naked as a popinjay.
And thus this fool, so lewd and squalid,
In half an hour was frozen solid.
And all the nation cried, 'Heigh-ho!
The King's deep-frozen in the snow!'

The Lion and Albert

★★

Marriott Edgar

There's a famous seaside place called
  Blackpool,
  That's noted for fresh air and fun,
And Mr and Mrs Ramsbottom
  Went there with young Albert, their son.

A grand little lad was young Albert,
  All dressed in his best; quite a swell
With a stick with an 'orse's 'ead 'andle,
  The finest that Woolworth's could sell.

They didn't think much to the Ocean:
  The waves, they were fiddlin' and small,
There was no wrecks and nobody drownded,
  Fact, nothing to laugh at at all.

So, seeking for further amusement,
  They paid and went into the Zoo,
Where they'd Lions and Tigers and Camels,
  And old ale and sandwiches too.

There was one great big Lion called Wallace;
   His nose were all covered with scars –
He lay in a somnolent posture
   With the side of his face on the bars.

Now Albert had heard about Lions,
   How they was ferocious and wild –
To see Wallace lying so peaceful,
   Well, it didn't seem right to the child.

So straightway the brave little feller,
   Not showing a morsel of fear,
Took his stick with its 'orse's 'ead 'andle
   And pushed it in Wallace's ear.

You could see that the Lion didn't like it,
   For giving a kind of a roll,
He pulled Albert inside the cage with 'im,
   And swallowed the little lad 'ole.

Then Pa, who had seen the occurrence,
   And didn't know what to do next,
Said 'Mother! Yon Lion's 'et Albert,'
   And Mother said, 'Well, I am vexed!'

Then Mr and Mrs Ramsbottom –
   Quite rightly, when all's said and done –
Complained to the Animal Keeper
   That the Lion had eaten their son.

The keeper was quite nice about it;
 He said 'What a nasty mishap.
Are you sure that it's *your* boy he's eaten?'
 Pa said 'Am I sure? There's his cap!'

The manager had to be sent for.
 He came and he said 'What's to do?'
Pa said 'Yon Lion's 'et Albert,
 'And 'im in his Sunday clothes, too.'

Then Mother said, 'Right's right, young feller;
 I think it's a shame and a sin
For a lion to go and eat Albert,
 And after we've paid to come in.'

The manager wanted no trouble,
 He took out his purse right away,
Saying 'How much to settle the matter?'
 And Pa said 'What do you usually pay?'

But Mother had turned a bit awkward
 When she thought where her Albert had gone.
She said 'No! someone's got to be summonsed' –
 So that was decided upon.

Then off they went to the P'lice Station,
 In front of the Magistrate chap;
They told 'im what happened to Albert,
 And proved it by showing his cap.

The Magistrate gave his opinion
    That no one was really to blame
And he said that he hoped the Ramsbottoms
    Would have further sons to their name.

At that Mother got proper blazing,
    'And thank you, sir, kindly,' said she.
'What, waste all our lives raising children
    To feed ruddy Lions? Not me!'

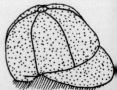

Bedd Gelert or The Grave of the Greyhound

★★

William Robert Spencer

Bedd Gelert, *meaning Gelert's grave, tells the legend of Gelert, a greyhound, given to Prince Llewelyn of Gwynedd by King John. Today, if you go to the village of Beddgelert in Gwynedd, Wales, you will find the grave of this faithful and brave dog.*

The spearmen heard the bugle sound,
And cheerly smiled the morn;
And many a brach,* and many a hound,
Obeyed Llewelyn's horn.

And still he blew a louder blast,
And gave a lustier cheer:
'Come, Gelert come, wer't never last
Llewelyn's horn to hear.

*brach – a hunting dog with a keen sense of smell

'Oh where does faithful Gelert roam,
The flower of all his race;
So true, so brave, a lamb at home,
A lion in the chase?'

'Twas only at Llewelyn's board
The faithful Gelert fed;
He watched, he served, he cheered his lord,
And sentinelled* his bed.

In sooth he was a peerless hound,
The gift of royal John;
But now no Gelert could be found,
And all the chase rode on.

And now, as o'er the rocks and dells
The gallant chidings rise,
All Snowdon's† craggy chaos yells
The many-mingled cries.

That day Llewelyn little loved
The chase of hart and hare;
And scant and small the booty proved,
For Gelert was not there.

*sentinelled – guarded
† Snowdon is the highest mountain in Wales

Unpleased Llewelyn homeward hied,
When near the portal seat
His truant Gelert he espied,
Bounding his lord to greet.

But when he gained his castle door
Aghast the chieftain stood;
The hound all o'er was smeared with gore,
His lips, his fangs, ran blood.

Llewelyn gazed with fierce surprise;
Unused such looks to meet,
His favourite checked his joyful guise,
And crouched, and licked his feet.

Onward in haste Llewelyn passed,
And on went Gelert too;
And still, where'er his eyes he cast,
Fresh blood-gouts shocked his view.

O'erturned his infant's bed he found,
With blood-stained covert rent;
And all around the walls and ground
With recent blood besprent.*

He called his child – no voice replied –
He searched with terror wild;

*besprent – sprayed

Blood, blood he found on every side,
But nowhere found his child.
'Hell hound! my child's by thee devoured,'
The frantic father cried;
And to the hilt his vengeful sword
He plunged in Gelert's side.

His suppliant looks, as prone he fell,
No pity could impart;
But still his Gelert's dying yell
Passed heavy o'er his heart.

Aroused by Gelert's dying yell,
Some slumberer wakened nigh:
What words the parent's joy could tell
To hear his infant's cry!

Concealed beneath a tumbled heap
His hurried search had missed,
All glowing from his rosy sleep,
The cherub boy he kissed.

Nor scathe had he, nor harm, nor dread,
But, the same couch beneath,
Lay a gaunt wolf, all torn and dead,
Tremendous still in death.

Ah, what was then Llewelyn's pain!
For now the truth was clear;
His gallant hound the wolf had slain,
To save Llewelyn's heir.

Vain, vain was all Llewelyn's woe:
'Best of thy kind, adieu!
The frantic blow, which laid thee low,
This heart shall ever rue.'

And now a gallant tomb they raise,
With costly sculpture decked;
And marbles storied with his praise
Poor Gelert's bones protect.

There never could the spearman pass,
Or forester, unmoved;
There, oft the tear-besprinkled grass
Llewelyn's sorrow proved.

And there he hung his horn and spear,
And there, as evening fell,
In fancy's ear he oft would hear
Poor Gelert's dying yell.

And till great Snowdon's rocks grow old,
And cease the storm to brave,
The consecrated spot shall hold
The name of 'Gelert's grave'.

Afterword

★★

Each week staff from The Reader Organisation read with over 200 children and young people in libraries, schools, community centres, foster homes, residential care homes, and alternative education settings. We have learnt a few things from our work: we know that the many effects of the shared reading sessions aren't the same for every child; we know that for some children engaging with the stories comes quickly, and we know that for some it takes longer, years even. Most importantly we see it making a positive difference every day, and the children we read with tell us what it is doing for them.

One young girl we read with lives a chaotic life and finds it hard to concentrate; focusing on reading for an hour helps her to relax and take a step away from the many things that have been happening that week: 'Reading makes me feel better because it takes my mind off my problems.' A ten-year-old boy is withdrawn and serious; sharing a great story brings him out of himself: 'I always enjoy the sessions because we have a good laugh.' For another girl it took two years of weekly reading sessions before she let her guard down and truly connected with the story; it was worth the wait: I could see the shift happen in her and know that if nothing else, she will always have the very real connection that she had at that moment.

That is what reading does: it makes connections between people, books, and the wider world. Stories are an integral part of all human existence; every day we are creating and adding to the story of our own life.

Reading and being read to ensures that we have a way of interpreting and understanding the world around us and our place in it. Being given the gift of reading at an early age grants young people an advantage and helps prepare them for the future. They can go forward into their future armed with a past and present full of knowledge and understanding and a tool for dealing with the many challenges that life will throw at them.

For some children it is slightly more complicated than this; they may have had difficult experiences in their past or be going through something in their present which they are finding hard to deal with. This can leave them feeling stranded and alone, disconnected from other people and the flow of life that continues around them whilst they feel as if they are left standing still. No words, no matter how kind or well intentioned, can instantly release a child from this isolation, but reading a story can; sharing a book together can help a child feel connected again in a way that reassuring words never can. Sometimes in life there is no easy answer to a situation, nothing we say can make a difference; these are the times when we need to be reading to and with each other.

Samantha Shipman
The Reader Organisation
Young Person's Project Manager

Read On

★★

A list of some of the novels, short stories, plays and poems that have helped to get older children hooked on reading.

SHORT STORIES

Free? Stories Celebrating Human Rights
Stories by multiple authors from around the world. The book includes such themes as asylum, law, education and faith in a way that will both inspire and entertain.

Paul Jennings
Unreal – Funny, weird and wacky short stories with strange endings.
Unbelievable – Quirky, bizarre, and very funny short stories.

NOVELS

David Almond
My Name Is Mina – A prequel to *Skellig*. This is Mina's story as she writes it in her journal before she meets Michael.

The Savage – A very special story of grief and hope told in words and illustrations.

My Dad's a Birdman – David Almond writes for a slightly younger age group in this moving story about a girl and her dad.

Malorie Blackman

Cloud Busting – A beautiful, funny and sad story told completely in verse.

John Boyne

Noah Barleywater Runs Away – Eight-year-old Noah runs away from home and, finding himself in an enchanted land where animals can talk, comes to a magic toyshop.

Frank Cottrell Boyce

Framed – Frank's books can make you laugh your head off.

Millions – If you found a bag with £229,370 in it, what would you do? This is the story of what happens to the boy who found that bag.

Roald Dahl

The Witches, Matilda, The BFG – In fact all Roald Dahl's stories 'work' for children.

Neil Gaiman

Stardust – Fairy tale for older children and young adults. Brilliantly imaginative, romantic, grisly and sometimes funny.

Coraline – A girl is trapped in a parallel world within her own house. Very very scary.

Sonya Hartnett
The Midnight Zoo – Two children carrying their baby sister in a sack flee from the Nazis in the Second World War. They take shelter in a zoo where the animals are trapped in their cages. Very moving.

Anthony Horowitz
South by South East – One of several funny and fast-moving detective stories about the world's worst private detective.
Granny – A wickedly funny tale about the granny from Hell.

Gemma Malley
The Declaration – In the year 2140, scientists have found a drug that prevents dying.

Michael Morpurgo
Private Peaceful – A young soldier thinks back over his life which has brought him to the trenches of the Western Front in the First World War.
An Elephant in the Garden – In Germany during the Second World War, an elephant becomes one of the refugees, forced to flee from the advancing Russian troops.

Andy Mulligan

Trash – Three friends try to earn a living sorting through rubbish on a dump in a Third World country. One day they find something extraordinary and from that moment their lives are in danger.

Patrick Ness

The Knife of Never Letting Go – The first in the trilogy *Chaos Walking*. An incredibly fast-paced book for older children who will find it impossible to put down.

Tom Palmer

Foul Play – Boys who like football but not reading have changed their minds after this book.

Mal Peet

Keeper – The story of how El Gato 'The Cat', once a poor logger's son, becomes the world's greatest goalkeeper.

Nicola Pierce

Spirit of the Titanic – The tragic story of the *Titanic* as told

by the ghost of fifteen-year-old Samuel Scott, who died building the ship.

Chris Priestley
Uncle Montague's Tales of Terror – Another brilliantly creepy book, full of menace, with unexpected twists in the tales.

Philip Pullman
Clockwork – A gripping, dark and terrifying fairy tale.

Louis Sachar
There's a Boy in the Girl's Bathroom – Bradley's teacher says he has serious behavioural problems. No one likes him, until a new teacher comes to school. Can Bradley change? Funny and thoughtful.
Holes – Fifteen-year-old Stanley Yelnats is found guilty of a crime he did not commit and is sent to Camp Greenlake – a place for bad boys. Perhaps surprisingly, this is a great story of family and friendship.

Brian Selznick
The Invention of Hugo Cabret – Some of the story is told in words and some in terrific pictures. Utterly original, this book is a powerful weapon against people who think books are boring.
Wonderstruck – Ben's story takes place in 1977 and is told in words. Rose's story, in 1927, is told entirely in pictures. Gradually the two come together.

The Houdini Box – The story of Victor, who meets his hero Harry Houdini, the world's greatest escapologist, is told in wonderfully detailed drawings.

Jerry Spinelli
Star Girl – The story of a girl who dares to be different.

PLAYS

Kevin Dyer
The Monster Under the Bed – Ben swaps places for the day with the monster who lives under his bed. Funny, exciting and thoughtful.

POETRY ANTHOLOGIES

Read Me Out Loud Paul Cookson and Nick Toczek
Revolting Rhymes Roald Dahl
New and Collected Poems for Children Carol Ann Duffy
My Dog Is a Carrot John Hegley
The Ring of Words ed. Roger McGough
Slapstick Poems Roger McGough
Read Me and Laugh: A Funny Poem for Every Day of the Year chosen by Gaby Morgan
Michael Rosen's A to Z Michael Rosen
A Spider on a Bicycle selected by Michael Rosen
Glass Bead Games a collection by Jacqueline Wilson
Wicked World Benjamin Zephaniah

Acknowledgments

★★

Every effort has been made to trace and contact all copyright holders. If there are any inadvertent omissions or errors we will be pleased to correct these at the earliest opportunity.

Joan Aiken: from *The Wolves of Willoughby Chase* by Joan Aiken, published by Random House Children's Books. Reprinted by permission of The Random House Group Ltd.

David Almond: from *Skellig* by David Almond. (©David Almond 1998.) Reproduced by permission of Hodder Children's Books.

Patrick Barrington: 'I Had a Hippopotamus' reproduced with permission of Punch Ltd., www.punch.co.uk

Hilaire Belloc: 'Matilda' by Hilaire Belloc from *Cautionary Tales* (©Hilaire Belloc) is reproduced by permission of PFD (www.pfd.co.uk) on behalf of Hilaire Belloc.

Frank Cottrell Boyce: *Cosmic* by Frank Cottrell Boyce. (Macmillan Children's, 2008) Reproduced by permission of the author and Macmillan Children's Books, London, UK.

Richmal Crompton: 'The Knight at Arms' from *More William* by Richmal Crompton. (Macmillan Children's, 2005) Reproduced by permission of Macmillan Publishers Ltd.

Roald Dahl: 'Emperor's New Clothes' from *Rhyme Stew* by Roald Dahl (Jonathan Cape, 1989). Reproduced by permission of David Higham Associates Ltd.

Philip Gross: 'White Ones' from *Off Road to Everywhere* by Philip Gross (Salt Publishing, 2010). Reproduced by permission of Salt Publishing Ltd and the author.

Russell Hoban: *The Mouse & His Child* by Russell Hoban (Harper & Row, 1967). Reproduced by permission of the author and Faber & Faber.

Ted Hughes: 'Amulet' from *Moon-bells and Other Poems (Poets for the Young)* by Ted Hughes (Bodley Head Children's Books, 1978). Reproduced by permission of the estate of the author and Faber & Faber.

Tove Jansson: ' The Invisible Child' from *Tales from Moomin Valley*, pp103-119 by Tove Jansson. (London: Penguin, 1973) ©Tove Jansson 1963. Reproduced by permission of Penguin Books Ltd.

Philip Larkin: 'Trees' from *Collected Poems* by Philip Larkin, ed. Anthony Thwaite (Faber & Faber, 2003). Reproduced by permission of the author and Faber & Faber.

Roger McGough: Extract from The Stowaways by Roger McGough (© Roger McGough 1986) is reproduced by permission of United Agents (www.unitedagents.co.uk) on behalf of Roger McGough.

Michael McLaverty: Michael McLaverty, *Collected Short Stories*, (Blackstaff Press, 2002) reproduced by permission of Blackstaff Press on behalf of the Estate of Michael McLaverty.

Michael Morpurgo: *The Silver Swan* by Michael Morpurgo (Corgi Childrens, 2001). Reproduced by permission of the author. Audio by permission of HarperCollins.

Brian Moses: The Ssssnake Hotel from 'Behind the Staffroom Door: The Very Best of Brian Moses' (Macmillan, 2007) copyright ©Brian Moses. www.poetryarchive.org/brianmoses

Leslie Norris: 'In Black Chasms' from *The Complete Poems of Leslie Norris* by Leslie Norris. ©Dr Meic Stephens.

LIST OF ILLUSTRATORS

THANKS

The Reader Organisation is extremely grateful to all authors and copyright holders who so generously and warm-heartedly waived or reduced their fee in support of the charity.

Grateful thanks to David Cookson who, in sickness and health, has gallantly battled through the jungle of Copyrightland in pursuit of permissions.

Sincere thanks to Lisa Spurgin and Fiona Macmillan for typing up the stories. Without you there would be blank pages.

The choice of stories and poems for *A Little, Aloud for Children* has been a team effort. Thanks to all the project workers at TRO who every day share books and poems with young readers. In particular Samantha Shipman, Sophy Povey, Patrick Fisher and Anna Flemming. Their advice and enthusiasm has been invaluable.

Huge thanks to Michael O'Shaughnessy at Liverpool School of Art and Design, Liverpool John Moores University for so enthusiastically involving his talented students in the illustration of this book. Thanks too to Bonnie Friend for all her contributions.

Last but certainly not least. we should like to offer heartfelt thanks to Alison Ritchie, Ness Wood and everyone at David Fickling Books for all their ready, skilful and kindly help with the preparation of this anthology and for their extremely generous support for The Reader Organisation in the publication of this book.